When the Past Finds You

ADRIAN J. SMITH

EREKA PRESS

To those who have experienced significant loss in their lives and who have struggled to grieve it...our grief may not look the same, but the pain is still there, no matter how many years have passed, and you are not alone.

CHAPTER

One

2010

"WHY ARE YOU SUCH A FUCKING BITCH?" Wil's voice charged through the full room.

Lynda stared at her, hard, as if Wil had hurled a glass to shatter against a wall instead of spitting a few curse words.

Shit. I meant to say that better.

Wil cringed inwardly, her face still a blank stare of fury as her stomach swam with shame. She couldn't believe she'd said that. Grandma was going to skin her alive. But defending her best friend was a necessity. She wouldn't stand aside and let Isla's stepmom be such a toxic force any longer. She was fed up with listening to her friend complain and be hurt by this woman. It *had* to stop.

"Wil, I will give you one minute to apologize before I send you home. This is my house, and I won't be spoken to like that." How she remained so cool and collected, Wil never knew.

Wil gritted her teeth, bearing down and refusing to budge from her point. For the last two years she had seen this family slip into the depths of hate, and she couldn't stand by and take it anymore. It was all Lynda's fault that they were falling apart. Wil directly stared into Lynda's caramel brown eyes, challenging her, like any good sixteen-year-old would.

The silence was thick, building on top of itself as each second passed, making it harder to breathe by the second. But Wil wouldn't give in. Isla and Aisling deserved better than this idiotic woman who had no idea what she was doing. Preparing to launch her next volley of attacks, Wil clenched her fists and opened her mouth, ready to say again exactly what she thought of Lynda's parenting—only this time better. She could manage to make Lynda understand these girls needed to be cared for instead of ignored, couldn't she?

"Get out." Lynda's command was low, her steely gaze hardening as the muscles in her face took on a different form. Fear consumed Wil. Every nerve in her body told her to high tail it out of there and get home before her grandma slapped her silly for being such a damn idiot herself.

"Why are you so mean?" Wil whisper-yelled, insisting that her point be made even though she knew she'd already lost the battle. *Fuck, I have to get better with words.*

"Get. Out," Lynda repeated, her jaw clenching with each syllable, but her sexy poise remaining.

If Wil pushed hard enough, would she strike out? Would Lynda hit her? Scrunching her nose at the thought, Wil dared herself to take it one step further. One more try to get her damn point across to make a dent in Lynda's thick skull. "They're not even *your* kids."

"Enough!" Lynda wildly boomed through the room, her voice a raw force that rushed over them.

Wil jerked, stunned by that kind of rage from a woman who was always so put together. Isla and Aisling stood to the side in the pristine white kitchen, their eyes bugging out of their heads. Lynda pointed at the door, her finely manicured finger showing the way to Wil's demise. No way would her grandma not find out about this. No way would Wil get out of it without getting her ass paddled.

Wil stepped forward, but Isla was quick and snagged her wrist, holding her back. Lifting her chin to stare at her forever friend, Wil held still, frozen on the spot.

"Get out of *my* house. Now." Lynda's breathing was heavy, her cheeks pink with well-contained fury.

Wil didn't want to admit defeat, but she had no recourse. Lynda had refused to answer her questions, refused to take the bait, and all Wil wanted to do was throw something else at her to prove her point—she was an awful mother. Wil lifted her eyebrows, rolled her shoulders, and knocked her chin up a notch or two.

"Quit being such a fucking bitch."

"Wil," Isla pleaded, tightening her grasp on Wil's wrist.

She hated that she couldn't stop herself enough to calm down and have a reasonable conversation. No matter how many times she tried, Wil couldn't make Lynda understand. They were left in the same place they'd been in for the last two years. Most days, she wished she never had to see Lynda again. But to be friends with Isla, she had to—at least for now.

"I'll see you around, Isla." Making the only decision she could to leave the argument with what little privilege she had left intact, Wil turned on her toes. Her black boots left skid marks on the white tile as she practically skipped her soon-to-be red ass toward the front door and slammed it shut for good measure.

2023

Confidently, Wil walked from her small office into the conference room. The tension in the office had been bad for the last few months but felt worse today. Something just felt off. Her shoulders were rock solid from stress as she stepped into the empty room.

These were her people, and it had taken her eight long years to cultivate her relationship with them. She would do anything to protect the balance she had created. She'd worked her ass off for the position she'd found herself in, and at twenty-nine, it was a coveted managerial role suited for her lack of temperament when it came to leadership.

The chair was cold as she slid into it, sitting at the spot right next to the head of the table. She left room for the firm manager, Millie, at the head to take charge of the meeting since she should be in today. Setting her yellow legal pad on the table-top, Wil prepared herself to hold her tongue and get her work done. The standard weekly staff meeting shouldn't be too jarring, but she always wanted to prepare herself in case something sparked her anger. She reined in that fiery torch she could never put out. While the team expected her bursts, she tried to only give them when deserved.

But Millie didn't walk into the room. Mr. Henshaw, the owner, came inside and carried a briefcase that he set down on the table. Wil's stomach plummeted, the stark retort on the tip of her tongue to ask what the fuck he was doing here, but she bit it back and swallowed it. The one person she couldn't be an asshole with was him.

Wil eyed him carefully. He didn't look nervous, but his gaze didn't meet hers either. Dread added to the tension she'd been feeling all morning, filling every available crevice in her.

Mr. Henshaw sat down in Millie's designated spot, and Wil knew in an instant, Millie wasn't going to be in today.

"Sir," Wil stated, her voice dropping down in an inquiry of what she didn't know. Being left in the dark was the worst feeling ever, and she'd had enough of that growing up with her parents in and out of jail.

"Ms. Powell." Henshaw nodded at her.

Wil clenched her jaw. She needed to word this question the right way to get information but also to not reveal how thrown off she was by the entire situation. She could control herself this time and not make a spectacle by failing to get her point across.

"Will Millie be joining us today?" Wil asked.

The door opened loudly as the rest of the team filed in. Henshaw cleared his throat, and Wil realized she had been staring and wasn't going to get an answer any time soon. Her shoulders drew together as she faced her team, waiting for any sign that Millie would be coming into the room. Bile swirled in her stomach, threatening to rise up. Wil pursed her lips hard, about to ask Henshaw if she could get Millie, when he cut her a sharp look and shook his head slightly.

"When everyone is seated, I'll explain."

"But Millie—"

"Won't be joining us today."

Wil stopped short in surprise. "Why not?"

Henshaw shook his head. Anger pooled together in her chest, covering the nausea and fear and raced to the front of the line. Rage was her safe spot, but it also would get her into a lot of damn trouble if she let it loose. She was about to speak when Henshaw stood up sharply. To stay quiet, Wil bit her cheek hard enough to feel the pain.

"Everyone knows we have been looking for a buyer for the firm for a while, and I'm pleased to announce that we have been acquired by Jolie Preston Investments." Henshaw spoke firmly and clearly, looking at everyone in the room.

The gasp was nearly audible, but it was dead silent. The tension in the room was thicker than Wil could ever remember it being. In fact, she only remembered it being that bad a few times in her life, including that one moment thirteen years ago when she thought she'd protect her best friend and failed miserably. She had to do the same here. These were her people.

"There are going to be some adjustments as we make this transition, but starting today, Jolie Preston will be sending in their own manager to learn about our company practices and to begin these transitions. The goal is to have the least amount of turnover possible."

Yeah, right. No company buy-out was without turnover, and Millie had been the first victim. Millie and she had an understanding they had spent the last eight years building, and without that safety net, Wil's job would be on the line. She could yell at Millie and nothing would happen because Millie knew she didn't mean it like that. But this new manager? *Fuck, I'm screwed.*

"Wil, I'm trusting you to show the new manager around in the next few days. Everyone else, business will be conducted as usual." Henshaw clapped his hands together, grabbed his briefcase, and held it in front of him like a shield against the inevitable backlash. "Any questions?"

He didn't even wait as he nodded at them and walked out of the room. As soon as he was gone, the tension snapped. Everyone looked at her. Wil had no answers, and the anger she'd clung to was gone. These people relied on her, and now was the time for her to be calm while she figured her shit out. Yes, she'd known they were trying to sell, but beyond that, she hadn't been told anything. And this? This was the worst possible way to tell everyone.

"What's going on?"

"Wil?"

"Did he fire Millie?"

Wil shook her head, the weight of everyone's fear resting on her already tense shoulders, and she had to fight it back. She wasn't ready for this, not being thrown to the damn wolves. She'd worked for her position, but this? This was outrageous.

Standing sharply, Wil put her hands on the tabletop and leaned over. Everyone quieted down as they stared at her. Her full lips parted, and she eyed them, carefully. "Look, I don't know what's going on. I'm finding this out just as you are. We all knew there was talk of a merger or a buy-out, I guess it happened. But...I'm going to make damn sure I figure out what's going on. Until then, buck it up, buttercups. We've got an office to run and clients to serve. Got it?"

The hard stare must have done something because their wide eyes turned to looks with a bit more confidence.

"Let's keep the gossip to a minimum today. None of us knows

anything. And until we know something, it's just going to be rumors. Understood?"

They all nodded.

"Right. Get to work." Wil straightened her back and watched as they filed out of the conference room, hushed undertones of questions and worries. Those feelings rampaged through her stomach too, but she didn't have time or energy to voice them. They wouldn't come out right anyway.

Returning to her office, Wil sat heavily in her chair with a sigh. Unfortunately, Henshaw refused to answer his phone. Millie refused to answer hers. In a last-ditch effort, Wil called Jolie Preston Investment's main offices and got nowhere. Sighing, she rubbed her temple, the ache in her head growing bigger by the second. She popped one of her migraine pills she always kept on her and stared at her email when an alert notified her to a new one.

Seattle Leadership Center—training, mentoring, and coaching for leaders in for profit and nonprofit business.

Wil narrowed her gaze at it, trying to figure out why she was getting such a random email with her name on it. Before she had a chance to do more than skim, a voice reached her ears, and a shiver ran down her spine—those cool tones, the precise consonants brought her right back to childhood. She froze. It had been eleven damn years since she had heard that voice. She must be dreaming.

Wil rounded her desk and walked out of her office. The hall was clear of people, and that voice was gone. Her heart raced. *Fuck,* she was going insane now, paranoid out of her mind. Running a hand over her smooth hair, Wil stepped back into her office and collapsed into her chair. With her eyes closed, she sat in the moment to attempt to collect herself.

In the span of the last two hours, her life had been flipped turned upside down. She had no idea what to do next other than the basics of her job, but she wanted to do more. She wanted to prove to Jolie Preston that she *could* be manager material, she could take on this entire firm and run it under their guidelines and not screw it up. These people trusted her.

Yet that stupid niggling voice in the back of her head told her it wouldn't happen. It would never happen. She would never be allowed to run the firm by herself, and she'd be damn lucky to find a job elsewhere. Henshaw had never let her run this place—he didn't trust her. While she hated that, she also couldn't blame him either.

Her cell phone rang, and she knew she wasn't supposed to answer it on the clock. Wil glanced at the door to her office and picked up her phone. She didn't really care right then, especially when she saw Isla's name pop up. She smiled at her best friend and brought the phone to her ear.

"Hey there—"

"Wil, I'm so sorry. I didn't—I didn't know. I'm so sorry."

"What?" Wil frowned and sat up a little straighter in her chair. The worry in Isla's voice was too damn much. She hadn't heard her this upset in a while. "Slow down, sis. What's going on?"

"I'm so sorry. You have to believe me."

"I believe you. Trust me, I do." Wil always would no matter what.

"Wilda, personal calls are not allowed during working hours."

That cold voice shook Wil to her core. Her muscles tightened up. Fear raced through her, piling into her stomach like a rock that weighed as much as the earth. Wil dropped her phone to the desk with a clatter, and she barely managed to reach down and hang up on Isla before she raised her chin to meet those caramel brown eyes she had never forgotten.

"Mrs. Walsh." Wil breathed out her name, not sure if it was a curse or a prayer. Probably a curse.

Lynda's lips pursed, lines around them and her eyes deeper than the last time Wil had seen her, nearly eleven damn years ago. Wil's heart went wild. She just stared—she couldn't make herself look away, or ask a question, or do anything. Lynda looked almost the same, the sleek curves of her body in the perfect skirt suit, the low cut blouse that was one button shy of being racy. Her sandy blonde hair was pulled back at the nape of her neck in a tight bun, highlights perfectly in place like they always had been.

Fuck, she thought, shame and fear warring inside her.

Lynda cocked her head to the side, her lips twitching as if she wanted to smile. "Aisling told me you worked in investing."

"F-for eight years," Wil stuttered, fear winning out. What the hell had happened to the strong ass woman she had worked years to become? The one who had stood up to this bitch and defended Isla?

A slow smile curled on Lynda's lips, her red lipstick matching the color of her pencil skirt. Wil had to swallow the lump in her throat. She knew Lynda could read her. She always could. Wil had never managed to hide anything from her—though she hadn't started trying until they were in high school and her damn crush reared its ugly head.

"What are you doing here?" Wil asked, finally regaining movement in her tongue and cooling her tone.

"I work here." Lynda's voice was so damn calm, so damn in control, so fucking sexy.

Wil paused. *No.* She couldn't go down that line of thinking again. She wouldn't let herself. She'd avoided that crush for years. "You work for Jolie Preston?"

"I'm your new manager."

Wil's heart sank. Nothing could have been worse. Isla must have found out, somehow, she had no idea how, but she must have. Isla had taken four years after high school to finally break off her relationship with her stepmom and now she was talking to her again? Wil gripped the edge of her desk sharply, holding on as tight as she could so she wouldn't fall on her ass and embarrass herself even more.

"Right," Wil whispered. "And you're starting today?"

"I am." Lynda's smile faltered, and Wil couldn't be sure, but she thought she detected a hint of concern floating through her gaze.

"Well, I'm your assistant manager." Wil's spine straightened, and she plastered on her best underling face. The hope of ever being the manager completely dashed from her mind, but she couldn't let that feeling of pity sink in, not just yet. Lynda knew everything about her, including her short as hell temper. She'd have to call Isla as soon as she got a chance.

"I've heard." Lynda's tone was drawn out, the last consonant ringing through the room sharply in her precise way. "I hear we have a lot of work to do."

Wil wasn't quite sure how to answer that. She knew changes were going to be made, but to consider it a lot? Henshaw ran a tight ship. To say they were completely inept would be an over-statement, although Lynda had only implied that, hadn't she?

"Tell me what you need."

Lynda's lip quivered, but she masked the look so quickly that Wil couldn't figure out what it was. She glided into Wil's office and sat in the chair across from the desk, crossing one knee over the other as her bright red skirt slid up, revealing bare skin. Wil gulped. *Fuck.* She had hoped that had gone away. Perhaps working with the stone-cold bitch would take care of the pesky crush she hadn't managed to obliterate.

"I'm going to need your policy books, any trainings you have for investment personnel, and an up-to-date schedule. We'll have to make some adjustments to it, I'm sure."

Wil's stomach clenched. They were already going to fire people. She knew it. She could only hope she wasn't one of them —at least not yet—because she really needed to find another job first. She couldn't be without the income. She worked too damn hard to be in this position to have *Lynda* throw her to the curb. Again.

Wil would just have to prove to her how good she was and exactly how she had changed.

Walking over to the bookshelf, Wil took the time and each step to put herself back together. It had been a long time since she'd been rattled this bad, and she needed to be able to keep that façade in place. No one could know the real her. No one could see the cracks underneath the mask she wore. And she definitely couldn't let Lynda see her because they would be right back in the past, and Lynda would send her packing.

Handing over the binders, she slunk to her chair and sat on the edge of it, perched as if she was going to get up and go again, which she supposed she was. She was now Lynda's right-hand-woman, and whatever she told Wil to do, Wil would do it. Even if she didn't like it.

Lynda flipped through the first big binder Wil had handed her. She did it so nonchalantly, as if she had the entire world at her command under her fingertips. Wil envied that. She had wanted to be like that for years. She'd admired how Lynda had always seemed to contain that amount of power, and she'd vowed herself to make changes to get her own anger in check because of it.

Wil dragged her gaze up and down Lynda's body. She may have aged eleven years since they'd seen each other last, but Lynda had lost none of the control she'd had then. In fact, Wil dared to believe she had even more now. When those eyes turned on her, Wil knew everything was on the line—her job, her reputation, and what little control she did have on her anger.

CHAPTER

Two

WIL'S FINGERS wrapped around the edge of the fridge as she bent over to stare into it. Nothing. A few containers of leftovers that were way too old to eat, two bottles of beer of which she snagged one immediately, and nothing more than a few packets of sauce from her favorite fast-food joint. Sighing heavily, she shut the door a little more forcibly than anticipated and rolled her shoulders to try and get rid of the still budding anger.

They had worked through lunch, which shouldn't have surprised her, but Wil struggled at the end of the day because of it. She'd spent more direct one-on-one time with Lynda in one day than she could remember ever doing before. Every understanding she'd had of her had only been confirmed in a short period of time—she was a bitch, she was immoveable, and she didn't care about anyone.

Sinking into her couch with her beer in her hand, Wil closed her eyes and took a deep breath to steady herself. She toed off her shoes, leaving them just under the edge of the coffee table, and spread her legs to relax. Her muscles ached from being so tense for hours on end, from the whiplash she had gotten that morning with Henshaw's announcement and Lynda showing up.

Damnit, I need to call Isla.

Isla had texted her several times, but Wil had only managed one text back during a bathroom break when she said she'd call later that night. She wasn't even sure what to say other than a long list of complaints about working with the evil stepmother neither of them liked.

Wil sat up a little straighter, grabbed her laptop and set it up on the couch while taking a long pull from her beer bottle. She deserved that at least. Pulling up a blank document, Wil created a resume, something she had never wanted to do. She had always wanted to work at Henshaw's as the manager, and she had spent eight years of her life moving toward that goal. Now that dream was shattered.

Lynda had shattered it. While Millie understood Wil's quick temper, Lynda didn't, and with their past, it would ruin any attempt Wil had at moving upward in the company. She didn't want to leave, and she'd work damn hard to avoid it if possible, but with the wicked witch in charge, she needed a backup plan.

Bitterness replaced the anger as she started inputting her work history. Wil set her beer down to grab her cell and called Isla, putting it on speaker so she didn't have to hold it and could go back to drinking.

"I wish I'd known sooner," Isla said as soon as the call connected.

"It's fine. You didn't." Wil sighed hearing Isla's voice, the regret, the exhaustion, the worry all wrapped up in a few short words. But more important than anything, she was comforted by it. Isla was her home away from home, and they had been through thick and thin together.

"But I didn't want you to be ambushed by it."

"I was, but not just by her. Henshaw didn't exactly tell us that he had sold out, and Millie had vanished. I can't get a hold of her." Wil wished she could have taken a few moments to hide away throughout the day, but she'd been tossed from one chaotic moment to the next, and now instead of sitting with and dealing with it, she was formulating plans of action.

"I'm so sorry, Wil. I wish I could drive down and be with you tonight."

Wil knew Isla would say that, and while she'd love to see her forever friend to just have someone to be there with her, it wouldn't be good for either of them. She wasn't at a crisis point yet, and that was when she would really need Isla there.

"You can't. I know you have summer school in the morning. Those kids need you." Wil finished the last fifteen years of job experience, the last eight of which were devoted to Henshaw. Gritting her teeth, Wil stared at his name on her screen—she'd been damn lucky to find this job and be able to work her way up in the company. Any other job she'd had, from the fast-food to the grocery store to the last investment firm, her temper had gotten in the way at every turn. It would happen again. Wil started on the education section with a heavy sigh. "I'm going to put out my resume, though."

"Are you? You don't even want to try it out with her?"

Wil paused. "You hate her, too."

"This isn't about me. It's about you, and I know how much you love it there."

"Yeah, I do, but I don't work for Henshaw anymore. I work for *Jolie Preston Investments.*" Wil scoffed. "It even sounds so pretentious. I won't fit in here."

"But what if you do?"

"I won't. Lynda and I have never fit together."

She hadn't ever wanted to see Lynda again after high school and had only put up with her because of Isla, but as soon as she'd been able to put distance between them, she had. For years Wil had avoided Lynda at every possible opportunity, and now she was stuck seeing her every day until something was resolved. Keeping that boundary in place had formed a rift between her and Aisling, however, and that saddened her. Aisling was like her little sister, and even though they weren't blood, Wil loved her.

"How did you find out?" Wil asked as she entered down to the next line to fill out her degrees.

"Find out what?"

"That she was the new manager?"

"Aisling. I don't know what to call it. Guilty conscience maybe?" Isla's tone dropped as she thought.

Wil finished her resume, sadness filling the empty spaces where anger had been so easy to snag even an hour ago. She hadn't been prepared for this. Leaving wouldn't be as hard as she thought it would, not now, but that didn't mean starting somewhere else would be easy. In fact, Wil knew it wouldn't. It would be impossible for her and Lynda to work together—it always had been. But now so much more was on the line than just her friendship with Isla. That was as secure as ever.

Reluctantly, Wil went to the Internet to find some place where she could submit her resume. She would be lucky to find another assistant manager position and not have to take a step down, and she'd be even luckier to find a place where she didn't get written up for being an asshole. But she knew she couldn't work with Lynda. They were like oil and water on a good day, and since that pesky crush hadn't seemed to fully disappear yet, she didn't want to put it to the test.

"What did Aisling say?" Wil asked, carrying on the conversation as she tried to drag herself out of the intense emotions raging through her.

"That Lynda had a new job and had mentioned you were the assistant manager."

"Well that confirms one thing I had suspected. She knew before I did."

"She wanted to surprise you, I bet." Isla's sharp anger at the end wasn't a surprise to Wil. They'd had issues since Isla's dad died, and they'd never managed to work through them.

"Probably knew I'd up and quit if I knew beforehand and she wanted sick satisfaction at seeing my reaction," Wil muttered, finding two firms that she might apply at. She copied the links and put them in a new document to keep track of where and when she was doing it, and what the results were. It was going to take her longer than she wanted to find a new job, that much she knew, the one with the right pay that meant she could still manage her bills and student loans.

"That might be why, but she's always been devious when it comes to things like that. You remember." Isla groaned, as if some particular memory had just hit her. Wil didn't pry into it, not needing to make this bitch-fest longer than necessary.

"Oh, yes, I remember very clearly." Will clenched her jaw, her molars grinding together. "I remember the hell she put you and Aisling through."

Isla didn't respond immediately, and Wil took that as confirmation of what she said. "What are you going to do?"

"I'm looking for a new job. I don't know when I can find one, but I'm looking, and I'm not going to stop until I can get out from under her. I'm not doing this to myself again, and I'm certainly not doing it to you."

"You working for her isn't going to do anything to me."

"Sure, it will." Wil stretched her back, taking a break from searching for open positions and having a sip of her beer. "You can't tell me that today hasn't already affected you, just the back-and-forth calls, the complaints, the tension that I have."

"I guess you're right." Isla's tone dropped, quieting at the end as she thought.

"Exactly, so continuing to work for her is only going to make that worse. Meaning it will affect you." Wil had nothing else to say on the matter. She knew she was right, even if Isla didn't want to admit it full out yet.

"So you'll find a new job, and then what?"

"Start over climbing up the ladder." Wil wasn't looking forward to that monumental task. It had been hard enough at Henshaw's, but Millie had given her the chance she needed and she'd been able to prove herself a worthy asset. Lynda would never see her like that.

"Why don't you just move up here? You can come stay at my house, and Cheyenne is so much cheaper than Denver."

Wil had considered it, but something had always kept her locked to Denver no matter how many times she had contemplated moving. Although, it was probably her own issues that kept her there. The thought hadn't even occurred to her that day to apply for a job in Cheyenne. "I can add it to my places to look at for jobs."

"You wouldn't work as much since I would be around, and that might be a good thing, you know. Maybe you could find someone—"

Wil snorted. "You know after the last person I dated that I'm not looking for that. I'm too much of a brute for a relationship."

"You don't know that. You two just weren't right for each other." An undertone of pleading in Isla's voice irked Wil even more. She was always trying to set her up with someone.

"I know it, sis. I'm not good relationship material, and if it happens, then it happens." Wil went back to looking, changing the filter to look in Cheyenne just to put Isla at ease that she had actually looked even if she didn't end up applying for anything.

"Regardless of dating, please really consider it this time. I'd love to have you be closer to me again. I miss you."

Wil's lips curled up at that—there was the real reason Isla wanted her to move there and one that was far more enticing than a relationship that would never happen. They had been best friends their entire lives, and not once had Isla ever made her not feel like family. Considering she had none anymore, Isla was her only family and where she went for most holidays. "I'll think about it. If I can get a job there, I'll be thrilled to move. Have to figure out how to break my lease, though."

"Ooof, that's never a fun adventure."

"It's awful." Wil had managed to find some sense of consistency in her life since her grandma had died seven years ago, but she was still very much alone. Isla was her constant, no matter what, and she wasn't willing to ever give that up.

"Hey, it's late and I've got to get up early, but I'm sorry about today, Wil. Really. I wish Aisling had called me sooner so I could have given you a fair warning."

"It was out of your hands, sis. You've got to stop worrying about things you can't control." Not that Wil couldn't stand to take her own advice on that one.

"You're right. You're always right about that." Isla sounded like she was almost smiling, but since Wil couldn't see her, she couldn't be sure. She'd call again soon to make sure everything was okay and that it wasn't just the shock of Lynda popping back up into her life again so unexpectedly.

"Then listen to me for once." Wil added, hoping Isla did this time.

"I'll try. Talk to you later."

"See you."

Hanging up, Wil finished her beer and searched for more firms she could seek out. There were a few she knew who might hire her in town even though they didn't have any openings, and she'd have to find time to personally drop off her resume instead of just emailing it in.

Wil shifted to stand, ready for a second beer for the night, when her cell phone rang. The firm's number popped up, and she reached for it before stopping herself. *Who the hell is calling me?* She was just about to answer when her stomach plummeted. Lynda—of course it would be Lynda, working late as usual. She would expect Wil to fall into line with that one no doubt. Sitting back fully, Wil answered. She didn't want to give Lynda any more ammo to fire her.

2006

The loud crack startled Wil awake, her heart racing as she sat straight up in the bed, the voices that usually initiated that crack didn't follow. She blinked to clear her eyes, finding Isla passed out next to her on the bed, the blanket half-covering her face as her beautiful blonde curly hair lay over the pillow.

Disoriented, Wil stayed put and tried to figure out what woke her up since it wasn't the neighbors arguing again. Another crack echoed through the house, shuddering the walls seconds after lightning struck down and lit up the room. Taking deep breaths to calm herself, Wil stared up at the ceiling of the very familiar room. It was practically her room during the summer months, and they were about to dive deep back into sixth grade —new school and new teachers.

When an hour had passed and she still couldn't fall back asleep, Wil slipped out from the covers and tried not to wake up Isla in the process. She made it into the hallway without any issues but was thoroughly confused when the lights were still on in the dining room. Rubbing her eyes, Wil stumbled her way toward the kitchen.

"Wil?" Lynda's voice perked up, soft but curious and surprised at the same time. "What are you doing awake?"

"The storm woke me up." Wil's voice was soft as the lie slipped from her lips. It hadn't been the storm, but rather a nightmare of listening to Ben beat Sadie again. She stopped short at the entrance to the kitchen and eyed Lynda over.

Lynda's gaze moved from the thick laptop in front of her to the large patio doors. Had she even noticed the storm before? Wil couldn't figure out what was going on behind that steely gaze. "It is getting loud."

Wil swallowed. "I didn't want to wake Isla up."

"Good thinking."

Wil nodded, her chin bobbing. Lynda and Patrick had been married for a couple years, but Wil still wasn't used to finding her in the house every waking second and never quite felt comfortable in her presence. They stared at each other awkwardly, Wil's shoulders tensing with each passing second before she pivoted and moved into the kitchen.

Grabbing herself a clean glass, she filled it with water from the fridge and snagged an apple from the basket on the counter.

She sat heavily at the table, next to Lynda's chair with papers strewn about the top of it and a laptop whirring.

"Why are you awake?" Wil asked, not quite sure what to say to this quiet woman who stared at her like she had no idea what to say or do.

"I was working on some problems for tomorrow."

"It is tomorrow," Wil answered with a slight snark. It was past midnight, so she was right, but it wasn't that far past.

"I suppose it is." Lynda smiled at her, hair piled on top of her head in a messy bun, her makeup taken off, and a warm sweater wrapped around her shoulders.

Wil bit into the apple, juices running over her lips. Lynda was always about the healthy snacks, and when she moved in that had been a significant change. Patrick had pretty much given them whatever they wanted before. But then again, he'd been a single dad just trying to keep up with three girls running around.

Lynda crossed her arms and leaned back in the chair, eyeing Wil as though she was a nuisance instead of a scared kid who couldn't sleep. Grandma had never done this when she'd crawled into her bed after being woken by the neighbors again. Grandma would stroke her long hair and keep her breathing slow and steady until they fell asleep together.

"I'm sorry the storm woke you up." Lynda stated, her gaze still not wavering from Wil's face to the point Wil was unnerved.

Wil shrugged the anxiety off as best as she could. "It's much quieter here than at my house, so it's probably just that."

"What do you mean?" Lynda grabbed her tea and sipped it.

"The upstairs neighbors fight a lot." Wil looked down at the table, not wanting to make eye contact.

"Just screaming and yelling?"

Wil shrugged. It was way more than that. She could hear the fists being thrown, when Sadie was tossed against the wall, but she didn't want to tell Lynda that. It was her house, and she didn't want anything to happen to it, or to get in trouble. Ben scared her most days, and she tried to avoid him when she could.

"Wil, is it just screaming and yelling?"

"No," she murmured into her apple, staring at the few bites she had taken so far.

Lynda said nothing, but her entire body was tense in a way Wil had never seen before. She took her time raising her gaze up, trying to figure out what Lynda was thinking, but she was a complete mystery. Even Isla couldn't figure her out on a good day. Bad days? Forget it.

Wil quickly finished her apple and her glass of water as they sat in silence. But Lynda never went back to working like she had been. Getting up to clean her mess, Wil stopped at the table and held her hands tightly in front of her and waited to see what Lynda would say and do next. "Thank you for the snack, Mrs. Walsh."

"What? Oh, yes. Are you going to try to sleep again?"

The concern was awkward and didn't sit right, as if it wasn't quite genuine. Wil stayed put for another moment with slow deep breaths. She'd expected Lynda to comfort, but she'd been met with nothing but cold awkwardness. But underneath it, Lynda seemed so disturbed by her neighbors.

Giving in because she was too tired to try and figure it out, Wil said, "Yeah, I think so."

"Okay."

Stepping awkwardly around the table, Wil turned her back on Lynda, the entire conversation doing nothing to set her nerves at ease or erase the dream that had woken her. Wil walked quietly to Isla's room, surprised when lightning struck just as she opened the door. The tree outside brushed against the glass window. That would have been what woke her up. Climbing into the bed, Wil turned on her side to find Isla wide awake.

"Where'd you go?"

"The storm woke me up," Wil whispered, trying to keep her

voice as quiet as possible even though Lynda knew she was awake. They weren't going to get in trouble for it. "I went out so I didn't wake you up."

"Dad says he's going to trim that tree every storm."

"And he never does it?"

Isla shook her head. "He always forgets or gets distracted with something else."

"Or someone," Wil muttered, thinking of Lynda's solemn look as she'd left the table. She'd seemed so disturbed by something. Maybe it was the neighbors, but it seemed more than that. "Did I wake you?"

"No," Isla answered, her voice just as quiet. "It was the tree, and the thunder."

"It's right on top of us."

Isla nodded and reached for Wil's hand, holding onto it tightly. "It scares me sometimes."

"I'm sure we can go out to the living room. I don't think Lynda will mind."

Shaking her head, Isla squeezed Wil's hand tighter. "No. Let's stay here. I don't want to deal with her tonight."

"Okay." Wil settled in even more, staring in her best friend's eyes. "Want to try to sleep?"

"Yeah. We should."

CHAPTER
Three

2023

LYNDA SETTLED into her chair in her office, setting up the few photos she brought with her every time she moved to a new building onto her desk. Rolling her shoulders to get the kinks out of the muscles, she snagged her coffee and took a long sip of the steaming liquid.

Lynda had known Wil worked here. She'd read her name in the employee list after she'd agreed to the position. She had hesitated at first, but the pang of guilt over her relationship with Isla had come back full force, and she couldn't resist the one person who could maybe bring them closer again. Just knowing about Isla from afar would be more than it had been for the last five years. And surely, how much could Wil still hate her? Eleven years was a long time to go without seeing someone, and no doubt they had both changed.

Lynda let the moment sink in before the rest of the office showed up. She hadn't changed except she no longer had two children under her care, and she no longer spoke to one of them. That still stung. She'd known Isla since she was eight years old, and when she started dating Patrick, she took on the responsibility of being an adult female figure in their lives. She'd never thought—Lynda halted as tears burned her eyes. She couldn't go down that thread of thought that day, or that week.

She was starting at a new office, and she needed to keep her focus on that, nothing else. Wil was only a distraction, and the day they had spent together working proved she wasn't willing to say anything beyond the profession. Lynda should have known better. For years, she'd gone into different firms Jolie Preston had bought out and rejuvenated, bringing them fully under Jolie Preston's umbrella. That put her in a precarious position of friend and foe to many, a line she was brilliant at walking except when it came to Wil. She had never managed to figure that girl out. But now she was a woman and a different person than she had been—tamer to start with.

People filed into the building slowly, but Lynda had already been there for hours. She wondered if Wil was even going to show up or if she'd call in and hide away or never show up. Then again, that wouldn't fit the Wil she had known for so many years. Isla and Wil had been best friends since the moment they'd set eyes on each other, and Lynda had come into the family with that relationship already attached to it. Wil lived across the street and one house down from them with her grandmother, and all three girls had spent more than one school evening, weekend, or summer day going back and forth between the two houses.

The knock on her door startled her, but Lynda looked up to find Wil's beautiful face looking at her filled with regret and perhaps an inkling of fear. Lynda had never wanted to instill that in Wil and had thought with their past they'd be able to push into a friendly relationship. Instead, Wil had done nothing to indicate they'd known each other for years. Lynda should have expected that since she was so close to Isla.

"There are a lot of questions from the staff," Wil implored.

Lynda waved Wil into her office and kept her voice firm as she said, "Shut the door."

Wil did as she was told and settled into the chair across from Lynda's desk, what used to be Millie's desk, but that had been the first necessary change Jolie Preston had made since they'd discovered Millie didn't have the leadership skills necessary to make the transition. Lynda drew in a breath, holding it tightly in her chest as she waited for Wil to begin with the questions. This young woman had grown so much in the time they'd known each other and even more in the time they hadn't seen each other. Although Wil hadn't walked away on the best of terms, she was still fiercely protective of Isla and Aisling—something Lynda could admire even if it caused her problems from the beginning.

"What are the questions?" Lynda finally asked, realizing Wil wasn't going to start the conversation.

"They don't know what's going on."

Lynda frowned. "The company was bought out. Didn't Mr. Henshaw tell everyone he was looking to sell?"

Wil shook her head. "He mentioned it once over a year ago, but only to Millie and me in a briefing call."

"Oh." Lynda folded her hands together, her elbows resting on the arms of the chair. She hadn't expected that, but it did explain the confusion when she'd first shown up. "I don't suppose Millie mentioned it either?"

Wil's eyes shot up to Lynda's face at that, a look of accusation in the gaze, which told Lynda more than words ever could.

"That's something we need to work on. There are reasons to keep certain information under wraps, but communication is key to having a company function and run smoothly."

"I agree." Wil seemed surprised by that, and Lynda could understand why.

For years all Wil had done was pick bones about what Lynda was doing wrong when it came to raising Isla and Aisling, what they didn't agree on, which was damn near everything. Wil had been an expert at picking at Lynda's one weakness. She couldn't corporate her way out of parenting. Lynda pressed her lips together tightly to keep from saying anything or sliding too far back into the past.

Lynda started again, "I'd like to run through the list of employees currently working here and do a private evaluation with your help. You know them better. Then we'll bring them in for an evaluation and set up improvement plans where necessary."

"You're not going to just fire them?" Wil's eyes widened, those dark brown colors nearly black.

Shaking the lost train of thought, Lynda raised her gaze as a pang of hurt lashed through her. She wasn't a monster, though many people thought she was. She was just damn good at her job and walking that line, which gave her the perfect skill set for these kinds of jobs. Still, for Wil to think that she wasn't compassionate with her insider knowledge to who she was hurt. "There are a couple who might be fired, but the majority seem to work well here."

"Who are the couple?" Wil leaned in, so interested in everything Lynda had to say, but she wasn't pressing for information either. Lynda took that as a good sign, that perhaps Wil would respect her position in this building rather than tearing her down at every opportunity.

"Bring me the employee files." Lynda sidestepped that conversation for another moment, needing the extra time to determine where Wil stood on their current relationship. The past was in the past, and Lynda had to keep reminding herself of that.

Wil frowned. "I'm not your assistant."

"I believe you are." Lynda raised an eyebrow at her, standing her ground. Wil was her assistant manager at the firm, but Lynda knew full well she wasn't a secretary. Still, she wanted to see how much Wil would do for information or when that fiery burst of anger would reveal itself again. Considering their past, Lynda suspected Wil still had her temper, but the way she had managed to steel herself against it thus far was intriguing. Like a fly to light, Lynda wanted to know everything about those changes.

Huffing, Wil stood up and walked out of the office with a sway to her hips. Lynda kept her gaze on Wil's ass as she left before she relaxed into her chair as she waited to see what would happen next. She needed to get to know the employees beyond what she'd already been given, and this would be the perfect opportunity for that along with picking through Wil's defenses a little more to learn about Isla.

Wil came back forty minutes later with a stack of paperwork. Lynda eyed her suspiciously as she set it down on the desk and went to close the door. Choosing to remain silent, Lynda watched every move Wil made. She was far smoother in how she walked now compared to when she'd been a kid with gangly legs and arms and always running into things. Now she was full of curves and knew how to use them, full lips that formed into a perfect pout when she was holding her tongue—something she'd never managed to do before.

"Here it is," Wil said as she sat back in her chair and looked directly into Lynda's gaze. "Where are we starting?"

"With your file."

Lynda eyed her carefully and ignored the stack as Wil only hesitated for a quick moment before grabbing the top file and handing it over. Lynda opened it and read, though this was the one file she'd been given when she agreed to take the position. She always wanted to know who her second was going to be and if they were going to be worthwhile. Finding out it would be one Wilda Powell had been a surprise and a burst of pride. Wil had managed to succeed when she hadn't been given the best of starts in life and that had to be from the grit she'd learned as a young child.

"Graduated top of your class," Lynda commented confidently, eyeing Wil over the top of the file. Wil had almost nothing but accolades in her file, aside from a small note from Henshaw about her temper on a couple occasions.

"Yes, ma'am."

Lynda looked up, surprised to hear the salutation. Wil had called her that as a child out of respect, but their roles had changed. "You can call me Lynda."

"I've never called you *that*, Mrs. Walsh." Wil's cheeks flushed pink, her eyes widening but locking on Lynda's face.

Lynda's heart raced hearing that again with a new intonation she hadn't experienced before, one that would have sent shivers through her if Patrick had said it. It had been so long, and even longer since Patrick... she had to stop that again. Pulling herself together, Lynda locked gazes with Wil. "Please call me Lynda."

Wil nodded. "And I still don't go by Wilda."

Lynda's lips quirked slightly, but she schooled it. Wil didn't need to know she'd done that specifically to get a rise out of her and see if there was the same reaction as there had been eleven years ago. "All right, Ms. Powell."

"Wil." Those dark eyes were once again locked on Lynda, and Wil raised a single finger into the air from the arm of the chair to make her point.

Unnerved by the depth of control Wil exerted, Lynda shifted her entire focus onto the file in front of her, the one she had memorized. She couldn't find an adequate response, so she focused on what she could. "I see you didn't waste your life away since I saw you last."

"No, ma—Mrs. Walsh. I did not."

"I'm pleased to see that." And she was, she'd been worried Wil's tendency toward angry outbursts wouldn't serve her well in life, but if yesterday and this morning was any kind of proof, Wil had learned to tame that anger. Or perhaps Wil's grandmother had been correct, and the behavior was only focused on Lynda herself. If that was true, Lynda could only hope she didn't become Wil's preferred target again. Though she'd survived it once already so she could easily do it again. It would, however, make the takeover next to impossible if they were to continue to work together.

"I've been working here for years, working my way up."

"I can see that," Lynda replied, nonchalantly, keeping her cool tone of voice so Wil wouldn't think anything of the comment. "Millie did an excellent job training you."

"Why did you fire her?"

Lynda raised her eyes suddenly. "I didn't."

Wil looked confused, and Lynda stared at her, waiting to see what question she would ask next, but when none came, she gave in and allowed a slight moment inside her mind.

"Millie was offered your position temporarily until proper training could be completed, but she saw it as a demotion and chose to find a new job. It was a coincidence that her last day was the first day we arrived."

Now she looked even more confused than before. "Millie's a good friend. She wouldn't do that without saying something."

Leaning forward, Lynda made sure to catch Wil's gaze before she spoke again. "Perhaps you don't know her as well as you thought you did. Or perhaps you're not as good of friends as you were led to believe."

"Wouldn't be the first time someone has turned on me." Wil's direct stare told Lynda exactly who she was talking about.

Normally she'd be able to sidestep this, but their years of history prevented it. Lynda clenched her jaw before purposely relaxing it. She had to maintain the image of control. It'd been the only thing she could do for years, and she'd nearly perfected it. Wil had been one of the few people to push her to her limits and cause her to break, but Lynda would hold her own this time.

Wil, however, while anger simmered under the surface, was next to impossible to read anymore, even with the years of knowing each other.

Lynda did the only thing she could—she changed the topic. "Have you heard of the Seattle Leadership Center?"

"What?" Wil shook her head, clearly thrown with the change in conversation.

A small burst of triumph lit in Lynda's chest, and she grabbed for her cooling coffee cup on the table, seeing the smiling picture of Patrick looking back at her. Holding her ground, Lynda didn't repeat herself, wanting to see how close attention Wil paid.

"I think I got an email from them yesterday?" A deep line formed on Wil's brow as she was deep in thought.

"Yes, they have training once a year. I've registered for the both of us."

"Excuse me?" Wil's eyebrows rose.

Lynda pressed her lips together hard, wondering if this would be the next outburst, but Wil schooled her features quickly. "The conference is in a few weeks, and I'm sorry for the short notice, but considering the circumstances of the buy-out, I wasn't allowed to share it with you prior to yesterday."

"You didn't share yesterday." There was that cool, smooth voice Lynda had come to find from Wil lately.

Sitting perfectly still in her chair, Lynda kept her gaze on Wil. "I sent you an email."

She could see Wil mentally work through everything that had happened yesterday, but she wouldn't be surprised if Wil didn't remember it. The day had been hectic, new, and overwhelmed with changes wrought without communication prior, so it was a wonder anyone had gotten anything done.

"What exactly does this conference do?"

"It's for businesses in leadership, so we can learn how to become better leaders. This specific conference is for managers or business leaders, so we can have an intense learning session." Lynda had gone for years, enjoying the networking, but she'd always dreamed of being asked to lecture. She kept going year after year solely for the right opportunity to arise.

"So we can be more like men, you mean."

Lynda's lips twitched, but she managed to contain the smile. "In some ways, yes, but also in how to use the natural abilities and advantages afforded to us by our sex."

A shiver ran through her at the last word, and Lynda couldn't quite figure out why. Normally, the thought of being in a building with so many people brought her anticipation because of the learning, but this time, being in tight confines with Wil for an entire week, had her on edge. It would either prove to be a decision she regretted or she would finally find that connection to Isla she wanted.

"We're there to learn how to manage and run companies, manage and work with people, how to effectively work through conflict, and put our own emotions to better use."

Wil narrowed her eyes suspiciously. "And you're giving me two weeks' notice?"

"Again, I couldn't tell you prior to yesterday." Lynda dropped Wil's file on the desk next to her computer and grabbed the next one on top. They needed to work on these employee files before the day was half over. She wanted to know who was working for Jolie Preston now, and it was her duty to weed out those who wouldn't be up to snuff.

"I have plans."

"Cancel them," Lynda stated easily, expecting Wil would fall in line. Going to the conference was an opportunity of a lifetime. Lynda had attended every year for the last five, and any time she could, she made sure the same opportunities were given to her assistant manager—Wil especially, since she hadn't had those opportunities growing up.

"I...I can't."

Dropping the new file on the desk loudly, Lynda stiffened her shoulders. "It's not optional."

"You can't make me go to a conference."

Lynda didn't answer, knowing the look she was giving was going to be enough. It always worked, although with their history—no, it had to work this time.

"Someone needs to stay here to make sure they can manage on their own without rumors running rampant." Panic swelled in Wil's undertones.

A plan had already been put into place. Jolie Preston always had back-up firm managers who would step in while someone else was gone, and this would be no different. Lynda always had a plan, business plans were just easier than learning how to parent on the fly.

Handing the file she'd been holding to Wil, Lynda waited a moment for Wil to read the name on it. "Do you think Jacob can handle it?"

Wil pursed her lips and eyed the file without opening it, surely working from her experience rather than what was on paper, which Lynda appreciated to an extent.

"I thought you didn't know anyone who worked here."

"Smart girl. I was given the files for the managers prior to accepting the position."

"So you knew I worked here?" Wil's stare was direct, and while it was a question, Lynda had a sinking suspicion she wasn't asking but rather stating.

"Yes." Lynda waited for the inevitable outburst, but it didn't come. Wil sat stoically in the chair as if she hadn't just been delivered another blow to her ego. "Jacob?"

"He can handle most of it so long as we set him up for success. He's never made the schedule before, so we'll need to do that, but if we're available for calls, I suppose he can manage."

"Good. And it's Jolie Preston's practice to always have a secondary firm manager available when another manager is out. Someone will be in here every day while we're gone." Lynda had plans for him in the future. She'd never wanted to come in and fire the lot of workers there. She'd wanted to come in and train them to her specifications, work the business to the best it could be, and then move on to the next takeover in a year or so, leaving Wil in charge. That had always been the plan. Wil, however woven into the strategy she was from the beginning, was still a wild card. If Lynda couldn't control her the way Millie had managed to, it could ruin Lynda's reputation and potentially leave her in the dust for future takeovers. That was why the week together would be intense, but the perfect place for them to iron out some of their differences as best as they could.

Lynda grabbed another file. "Let's start with the investors first."

"Sure."

They spent hours together, and the conversation went smoothly. Still she kept waiting for the inevitable burst of anger to slash through her and wipe her out in a flash. Wil had been so good at that when she was a child. As Wil left her office mid-afternoon to complete her own duties, Lynda had hoped they'd be left with a sense of strength between them. Instead, the chasm only felt wider and deeper.

LYNDA'S HEELS clicked across the sidewalk as she made her way into the restaurant. She wouldn't take more than an hour for lunch. It wasn't that she didn't trust Wil to run everything while she was gone, but the firm was so new to her that she didn't trust anyone else while they were both out to lunch.

She stopped as soon as she was inside the main doors, finding her college friend, Camryn, standing near the side of the lobby area. God, she needed this lunch to take off the stress of the last week. She hadn't been able to schedule anything until Monday, and she needed it sooner than that.

"Hey," Camryn greeted, a bright smile on her lips.

"Hey. Laura here yet?" Lynda tensed her shoulders and resisted the urge to look at her phone to check her messages. The restaurant was deliberately close to the firm so she could leave at any point and make it back quickly.

"Late as always."

Lynda sighed. Now was not the day for Laura to take her time. She needed them. "Of course, she is. Do we have a table yet?"

"Few more minutes."

Lynda grabbed her purse strap on her shoulder and straightened her back. She wasn't even sure how to broach the topic of Wil with them. When she and Patrick had gotten married, they'd warned her about having stepchildren, about the complications that came with that relationship. The warnings hadn't been enough despite how many of them she listened to. She hadn't been prepared to be the sole parent for two young, impressionable girls.

"Everything going well with the new takeover?" Camryn perfectly segued into it, but Laura wasn't there yet, and Lynda valued her opinion so much that she wanted to wait.

"We can talk about that when Laura gets here."

"That bad?" Camryn raised her eyebrows in surprise.

"Not bad exactly, but I have some concerns I'm not sure how to work around. You'll likely be more helpful with that." All those conversations about Wil when she'd been a child came back to mind, all the advice Lynda had sought out in order to make a bad situation better. Neither would believe that they were working together.

"Interpersonal issues?"

Lynda resisted the urge to smile at the irony but failed. "Yes."

Camryn blew out a breath. "You have to expect some of that when you go into a company and redo everything."

"I do, and I plan for it, but this one I wasn't exactly able to plan for as much as I thought. Oh, here she is." Lynda smiled as she caught sight of Laura through the front window of the restaurant.

Laura stepped inside, perfectly done up as she always was. Lynda had no idea when they'd gone from college students to professionals or young parents to parents with adult children. She barely remembered it anymore, but the three of them were dressed to the nines in their work clothes, makeup on, and battle ready for the day. In college, Laura had been the one to throw her hair up in a ponytail. She didn't start wearing it down until

Rodney. Lynda wrinkled her nose at the thought of him. She'd never liked him.

"I have your table ready."

Lynda's attention swung back to the hostess in uniform. She remembered working those jobs when she'd just been starting out and going through school. It'd been worth it in the end, but not something she ever wanted to go back to doing.

Lynda waved Laura over, and they followed the hostess until they were seated. With drinks ordered, Lynda tensed again, trying to figure out exactly what she was even doing there. She should have given the job to someone else, someone who could deal with Wil. Because despite the eleven years that they hadn't seen each other, that same tension remained between them. Wil despised her. She'd debated whether it had been ethical for her to accept the position fully without telling her boss, Jessica, but she'd done it anyway. The chance to find some way to get in touch with Isla again, find some way to break that ice that had formed over their relationship, was too tempting to give the opportunity up.

"Lynda was talking about work," Camryn supplied, no doubt wanting to know the dirt Lynda brought to the table.

Lynda would have to thank her later. Laura perked up at the idea of business discussions, like she always seemed to do since she hated discussing anything family related. Lynda was going to have to choose her words wisely since this would involve Patrick and the girls, a sore subject for Laura all around.

"I took over another firm last week. It's been a bit of a disaster in some ways. The previous owner didn't tell anyone he had sold." Start with the business and move into the personal issues—her tactic for the afternoon.

"He didn't?" Laura's eyes grew wide. "That must have been a shock for them."

"Still is. But that's an issue I can work with."

"What's the one you can't?" Camryn reached for her water

but kept her eyes glued on Lynda, knowing there was way more to the story than she'd shared so far.

Lynda pressed her lips together hard, trying to get the words out in a way that would make the most sense. "Do you remember Wil? Isla's best friend who lived across the street."

She could tell both had to work to remember. It had been a decade since Lynda had really mentioned her, and certainly not in the last five years since Isla had stopped talking to her.

"She's the one who gave me a lot of problems after Patrick died." She tried to downplay the hurt Wil had caused, wrapping it up in her grief over losing Patrick, but didn't quite manage it. The sting from the past seemed to hurt worse than it had in the last decade. Lynda pulled herself together and pushed those unruly emotions to the side.

"Oh, right." Laura tapped her fingers on the tabletop in quick succession, her nerves over the children-conversation obvious to those who knew her. "It's been a long time since I've heard her name."

Lynda steadied herself, her hands shaking in her lap to the point she had to wrap them together. She couldn't tear her gaze from them when she finally confessed, "I haven't seen her in about a decade, but she works at the firm."

Laura's eyebrows rose, and Camryn clenched her jaw.

"How?" Camryn asked.

"That's a conflict," Laura stated, her thin lips pressing together tightly.

Lynda put her hands out to stop them from saying anything else. She needed to get this explanation out. "After Patrick died, it got bad with Wil. I never was able to figure it out beyond her wanting to protect Isla. The names she called me, the hurtful things she said..."

Lynda's eyes burned with unbidden tears, and her shoulders tensed at the memories. Camryn touched the top of her hand in support, and Laura shook her head, no doubt still in shock.

"I never made the right decision for her, no matter what I

did. But she also wasn't my kid, and I had to focus on Isla and Aisling."

"You did," Laura agreed.

Lynda held back the wash of grief. If Patrick had been there, none of this would have happened. Everything would have been calm, and he would have known exactly what to do. He always had known because he was a natural parent. Lynda had to work for it every second.

Camryn squeezed Lynda's forearm in support.

"She's my new assistant manager."

A tense moment fell over them. Lynda shuddered under the scrutiny, still not sure what the right decision had been. She'd told herself why she agreed to the job, but with each passing day, she believed it less and less.

Laura was the first to break the silence, her voice wavering as she asked, "How's that working out?"

"It's not quite the nightmare it could be. We haven't gone backward in time ten years, but it's not easy either. I have to justify everything I say to her, and I have to walk boundary lines I never knew existed. She's just as stubborn as she was as a teenager, but she's changed, too. I still think she hates me."

"Has she told you that?" Camryn's voice was nearly a whisper, though Lynda had no idea why.

Shaking her head, Lynda looked at her long-time friend and found the compassion she had been seeking all week. "No, she hasn't. Not yet anyway, but I can't stop waiting for the façade to break and the Wil I knew to reemerge and take over. It's like every time I know I'm going to have to push her, I keep waiting for the other shoe to drop and the rage to emerge."

"But she hasn't done that, right?" Laura pressed.

"No, not yet. In some ways, I think she's grown a lot."

"Do you think she will?" Camryn squeezed her arm before letting go.

"I don't know." Lynda rolled her shoulders and rested in her chair. Just talking about it with someone made everything that much easier. "She's not the same person she was when she was a teenager, nor the last time I saw her. I should have anticipated that."

"Why did you take the position if you knew you'd be working with her?" Camryn smiled at the waiter as their food was set in front of them.

Lynda had been asking herself that same question since she'd found out. She could have gone back to Jessica and told her to find another firm, but she hadn't. She had an answer floating around in her mind as to why, but she wasn't ready to share that, not in a capacity that she wanted it confirmed by either of them. It was purely a selfish reason. She wanted Isla, not Wil, but Wil was the way to Isla. Lynda had been too scared to try and contact Isla for years, but to know if she was ready for it? That would change everything.

"I don't know," she murmured, staring at the plate in front of her. Her appetite had come back a bit since being with them, a good sign for sure.

"I suggest you work on figuring that out." Camryn was always wise with that kind of advice.

Goosebumps raised along Lynda's arms, and she suspected Camryn might have figured out why she'd agreed to work with Wil in the first place. She was thankful, however, that Camryn didn't push the pain point.

"As for the business," Laura started just as Lynda knew she would. "You need to put up some boundaries very quickly as to what kind of behavior you'll allow and what you won't. You also need to make sure that she understands in this new capacity you won't put up with what you did when she was a teenager."

Lynda sucked in a deep breath. She had put up with a lot, more than she had ever shared with them, and Laura was right. Those boundaries had to be in place because she couldn't go through what she had back then. "I think she knows that."

"And you should tell Jessica."

Cold washed through Lynda at that thought. She should have

told her as soon as she'd known, but she'd kept silent on that front, and now she was in over her head on that one. This could cause so many issues for them both, and it would all be her fault for allowing it to even happen. She'd told herself this time would be different, that they could manage to work together without all that baggage. Guilt filled her to the brim.

"I should have said something as soon as I found out."

"You should have." Laura gave her a hard stare. "But now isn't too late."

There could be a time when it was too late, Lynda knew that. Yet, she still didn't relish having that conversation. Open communication was something that she always prided herself on, but she wasn't sure she was ready for this.

"You need to have a plan—"

"I get it, Laura." Her defenses came up in an instant. Slowing herself, Lynda shook her head and frowned, hoping that would make it better because Laura was right. She softly murmured, "Thank you."

"You're welcome." Laura nodded. "For the record, I think everything will work out as it should. You can hold your own against her. You always did."

It was a vote of confidence, but Lynda didn't think Laura was right to have it. She hadn't been there when she'd broken down in tears after Wil had left several times, when she'd dreaded seeing her walk across the street and come to the front door. Laura wasn't one for emotions, so when she'd needed the comfort of a friend, Laura hadn't been her first call.

"I think we'll be fine. It was a bit of a surprise for both of us." Lynda swallowed back the comment. The shock for her had come when she'd seen Wil's file on her desk, not when she'd walked in on the day of the takeover. Burying the discomfort, she focused on the plate of food in front of her.

"How is Wil handling it?" Camryn asked.

"That I don't know. She's far more mature now than she was,

and she honestly hasn't brought anything up other than work and business. But she's been guarded and quite defensive."

Camryn shrugged. "That's a really good sign then."

"It is," Lynda agreed, still unsure if this had been the right step for her. There were a few more open firms she could have gone to, but they were outside of Denver. When they'd bought out Henshaw's entire business, they'd gotten three firms in the greater Denver area. This one was the closest to her home base, and she had seniority which had been why she was given it when she made the request.

"It'll be fine." Laura tried to sound reassuring, but she didn't quite manage it. She was someone who had built up her walls since her divorce, and Lynda and Camryn had been privy to watching her close in on herself. Neither had been thrilled with it, but Lynda had been dealing with Patrick's death at the same time, so she hadn't been focused on her friend's pain, only hers.

2008

Lynda sat at the kitchen table, her heart shattering into a million pieces again. One year—she couldn't believe it had been a year. "And I still miss you like crazy."

Tears brimmed in her eyes, and she did nothing to stop them from falling down her cheeks. Her eyes burned from the amount of crying she had done that day. She hadn't been prepared for it. She had wanted to sail through the anniversary without being affected so she could help the girls, but she hadn't managed it.

Aisling had stayed home from school, too much of a mess to even attempt to walk into the building. Isla had gone, stoic as ever. Lynda admired that in her some days and hated it on others. The house was his. It wasn't hers—it never had been— but she'd agreed to move in there to give the girls as much consistency as possible, and when he died...

She broke again at that thought.

When he died the year before, she couldn't bring herself to

leave. The closet floors still smelled like him. Sometimes, on her worst days, she would crawl in there and curl up in a ball, letting every emotion out she possibly could. She never let Isla or Aisling see her. They didn't need that added weight in their lives. They had lost their father, the only living parent they had, and they were stuck with her, the stepmom they hadn't always wanted.

Dragging in a quick and shattering breath, Lynda stared blankly across the living room to the window into the back yard. It hurt so damn much. Nothing had prepared her for this. She wasn't sure anything could. Her hand shook as she brought her wine glass to her lips. One glass was all she'd allow herself that night. Isla would need her when she broke, and Lynda knew she would. She did every time she tried to hold back her emotions like this.

And Lynda had to be sober enough to handle her. Bitterness swelled in her chest because she couldn't just wallow like she wanted to on days like this. She had to be the responsible one, the parent, the one who stood between devastation and hope.

A blur of motion out the back window caught her attention. Lynda blinked away her tears, wiping them from itchy, swollen eyes with the side of her hand as she tried to make out what it was. Standing, she walked barefoot across the living room and held her breath.

"Wil," she whispered.

Wil, in all her infinite wisdom, stood outside Isla's window. She had to stand on her tippy toes to reach the bottom of the sill, but she managed to tap against the glass lightly. Lynda stayed as still as possible, not wanting Wil alerted to her presence, to the fact she was watching. Her hair was in two long braids down her back, the light hoodie she had on keeping her warm from the chill in the middle of the night.

Wil knocked again, and Lynda heard Isla through the walls moving out of her bed to see what was going on. The window slid open, and she couldn't make out what they whispered to each other. In a matter of seconds, Wil moved to the patio and grabbed one of the plastic chairs they had in the back, setting it against the wall of the house and just under the window to Isla's room.

The pop was unmistakable as they took the screen off, the scuffle as she climbed in. Lynda rubbed her lips together once Wil disappeared from her view. She gave it a few more seconds of silence before turning back to the kitchen and grabbing the phone off the receiver.

Lynda leaned against the wall for a second, gathering her thoughts and clearing her throat so she didn't sound like she had been crying—if that was even possible. She dialed the number she knew by heart.

"Hello?"

"Joyce, sorry to call so late." The rasp of her words sounded foreign in her ears. When had she lost her voice? "It's Lynda."

"What did the girl do now?" Joyce sighed heavily, assuming Lynda was calling to tattle on Wil again.

"Nothing, I promise. I just... I wanted to let you know that she is over here. Snuck in Isla's window, but I promise you, it's okay. I think... I think Isla needs her right now." Her nose burned as tears prickled at her eyes again. She needed someone too, someone who understood what she was going through, and while Joyce had been that, Joyce hadn't lost her husband when he was young or when their children were barely teenagers.

"She snuck in the window?"

"I don't think she wanted me to know she was here, but I'm okay with her staying the night if you are. I don't know what her plans are for going home."

Joyce grumbled. "If you think Isla needs her."

"I do," Lynda confirmed. "She was very closed off today."

"Wilda said as much when she got home from school."

Lynda swallowed hard. Playing the parent to two kids who weren't biologically hers, two kids who she didn't know until they were already in school was harder than she had ever imagined. Being alone with them now scared her every single day. Most days she was pretty sure she couldn't do it. Then she remembered Patrick. The sweet man and husband he had been, the wonderful father who seemed to always know the right thing to do and say with the girls. He had planned for this, and he'd told her she could do it when he'd asked her to raise them if something ever happened to him.

With that confidence in mind, Lynda answered, "I think she needs it."

"Okay. Send her home in the morning for clothes. They're good for each other." Joyce's voice softened, understanding in the words.

"I will. And thank you, Joyce."

Lynda was about to hang up when Joyce's gravelly voice reached her. "You come over here, too, if you need."

The compassion nearly broke her.

"I'm serious. You don't need to do this alone."

Lynda dragged in a shuddering breath, a sob on the cusp of tearing through her. "I know. Thank you."

They hung up, and she was cast into silence. As much as she appreciated the offer, Lynda wouldn't take it. This grief was their own to deal with, and no one else needed to be thrown into the chaos it caused. Lynda grabbed her wine glass and dumped it in the sink before she cleaned it and set it to dry. Her hands still shook. She hadn't been able to stop that all day. She and Aisling had spent hours on the couch, watching random television and sharing memories of Patrick.

Damn it hurts so bad still. It shouldn't hurt this bad, right? A year should be plenty of time to heal from this. Her friends had even hinted about her dating again, so why was she so hung up on him? Why did it feel like the cops had just shown up yesterday to tell her he was gone? With a tight chest, Lynda sauntered toward her bedroom, passing by Isla's on the way. She stopped just outside the door when she heard their voices, this time clearly.

"Your daddy loved you, Isla. He loved us all."

Wil was right. He had loved any child who came into that house, whether he saw them again or not. Patrick was someone who was built for parenthood, unlike her, and she knew there was no way she could live up to a ghost like him. *A saint like him*, she corrected. She'd never wanted to be a parent, and she'd always assumed he would be there. She'd even made a joke about how he couldn't die until the girls were out of the house.

"I miss him," Isla murmured, her voice thick with desperation.

Lynda leaned against the wall, her hand barely keeping her steady as she broke, the final string holding herself together snapping. She melted into the wall, using it to hold herself up.

"We all do. Everyone in this house. He's someone worth being missed. You know what?" They got quiet for a minute before Wil spoke again. "It's okay to be sad and happy at the same time, you know. And it's okay to be mad at him for leaving. He did you dirty on that one."

Hot trails of tears streaked down Lynda's cheeks.

"You can scream and yell at him and be all sorts of mad. And you can be absolutely depressed because you'll never see him again. Because he's going to miss out on the rest of your life. But, Isla, it's not good to keep quiet about it all." The earnestness in Wil's tone made the emotions in Lynda's chest grow heavy as a stone.

Lynda wished any of her friends had told her that. It was the most beautiful thing she had heard in the last year.

"Lynda doesn't miss him," Isla made her point strongly.

"Oh, she does," Wil whispered. "I promise you she does. We just can't see it because no one can. Only Lynda."

Shuddering, Lynda clenched her fists tightly and shook her head. They were both absolutely right, and despite how many times she had tried to get closer to Isla, she wasn't able to break that wall between them. She wasn't capable of it, even Wil understood that. She shouldn't be able to, but she did, and that scared the shit out of Lynda. Breathing heavily, she held her hand up to her mouth to keep from sobbing. She couldn't be the parent they needed—she wasn't equipped for it, and they didn't want her.

Her toes sunk into the carpet as she finally made her way into her bedroom. With the lights off, Lynda stared at the closet in the streams of moonlight. Why did the night have to be so beautiful when it was one so full of pain? Stepping up to the doors, she pulled them open hesitantly, finding all of Patrick's clothes still hung up on his side. She hadn't been able to part with them. Not yet.

With fear in each step, Lynda went into the closet and fell to her knees. She curled up on her side in a tight ball. Taking a deep breath, she closed her eyes and waited for his scent to overwhelm her just like it had the last time she'd done this. But it didn't. She was filled with her own perfume, with the tinge of dust. Her eyes burned as she unraveled. She lost him all over again.

CHAPTER
Five

2023

LYNDA STOOD at the head of the conference table, ready and prepared for the weekly staff meeting. Wil had been competent so far in the short time they'd been working together, but that didn't mean something else wasn't going to happen in the coming week that would set her off. When she'd been younger, Lynda had never managed to figure out what those triggers were.

As the staff filed in, Lynda stayed standing, with her arms wrapped around her belly, and a slight lift to one hip. They all looked at her as though she were the enemy, and she agreed that she was. Anyone coming in from an outside agency or firm would immediately be put into the hostile category. Though, she hadn't fired anyone yet, and she hoped that would ease some of their nerves so far.

Taking a stack of papers, Lynda shifted them from one person to the next until they were passed around the table. "This is the schedule of projects for the upcoming week and who is assigned to what from my understanding. We have a few projects that are coming to an end, and if your name is with an asterisk,

I'll need you to come see me before the end of the day. Next week, we'll have access to the online system Jolie Preston uses, and all of this will be electronic. Training will begin for each of you on how to use it."

Wil stared at her directly, eyes locking together, but her mouth stayed shut and silent.

"I ask that if you have any issues or questions concerning where the firm is going from here or any policy changes that are happening that you come and speak with me directly. My door is open to all of you, and I want you to know what's going on."

She knew what was coming next wasn't going to please everyone. It never did, and changes in policy always worried those who weren't immediately a part of the conversation. Lynda shifted her gaze around the room, touching on each of her staff who was present. It was a small firm, one of the smallest that Jolie Preston had taken over in her time with them, and they totaled less than twenty for the managers.

"We are going to go through some of the standard practices in this company that need changing, including how the chain of command works. This is so communication can increase and improve before we completely run on our own."

They all hardened instantly, glares lobbing her way. Wil glanced at her and then looked at the others, likely judging their reaction. Lynda couldn't tell if she would come to their defense or hers.

"I know these are unnerving times, when you feel lost because you don't know what's going on, but I promise there is a method here. Beginning with the standard operating policies will allow us to build a firm foundation."

"This is ridiculous!"

Lynda missed who had said it, but she tensed, her shoulders hardening in defense. "This is the way this takeover will work. If you don't like it, there's the door and I'm sure you know how to use it."

She was met with silence, and when she risked another look

at Wil, she found her with a hard look on her face, daggers coming from her eyes, her arms crossed, lips pulled tight. She was ready to defend her team, which would be another argument when the rest of the managers were out of the room and it was only the two of them—assuming Wil could hold her tongue that long. Unease filled her as she grasped for the next step.

"I want each of you to report to Wil. Give her the strongest and best update of the day, include the failures and the successes and where you believe improvements can be made. Wil will then report to me. If you think there hasn't been adequate reaction or the issue hasn't been dealt with sufficiently, then I want you to come directly to me. Understood?"

She waited for confirmation from each of them. "Right, any questions?"

When they left to go about the day's work, Wil stayed put, her hands on the table and her face down. "They don't like you."

"They don't have to like me," Lynda answered as she gathered the papers stiffly, her movements rough as discomfort settled in the pit of her stomach. She'd anticipated this, but she hadn't been fully prepared for it either. "They have to listen to me and respect me, like I do them."

Wil snorted slightly, but she didn't say anything, lending to the fact that she had far more control now than she did when she was younger. A change Lynda was quite proud of, though she wouldn't mention it. She didn't need to dredge up the past any more than Wil did.

"How are they going to respect you if they don't know you?"

"This is a small firm. We'll all get to know each other rather quickly, don't you think?" Lynda held the folders of papers in her arm, staring down at Wil. She had been waiting for this to happen, yet each time Wil touched on the anger, she backed away like an expert.

"I think they need some time to adjust."

"Everyone needs time. Unfortunately, not everyone can take the exact amount of time they need. Sometimes we must run to catch up." Lynda raised an eyebrow, hoping Wil wouldn't push her to say more. "We need to talk about Jacob."

"What about him?"

"My office." Lynda walked out, not waiting for Wil to catch up.

When she reached her office, she set the papers on her desk and turned around to lean against the edge of it as she waited for Wil to join her. Wil stormed in, rage lighting her features as she slammed the door. Lynda jumped slightly at the loud bang but managed to keep her composure.

"Are you firing him?" The question was out before Lynda even had a chance to explain.

"No." She crossed her arms and held her ground, waiting for Wil's next outburst.

"Who's getting fired?" Wil's eyes were wild with anger.

Lynda had seen this before, she was used to it from years ago, and she could handle this Wil. She kept her voice calm, making sure that Wil understood she was in control and it would take more than a few angry words thrown at her for her to lose it. "No one is getting fired, not today, anyway."

"Then what the hell are we doing here?"

"Sit down, please." Lynda motioned to the chair in front of her smoothly, still keeping her voice calm.

"Are you going to sit?" The bite in Wil's tone was there, but Lynda detected a weariness in it as well. She would lean into that as much as possible.

Lynda stayed perfectly still, wondering if that was what this was all about. The power in the room and who had it. By remaining standing through the staff meeting and potentially through this one, she was the one in charge. By sitting, they would be on more even footing. Lynda acquiesced and slid into one of the chairs on the other side of her desk and waited for Wil to join her.

She crossed her legs, her shoe falling off her foot slightly now that it was elevated. She kept her back ramrod straight and sat fully in the chair, so she was ready to stand as soon as she needed to. Wil reluctantly lowered herself into the chair only a few feet away, her gaze dropping from Lynda's face down to her legs. When she looked back up, she had that same flushed expression she'd had last week.

Now that they were seated, she waited to see what Wil would do next. She was the one who had the most pull in the firm, but Lynda was in charge. Wil had power, even if she didn't recognize it. At that point, all Lynda had was authority. If they failed to work together, everything would fall back on her, and that would be something she would have to contend with. It would be easier with Wil on her side to complete this takeover. It would take her less time, which meant she could move on to the next one. She had never failed before, but this was supposed to be an easy break after her last takeover in Boulder, a respite that she needed.

"What did Jacob do?"

"Nothing," Lynda answered swiftly, wanting to make sure this wasn't about an issue she had with him but rather one she wanted to prevent. "I want to make sure he is set up for success."

Wil eyed her suspiciously.

"In the last week, I've realized that aside from yourself, no one else has received extensive training. Am I correct in assuming that?"

Wil seemed to take a moment to think before answering, though she was very careful in the words she chose, that was for certain. "Millie handled the training."

"And do you think it was adequate training?" Lynda wasn't going to give her an out. Millie didn't work for Jolie Preston, and she wasn't at the firm anymore, so there would be nothing in it for Wil to defend any longer.

"No," Wil simply answered. "But I didn't train them, either."

That was an interesting development. Lynda pressed her palms onto the arms of the chair, the cold from the wood seeping into her skin and reminding her of the delicate line the two of them walked. "Why not?"

"I wasn't in charge of training."

Lynda pursed her lips, trying to read through the lines of what Wil wasn't saying. She held Wil's gaze and took the plunge. "Because you couldn't be trusted with it or because you don't have the skills to do it?"

Wil blanched. "I have the skills."

Lynda knew she did. She'd seen Wil's resume and work history, and she'd seen Wil interact with everyone in the past week. What she suspected was Wil lacked an ability to keep her temper when frustrated with mundane things, which would not be ideal for training others.

"Then why weren't you given the go-ahead to train?" Lynda sat still, keeping her gaze firmly on Wil until she had an answer.

"As you very well know, I have a short fuse sometimes."

Lynda resisted the urge to smile but barely. "So since you weren't ideal to train, Millie didn't pass on that responsibility to anyone else? Seems like a massive failure on her part as a manager."

"Millie was the best manager." Wil's defense rang true in the room. She may have been a willful child, but she was always loyal to a fault.

Sighing lightly, Lynda relaxed. "You and I both know that no one is perfect, and while you may have learned a lot under Millie's mentoring, she was not the best manager. She had faults of her own. Don't make her faults yours."

Wil held her ground for another few seconds before she relaxed, giving in. Lynda was glad to see it. In the eight years Wil had worked there, she had issues, most had been at the beginning of her tenure, and she suspected Wil had learned to tame her temper throughout those years and was far more capable now than when she'd first been hired.

"Now, about Jacob." Lynda uncrossed and re-crossed her legs, that same look appearing on Wil's face as she leaned back in the chair. She wanted to know more about what was behind that intense gaze, the flush, the embarrassment that seemed to be striking her, but intuitively, Lynda knew she couldn't ask.

"What about Jacob?" Wil clenched her jaw, still tense as ever as she locked their gazes together.

Lynda raised an eyebrow and held that tension firmly. "Don't you think we should train him so he can succeed?"

"It might help."

"Right, so let's do that. He has the knowledge from what I've seen. The accounts he supervises are stellar. But he lacks management drive and tact when it comes to dealing with those under him."

Wil didn't disagree.

"We need to teach him how to be a better manager and leader." Lynda leaned forward and snagged a notebook off her desk along with a pen. She didn't want Wil to leave before they had a plan of action in place to begin training at least the top managers. They needed new systems in place for mentoring.

"Maybe you should take him to this conference instead of me."

Lynda was thrown off by the vehemence in Wil's tone. The conference was an opportunity Wil deserved to have, and she hadn't backed down from that argument when she'd fought for Wil to go prior to the takeover. She had thought about bringing both Wil and Jacob but had largely only fought for Wil.

She had wanted one-on-one time with Wil since she'd known they would have issues to resolve and the past to work through. Jacob would have been an intrusion into that. Wil was also her second and needed to understand quickly how Lynda worked so they could best keep the team together. She had almost canceled the entire thing herself and stayed to get actual work done. As it were, they would be working while they were in Seattle anyway.

"I think you deserve to go to the conference, since you've never been to one in the history of your tenure here."

"No one has," Wil snapped.

"A problem we must rectify. Jolie Preston is all about endeavoring to provide learning opportunities for its employees. Every one of us."

Wil's lips parted as if she was about to speak, but she held back. Something else that was different. She was thinking before answering, and Lynda had never seen her do that before. Not in their entire history of knowing each other. The change was startling in a lot of ways, and she struggled to understand that this was the same person as before. It would make their working together much easier, if only they could get past whatever barrier was between them that Lynda hadn't been able to name yet.

"I know I sound like I've drunk the water, but I've worked for Jolie Preston almost my entire career, and this company isn't like any other firm out there. I promise you they care about their employees in ways others don't."

"Yeah, sure, whatever." Wil rolled her eyes and crossed her arms, sliding down into her chair.

Lynda resisted the urge to comment on Wil's petulant behavior. She settled the notepad back on the desk. "I know this conference is soon, but it only happens once a year, and timing isn't ideal."

"It's next week."

"I understand, and Jacob will be in charge here for the week while we're both gone, along with the assistance of another branch manager. Do you think he can handle it?" Lynda wanted to know Wil's honest opinion, but she wasn't sure she was going to get it. Wil had protected every one of the employees so far, but this would very much be throwing Jacob to the wild.

"He'll be able to reach us if he needs."

"He can," Lynda agreed. "Do you think he will?"

"Yes. Jacob has never been shy about asking for help."

That was one of the things Lynda always looked for in someone that she wanted to promote up into manager or further along the managerial ranks. If an individual was willing to ask for help, or ask questions when they didn't understand something, then they showed the promise of being able to learn and being teachable.

"Then let's make sure he can succeed while we're gone, and let's make sure he can succeed in the future. I want a full plan for bringing him up to speed and how training will trickle down from there."

Wil seemed to seriously contemplate that. "Mr. Henshaw and Millie never left me fully in charge when she was gone."

"Never?" That surprised her. That was exactly the purpose of an assistant and chain of command. If Lynda was gone, she had to be able to trust that Wil was able to take over, but if neither of them had trusted it was either because Wil couldn't handle the situation or because they were both micromanagers who had an ego.

"No. I never had any issues that I couldn't handle while Millie was gone, but Mr. Henshaw frequented during those weeks."

"Why?" Lynda's question was direct, but she wanted an answer. Knowing the nuances of what the firm was like before she took over would help her iron out the issues for the future.

Wil again took her time answering, as if searching for the perfect words that would keep her out of trouble and not taint the relationships that she had relied on for so many years. Lynda understood the complexities that came with these types of conversations.

When she didn't answer, Lynda tried again. "Is it because of your temper?"

"No," Wil ground out, firm in answer.

"Then why?"

"Millie is a bit of a control freak, and Mr. Henshaw adores her, so anything she said went. She knew that if I was left totally in charge then she wouldn't have her fingers in anything happening that week because I believe a vacation is vacation and she shouldn't work during PTO. She didn't like that, so she made sure she still knew what was happening while she was gone."

"Ah." Lynda had seen many managers like that through the years. In fact, she was known to be one of those. Then again, she normally worked in conditions where she was taking over another firm and working with new people who were new to the company. It would be entirely different, and had been in the past, when she was working with the same employees for years. Then they had a respectful understanding of each other and how the others worked.

"Let's start with making sure Jacob understands the facets of your position and mine. He doesn't need to know every little detail, but understanding what we do will tell him exactly when he needs to ask for help."

"That's it?" Wil loudly asked, that same anger Lynda had seen before underlying her tone.

"Yes. I don't see an issue with your anger, and I'm certainly not Millie. Please form a plan for bringing Jacob up to speed and send it over to me."

"We're really not going to talk about it?"

"Talk about what?" Lynda had been ready to get back to business and end the conversation. She had gotten what she wanted out of it, not only a confession from Wil about her anger issues, but also a plan that would be put into place shortly to deal with the training issues.

"Why am I going to this conference?"

Lynda parted her lips to say something but stopped herself. She was tired of regretting the past, her actions and Wil's, and she just wanted to move forward. She also wanted to prove she wasn't the monster Wil thought she was. "As a manager, you need to continue educating yourself on how to be a better leader."

"And you do this regularly?"

"I attend this particular conference every year I can." Lynda lifted her toes, making her shoe wobble on her foot. Wil's gaze dropped to her foot, swallowing hard, before she slowly looked up every inch of Lynda's body. This time there wasn't a flush in

Wil's cheeks but a purposeful stare that Lynda wanted to know everything about. The conversation had eased up from the tension, and she felt lighter about it already. Still, she knew she had a phone call coming up that she had to make that she was less than thrilled about.

"Jacob can go instead of me."

"He's not the assistant manager." To her it was a simple fact of who would attend. "I wish there was more time between the buy-out and the conference, but it only occurs once a year. The timing isn't ideal, but I promise you that it'll be worth it."

"It's not that," Wil muttered.

Lynda furrowed her brow in confusion. "Then what is it?"

"Nothing. It's fine. I'll talk to Jacob this afternoon and send you that plan."

"Before the end of the work day, please." Lynda liked the way Wil skirted around the topic she wanted to avoid. They were both experts at that it seemed.

"Good. Thanks." Wil stood up and left the room far less angry than when she'd entered it.

Lynda sat for a moment longer before standing and moving around her desk to sit in her chair properly. She blew out a breath before she checked the time. She needed to call Jessica even if she didn't want to. And she needed to do exactly what Laura had advised her. It was the right call to make.

With the phone pressed to her ear, Lynda waited for Jessica to answer. She rarely didn't, and only when she was in an important meeting that sucked up all her time. It was on what had to be the last ring when Jessica finally answered.

"Hold on a minute, Lynda."

Before she could even answer, Jessica put her on hold. Her stomach tensed as she waited for the difficult conversation. She watched her employees walk by the door to her office, not talking to her. She heard the gossip that was going around about her. She usually did, but it had been worse this time around. Although none of it seemed to come from Wil herself, which was a surprise. Wil had special information on her and could easily ruin any relationship she was attempting to build. Still, Wil had remained entirely professional throughout the entire last week. How long that would last was anyone's guess.

"Lynda, what can I help you with?"

"I wanted to give you the update on the first week."

"And?"

This is what she loved about Jessica—straight to the point. It was a skill they both had. "It's going as well as expected. There's resistance, and lack of communication. I think that's the real crux of the issues here. No one told them the company sold until we arrived."

"Are you serious?" Jessica's voice rose in surprise.

"I found out a few hours into being here. It'll make this transition more difficult in some ways, but a week in is still the honeymoon period."

"It is. I have faith in you, Lynda."

Lynda snagged her pen off the desk, flitting it between her fingers before she dropped it and steeled herself for the next part of the conversation they needed to have and the part Jessica wouldn't be expecting. "There's one other thing I need to talk to you about."

"What is it?" Jessica tapped away at a keyboard, the echo of it through the phone line normal. They always multitasked when they talked like this.

"The assistant manager, Wilda Powell, is an old friend of my stepdaughter's."

Jessica paused and the typing on the keyboard stopped. "Of Aisling's? Why didn't you tell me?"

"No." This was the part Lynda was going to struggle with. She barely talked about Isla. It hurt too much to mention her most days, and since there was no current relationship between them, she didn't talk about her to people who didn't know her when she was a child. Jessica was new enough to Jolie Preston that she hadn't been around then. "My other stepdaughter, Isla."

"I didn't realize you had two."

"We're estranged. Wil and Isla were best friends growing up. Still are from my understanding." Lynda played with the pen again, needing something to distract her hands so she could get this out. "I only share this because when Wil was a teenager and throughout college, her relationship with me was quite antagonistic. Since there is defined history between us, I thought you should be aware of the situation."

"Is it still antagonistic?"

"To an extent, yes, but I'm sure that has to do with who I was to her." Lynda resisted the urge to delve in deeper or potentially cause more issues between her and the firm in the long run. Had Lynda been anyone else, she was sure Wil would be acting differently. She wasn't the same person she was eleven years ago, and Lynda supposed she wasn't either. She was just finding her footing with parenting, only for it to be in time for Isla to move out and go to college. "I think we may have found our way over that hurdle, but a week is still a week, and I suspect I'll know more after the conference."

Lynda hoped she did learn a few things while they were in Seattle. If anything, she wanted to come away with a better understanding of who Wil had become compared to who she was.

"Right, you leave Monday, don't you?"

"Yes, in the evening." Lynda was tempted to check the time just to be sure, but Jessica didn't need to know that. "An entire week with the two of us secluded will give me the time to learn if we've worked through those issues."

"For the record, I hope you have. We don't need any more complaints made about you."

"I understand." Lynda balked slightly at the thought. She had complaints from each place she worked at, but it was expected in the type of jobs she took. Still, one more ethical inquiry into her conduct and she wasn't sure she would have a job anymore. Not to mention, finding another position in investment management with that kind of record would be impossible.

"Lynda, I'm serious. If this merger fails to go through and we have to shut down that firm, we'll be out all the money we paid for it. That'll be on you, not me."

Lynda cringed. This was supposed to be an easy takeover, not one that caused issues. Her past relationship with Wil was causing more problems than she had anticipated.

"This was supposed to be a safe bet for you, some place you could go to work and not get into trouble, and now you're telling me this? Lynda, you're smarter than that."

"I know." Shame filled her. She should have known better, and like Laura had told her, she should have told Jessica about her background with Wil as soon as she'd found out.

"I expect better from you."

"Give us the conference week to figure this out," Lynda pleaded. "Since she had no idea about the buy-out, she's been thrown for more than one loop with me being here."

Jessica held the silence, and Lynda's stomach twisted as she waited for an answer, for some kind of acceptance of the plan she had put into place without Jessica knowing it from the start. She had made so many mistakes already.

"You get the week to figure this out, and if anything happens on that trip that shouldn't, it's your job, Lynda. I'm not going to protect you over this one."

"I understand." Lynda dropped the pen again and closed her eyes, the full revelation of what she'd done sitting on her shoulders.

Jessica sighed. "You could have handled this so much better."

"It'll be fine. I promise. Nothing questionable will happen."

"It better not." Jessica groaned, but Lynda sensed the break in the conversation and chastisement. "Who do you have coming in while you're gone?"

"Devon."

"Well, at least he doesn't have any ethical issues to be concerned about."

Lynda's chest tightened with the harsh criticism.

"Keep me updated. You have the week to resolve this."

"Okay."

"I'm serious, Lynda. Fix it." Jessica hung up without another word. Lynda rubbed circles into her temple and closed her eyes as she took a deep breath to steady herself. That hadn't been as bad as she expected.

CHAPTER

Six

WIL BUMBLED her way through the aisle in the center of the airplane, trying not to hit anyone with her rollaboard. Lynda walked ahead, her chin raised as she looked for their seats. She pulled her suitcase behind her with her purse clasped tightly against her side and over her shoulder. Wil tottered slightly when her toe caught on her heel and she nearly fell over.

"Fuck," she muttered under her breath as she caught herself.

Her hands still shook. Even the beer she had drank while they waited on their flight hadn't helped with that. Clenching her jaw, Wil righted herself and squared her shoulders. The bustle on the plane was unbelievable and nothing like she had ever seen before. She focused on the sway of Lynda's hips from side to side as she walked in her heels.

If she could keep her sights on Lynda, then she wouldn't get lost. And if Lynda stayed in front of her, she wouldn't see if Wil fell flat on her face. Snorting, Wil shook her head—that was a stupid idea. All of it was a stupid idea because staring at Lynda's ass only conjured other images she didn't want in her mind. That had been half the point of the alcohol to begin with.

"Here we are." Lynda turned around sharply, and Wil stumbled into her suitcase.

She resisted the urge to curse again, thankfully. It took some maneuvering, but Wil managed to get both suitcases in the overhead compartment and then sat next to Lynda. Wil pressed her shoulder against the window, trying to put as much space as possible between them. Lynda crossed her legs, that damnable skirt riding up again and doing stupidly silly things to Wil's stomach. Booze was a bad idea. She should have rethought that one.

Looking away from Lynda, she glanced out into the dark sky outside. Lights from the building and the vehicles moving all around them lit up the tarmac. Wil's stomach roiled, this time with nausea as her nerves hit full force. She couldn't do this. She should have told Lynda she had never been on a plane before.

Immediately, Will closed the shade, not wanting to see their assent into the air and panic even more than she already was. Fear settled into her stomach as the flight attendants came through and checked everything. She had no idea what to expect other than what she'd seen in movies, and this was nothing like that so far.

Listening intently to the directions in case there was an emergency, Wil faltered. She should get off the plane. She should tell Lynda she couldn't do this, get off, go home, and seriously start looking for another job since she couldn't do this one anymore. But she also couldn't get out. She couldn't crawl across Lynda's lap along with the other stranger's lap and claw her way to the front before they shut the door.

Wil's ears popped. *Damnit, now it's really too late.*

She couldn't let Lynda know how wasted she was or how weak she was or how damn afraid she was. Wil's thoughts skittered through her brain a mile a minute as she tried to grasp onto one single thread to just make herself stop the spiral. Her phone dinged her in pocket, and Wil had to shuffle to get it. The text was from Isla.

She was just about to open it, when she realized Lynda had caught sight of Isla's name on the screen. Turning her phone slightly, Wil opened the message and read it quickly. She quickly wrote back that she would need Isla to stay up late or get up early so she could calm down after this flight. Before she could get an answer, a throat clearing caught her attention.

"Phones need to be off."

Wil clutched the phone in her hand as she stared up at the flight attendant. "Yeah, that's just what I was doing."

She didn't wait again as she put her phone in airplane mode and shoved it into her pocket. The belt pressing against her bladder did nothing to help her. She should have gone pee first, but instead, she was stuck against the window with no way out and the flight attendants had told her multiple times already she couldn't move. With the look the last one had given her, she wasn't going to try them any time soon.

Bouncing her toes on the floor, her hand on her knee, Wil closed her eyes and tried to take deep breaths without alerting Lynda to the fact she was doing it. She couldn't let her know what was going on—she had to keep up the front that she had her shit together. Wil worried her fingers together, looking around with her eyes wide open. Lynda just sat there with a book on her iPad as if nothing was amiss or odd or new. Which it probably wasn't. Wil scolded herself for that thought. Lynda had likely traveled by plane so many times in her life that this was nothing. It also probably never occurred to her that Wil hadn't done this before.

Wil tensed her legs, then had to work hard to relax them. As soon as she managed that, they were tense again. The plane jerked back as they moved, and Wil grabbed the hand rest, her knuckles whitening as she practically strangled the thing. She happened to catch Lynda's glance toward her then, first at her hand, then slowly trailing up her arm to her eyes.

She wanted to blink and look away, but she couldn't do it. Lynda held her gaze, those caramel eyes searching for something deep in her soul. Her lips remained thin, calm, her chest a steady rhythm. It took Wil a moment to realize that her own breathing was evening out. Lynda parted her lips to say something, but Wil shook her head.

"Don't," Wil whispered, embarrassment sweeping into her chest and causing tears to sting in her eyes. "Don't say anything."

Listening, thank the fucking Lord, Lynda leaned back into her seat, put her iPad in her lap, and slid her hand on top of Wil's, curling her fingers. Her hand was so warm. Wil had expected it to be cold for some reason, but the connection gave her something else to think about, something nice instead of all the fear and worry ricocheting through her brain.

They were finally moving forward instead of backward, and Wil's heart moved out of her throat and back into her chest where it belonged. A clammy sweat came over her, but she wasn't sure she was willing to risk a move to turn the air on. Wil counted to ten before she relaxed her hand and flipped her palm upward and laced their fingers together. That touch rooted her as the plane reached the runway.

The physical connection steadied her, centered her, calmed her when they sped up, the force making her shoulders hit the back of the chair. Wil clenched her eyes shut tight, wishing she could be like Lynda, that she could never experience this again, that she could be cool, calm, collected. The perfect manager. The perfect woman.

When they evened out, Lynda squeezed her hand lightly and leaned in. Her voice was so quiet that Wil barely managed to hear her over the roar of the engine, but her breath was hot against Wil's ears. "It should be smooth flying from here on out."

"Thanks," Wil managed to breathe out the word.

Lynda waited until Wil relaxed to open up her iPad again with her book, balancing it precariously on one knee while she still gripped onto Wil's hand. Wil eased into the plane ride as soon as they seemed to level out. She took long, slow breaths until she felt every muscle relax one by one. She wasn't sure how much time had passed, but she managed to pry her hand from Lynda's so they were no longer tangled together. Instantly, she missed the contact, but she couldn't let Lynda think she was so scared she wouldn't be able to fly home.

Now that she had time to think about her body, Wil cringed. Her stomach lurched from the beer she drank not settling, and her bladder once again yelled, reminding her she needed to relieve herself. She still didn't want to climb over both of them—especially Lynda.

Lynda leaned in, a gentle touch to Wil's forearm that sent shivers of a different kind through her. Lynda tilted her head slightly until Wil made eye contact, searching for something that she apparently found.

"You could have told me you were a nervous flier." Lynda raised an eyebrow as if expecting an answer to a question she didn't ask.

Wil took a moment before she confessed. "I didn't know."

"What do you mean?"

Wil closed her eyes, that same embarrassment as before washing over her. "I've never flown."

She managed to look up into Lynda's face, nonplussed by the surprise reflecting in Lynda's gaze. She'd expected that. Everyone assumed that normal people of her age had flown and been places, but unless it was within a few hours of Denver, Wil had never been there.

"I didn't know that."

"You wouldn't." That venom was back, and Wil once again wished she could control it where it concerned Lynda. She took two steadying breaths before trying to speak again, glad that this time she didn't let her anger win out. "Your family went on annual trips."

"And you didn't," Lynda surmised, staring directly ahead at the small screen on the back of the seat in front of her. "Doesn't seem to have made too much of a difference, Wilda. We've both ended up in the same place in the end."

The lump in her throat grew bigger. Lynda and she may have ended up in management in investing, but Wil would never be

Lynda. She would never master the aloof leader that Jolie Preston wanted from her, and even though they were sending her to this conference, she would never be what they wanted. She knew that. Deep in her soul, she knew she'd never measure up, no matter how much she wanted to.

They hadn't ended up at the same place in the end. Wil had just managed to fool everyone into thinking she belonged there.

Wil said nothing, and after another minute, Lynda picked up her iPad and began reading again. Wil glanced over several times to see what it was, but her nerves made it too hard to be able to focus. She was glad Lynda hadn't chosen to do work while flying because she wouldn't have managed to get anything done.

With a bolstering breath, Wil undid the buckle on her belt. "Do you mind?"

Lynda's chin lifted up, confusion in her gaze until she realized Wil was half-standing in the seat. "Oh."

The shuffle of them from the seat to the aisle was annoying, but Wil didn't have another choice. As soon as she reached the aisle, she looked down at the end of the airplane and to the bathroom. She walked as quickly as she could until she reached it and locked herself inside. After taking her much needed piss and washing her hands, she closed her hands and leaned against the cold metal.

"Deep breaths, Wil. Deep breaths."

Grandma had used to repeat that to her when her anger got the best of her, and while she wasn't ticked off at the moment, she was nervous as hell. She clenched her eyes tightly as she found her balance now that the alcohol seemed to be slowly dissipating from her blood stream. She would need to get some water as soon as possible, and hopefully she wouldn't have to get up again during their flight.

One more time through the mantra and Wil straightened her shoulders. She bent over the sink and splashed cold water onto her face, the droplets hitting her tongue and cooling her embarrassment. She should be better than this by now. They had managed to make it two weeks without fucking up, but this week would put Wil's patience to the test.

"Damnit," Wil muttered. She had to go back there, slide back into her seat while disturbing the entire row, and somehow make it through the rest of the flight with a buzz that was clouding her ability to hold her tongue.

Unprepared, Wil stepped out of the lavatory and made her way back to her seat. As soon as she was situated, she buckled herself in like the flight attendant had told her to. Lynda shot her a curious glance, but Wil ignored it and folded her hands in her lap.

Taking a page from Lynda, Wil drew in on herself. She talked to herself repeatedly about maintaining her persona, the one that she wanted to have. Wil had been so impressed with her until Patrick died. Then it had been nothing but cold from her when the girls had needed everything else. She had changed in a flash, and Wil had been left to pick up the pieces that were Isla.

Yet, this woman who sat next to her was so different than *that* Lynda. This woman was her boss, but she also had been kind to her. Swallowing the lump in her throat, Wil centered herself again. This Lynda knew when to help and when to back off, and she'd listened to what Wil had needed in the moment.

Wil's heart raced at the thought that they were two different people now with pasts that had collided and futures that were unknown. Neither knew who they were no matter how much they assumed they did. She needed to talk it out with Isla if she could. Keeping her eyes closed, Wil ignored the woman next to her as best as she could. Finally she drifted off to sleep.

"Hello?" Isla's sleepy voice reached her ears.

Wil's nerves were frayed. "I'm never flying in a tin can again."

Isla chuckled. Wil paced her hotel room, having finally

gotten to it and being unable to get rid of her nerves. Landing hadn't been any better than taking off, and she could feel the pity leaching off Lynda in droves.

"I'm serious."

"You have to fly to get home."

"I'll fucking drive. I'll rent a damn car, and I'll drive it back to Denver."

"You won't, but you can think that for now." A rustling sound echoed through the line, and Wil knew she'd caught Isla asleep and she was likely lying in her bed. Isla was an hour ahead of them, and she winced, thinking that she'd woken her up when she had to get up in a few hours anyway.

"I'm sorry about calling so late."

"Don't be. You texted. I knew you'd call when you got there."

Wil breathed out a sigh and flopped onto the bed, pushing her shoes off her with her toes. "I don't know how people do this."

"Did you puke?"

"No." Though the thought had occurred to her. She covered her eyes as she laid fully on the bed, still in her dress clothes from work that day. "What was I thinking agreeing to this?"

"To a conference about leadership? Probably that you'll learn something useful."

"Not that." Wil frowned, turning to stare out the window at the city lights outside. Her shoulders relaxed in a way that she knew would happen once she was talking to Isla. "I mean being here for a whole week with *Lynda*. You know I don't exactly make friends easily, so she's the only one I know, and I don't really want to be in her vicinity longer than necessary."

Silence reverberated through the line, and if Wil didn't know better, she would have thought Isla had gone back to sleep. But she did know better. Taking a deep breath, she waited for the next step in the conversation, for Isla to tell her to shut up and suck it up, for the tension that would no doubt be present because they were talking about her dreaded stepmom.

"I think you need to put yourself out there and make some connections. You said you were looking for a new job, maybe someone there works in finance and you can apply with them."

Wil raised her eyebrows in surprise. She hadn't honestly thought about that. She'd been so concerned with being stuck with Lynda for days on end that it hadn't occurred to her. "Not a bad idea."

"As for Lynda, you're going to have to do what you never managed when we were in high school."

"What's that?" Wil cringed, already feeling as though she knew what was coming.

Isla laughed a little, the sound of her rolling and changing position again on the bed loud through the phone. "You're going to have to shut up and hold your damn tongue."

Wil snorted. "Fuck, I tried to do that every time I talked to her back then, and I just couldn't make myself."

"I know," Isla cooed on a yawn.

Wil wrinkled her nose. "I should let you get to sleep."

"Yeah, you should. But you know what?"

"What?"

"You can always take a page from my book if you want to break that tension and not be an asshole to her any longer."

"Which is what?" Wil rubbed her forehead just above her eyebrows, the exhaustion from her nerves playing havoc for hours finally settling in.

"Pull a prank."

"Fuck no. She'll kill me, and I very much value my life." Though the thought of Lynda bending her over her knee and spanking her was a fantasy she'd had before. Clenching her jaw, Wil shook her head. She couldn't have those thoughts, not ever again.

"To be fair, Wil, there were plenty of times she could have skinned your hide growing up and she didn't."

"Well, she's more moralistic than I am."

"Yeah, had nothing to do with the fact she'd have to get dirty to do it." Isla laughed again.

They settled into a calm quiet, something that helped ease all those nerves Wil still had lingering in her bones. "I wish you'd been on that flight with me."

"Me, too." Isla yawned again, this time long and hard. "I need to get some sleep, sis."

"I know you do. I'm going to shower the plane grime off me and crash myself."

"You better tell me every detail if you pull a prank on her."

"You know that's not happening. I don't even know why you're thinking about it." Wil sat back up and started to undo the buttons on her blazer and vest. "Like I said, I value my life."

"As you should. Text me tomorrow."

"It is tomorrow."

"Don't be an ass to the only person who loves you."

Wil's heart clenched hard at that because Isla was right. It had been a running joke of theirs for years, and each time it stung. She'd never said anything about it, though, because the truth of the words was so strong. No one loved her except Isla. Grandma had, but she was long gone. No one else had ever stood by her.

"Love you, too," Wil answered, choking back on the emotion threatening to burst.

"Talk soon." Isla hung up.

Wil took a moment before she finished stripping and walked naked to the bathroom. A good hot shower would relax her enough that she might be able to get some sleep. Maybe. If she could stop thinking about being spanked by the woman in the room next to her.

CHAPTER

Seven

THEY HAD ARRIVED LATE ENOUGH into the night, well after midnight, but they'd gotten to the downtown hotel in time for Lynda to fall into her bed and collapse from exhaustion. Being on point for that length of time was hard, and she craved the quiet so she could reset. Unfortunately, the alarm on her phone came far too early, and she needed to get up and dressed for the first day of the conference.

Lynda kept her ears tuned to the room next door, wondering if Wil was awake or not. She walked around her room in nothing other than a silk robe she'd brought, dealing with her hair and her makeup as she went. The coffee had been strong enough, but she was going to need multiple cups throughout the day to keep going until she could catch up on some rest that night.

Checking her watch after getting dressed, Lynda pressed her lips together hard. She had two minutes before she needed to be downstairs to meet with Wil to go through some of the portfolios the investors had put together as samples. They'd brought too much work with them, she knew, but it was impossible to get away for an entire week so close to the takeover. It would, however, force her and Wil to figure out how to work together, and that was a chance she was willing to take.

The knock on her door startled her. It wasn't the door in the hall but rather the adjoining door. Lynda's heart thundered as she slipped into her black stilettos and smoothed down her skirt. She opened the door, finding Wil standing on the other side with a Starbucks cup in hand and a curious look on her face.

"Your...uh...shirt."

Lynda cocked her head to the side, keeping her cool, until she glanced down and found her blouse unbuttoned halfway. She'd been right in the middle of that when Wil had knocked. Trying not to get flustered, she didn't even reach to fix it, staring back at Wil with a determined look.

"Are you ready?" Lynda swallowed down her embarrassment.

"Yes," Wil replied. "Are you?"

"In a minute." Lynda stepped into her room, leaving the door open so Wil could come inside. She reached up then and slid more buttons in place, hiding the beige bra.

When Lynda looked back to meet Wil's gaze, she was surprised to find Wil's eyes not on her face but on her chest, on her hands as they pushed the button through the fabric, her cheeks flushing, and her lips parted. Lynda had seen that look so many times in her life, and yet, she never expected to see it from Wil.

She had no idea how to snap Wil out of it without also embarrassing her or pointing out what she was doing, because she was pretty sure Wil was so lost in thought that she was completely unaware. Lynda finished buttoning her blouse, needing the material to cover her skin before they began this conversation. The awkward tension grew in Lynda's stomach until she had no choice but to say something about it.

"Do you have the files?"

Wil blinked harshly, her gaze immediately moving to Lynda's eyes. She cleared her throat. "Oh, yeah."

"Good, then we can work over breakfast." Lynda grabbed her jacket and put it on, doing up the sash that sat in the middle of her belly. Again, Wil's eyes were locked on her fingers, that same lustful expression. Lynda paused, this time lost in what to say again.

She'd had people give her those looks before, but this time was different. This was Wil, not only her subordinate, but a kid she'd known nearly her entire life. She tried to find the discomfort she knew she should be feeling, but she couldn't. She wanted nothing more than to hold this moment of tension and see where it led. Her heart raced as she watched Wil's rapt attention. Lynda moved her hands to her sides and waited as Wil dragged her gaze up her body and their eyes met. Her stomach fluttered, and breathing was harder than it should be.

Lynda's fingers tingled, needing something to do to distract herself. Because if she didn't, she had no idea what was going to happen. Her lips parted, and she shifted to take a step backward, breaking the moment.

"Breakfast?"

"Yeah." Wil snapped out of it and walked toward the main door to Lynda's room. Lynda grabbed her purse and slung it over her shoulder as she followed Wil out of the room.

Wil had chosen a nice pantsuit to wear that day, the lines of her body accentuated by the pinstripe material of her pants. It was a good choice for her. Lynda wanted to comment on it, but she bit her tongue instead, deciding that talking about her employee's clothing choices would be an ethical gray area. She had to avoid those at all costs, and this morning was already too many of those moments wrapped up in one. If Jessica found out about anything that had happened in the last fifteen minutes, her career would end.

They were silent as they stepped into the elevator and took it down to the main floor. They walked to a small restaurant and were seated immediately. Lynda ordered a coffee, and Wil stared at the one she still held in her hands oddly before setting it on the table. Before Lynda could ask, Wil had the files and was spreading them out so they could look through them.

"I have the report from Jacob here," Wil handed the top sheet over.

Lynda took it, more curious than ever what was going through Wil's mind at that moment, and the entire morning. Something about her seemed off in ways it hadn't before. Lynda ran her fingers along the mug as soon as the waiter filled it with coffee and watched Wil as closely as she listened to what she was saying.

"And here is the report from the others."

Lynda took each set of files and laid them in front of her, skimming through them. Wil had done well in preparing their morning meeting time. She'd rather be spending the morning at the conference, but they did need to get through this. If she could train Wil to take over her position when she left, then she likely would want to train Jacob to be second to Wil.

"You've done a lot of work preparing for this, thank you." Lynda flicked her gaze up to meet Wil's over the sheets of paper, but Wil shook her head.

"No, ma'am, simply doing my job."

Lynda shuddered, keeping her gaze on Wil as she watched the walls that had been gone that morning move right back into place. "This is more than your job."

"It's not," Wil countered.

Lynda wasn't going to fight her on it. She picked up her coffee, took a sip, and focused solely on the work in front of them for that morning.

~

The first day of the conference had been good, but Lynda was distracted. She hadn't even managed to pay attention during the anger management lecture she'd sat in on. Wil hadn't either, from what she could tell. They'd resorted to sliding a paper full of notes back and forth between each other at least fifteen minutes in.

Hours later, she paced her room. They'd done dinner together, with work floating between them, and when she'd told Wil goodnight and headed into her room, she hadn't expected the ache of loneliness in her chest to hit her. She rubbed at the raw feeling and closed her eyes, trying to let it sink in, but it was so overwhelming she had to stop.

Straightening her back, Lynda glanced out the window to downtown Seattle, wishing she was out there and enjoying the time with other conference goers, but at the same time, she knew she would make for piss poor company. Dragging in a ragged breath, she wondered not for the first time what Isla was doing in the last few years since they had spoken. Aisling kept her updated to an extent, but there was no detail in it.

She was so far removed from both her stepchildren's lives. Aisling let her in a little more, but even then, they only talked every few months. Her own family had all but abandoned her when she'd married Patrick. They'd told her she was insane for marrying an older man who already had children, that she would live to regret it, and in some ways, she did. She'd lost him far too soon.

Walking to the bathroom and back to the window, Lynda sighed. She needed to do something to burn off the energy. As she paced again, she stopped in front of the adjoining door between the two rooms. Wil had said she was going to be in her room all night. Closing her hand into a fist, Lynda hovered it over the door and knocked before she realized she needed to have a damn excuse for asking Wil to join her.

The door opened before she could think of a reason why she may have accidentally knocked in the first place. Wil looked up at her with those dark eyes full of curiosity, and dare she say, a fleeting moment of concern flashing through them. Lynda's voice caught in her throat at the beautiful presence of this woman in front of her. She had no idea what to say.

"Did you need something?" Wil asked, a hint of frustration in her voice.

"Oh...um...yes. I'd like to go over the Johannes Press file."

"We did that at lunch."

Right, they had. Lynda had forgotten in her haste and impulse. She moved to stare out the window, hoping that Wil wouldn't catch the tears threatening to flood her eyes. She blinked them back and focused on Wil again. "I'd like to go through it again."

"Sure." Wil huffed, obviously frustrated now. She stepped away from the door, presumably to grab paperwork.

Lynda moved to the small desk in her room and cleared a space for them to get work done. She pulled over the footstool to the chair and sat down in the office chair herself. She waited patiently for Wil to arrive. She didn't care what they worked on, but she needed someone else there to keep her from her own fears and problems.

Wil settled her laptop onto the desk and pulled up the information. "I think it's perfect. We don't need to change it."

Lynda narrowed her gaze at it. Wil clucked her tongue and grabbed the reading glasses sitting on top of the nightstand, handing them over. She didn't sit on the footstool and instead leaned over Lynda's shoulder to eye the computer in question.

"You can go over it a million times, but there's always going to be someone who isn't happy." Wil's breath rushed over the back of Lynda's neck, sending shivers through her body. Lynda realized belatedly that she was in her robe and not dressed for working with her lower manager. She was making more of a mess of this by the minute.

"I know," Lynda whispered.

"Why did you really call me over here? Because I don't think claiming you want me to work while sitting like royalty in your robe is going to go over well with HR."

Lynda sucked on her tongue as Wil pointed out the obvious. Wil was always so damn good at finding that one thing that worried her. Lifting her chin, she raised her gaze to Wil's eyes and was glad to find Wil looked directly back at her and not at her body. She knew what she wanted to say, but at the same time, she couldn't quite make herself confess the emotions roiling around in her belly that she didn't want to admit to.

"I can just leave—"

"Please, don't," Lynda murmured.

Wil didn't move, still leaning over the back of the chair and looking down into Lynda's eyes. Lynda stayed put, trying to find a way out of the intensely intimate moment, a time when she was worried she'd confess everything Wil never wanted to hear.

"When's the last time you talked to Isla?" Lynda grasped for the one safe conversation they always had. She knew Wil would do nothing to hurt Isla, and she could use the distraction.

"That's a bit of a personal question for a work-related conversation, isn't it, Mrs. Walsh?"

Lynda swallowed the lump in her throat and pushed beyond Wil's comment. This had been part of her intrigue into working with Wil, and it was high time they get to that. It was the main sticking point for the loneliness she was struggling with. Being so near Wil had brought up the broken promise to Patrick, the harm she had caused the girls by inevitably failing them as their sole remaining parent. Why had she been the one left alive? Lynda stepped out of her own pain for one brief moment, hoping to share it with someone who would absolutely understand. "I haven't talked to her in years."

"Five years. Since March twenty-first," Wil supplied. "I do actually talk to her."

"Right." Lynda shifted then, putting some space between them. She stayed in her chair and faced Wil full on. She knew why Wil was angry with her for that. Wil had never hidden her reasons for being protective, but Lynda had always suspected there was something else behind it. They had made it this far, and Lynda wanted to take it one step further. "Would you stay for a drink?"

Wil narrowed her gaze as if judging her, and Lynda supposed she was. Everything had been professional between them, and she was changing the parameters—she was outright walking across that line she'd told Jessica she wouldn't. "Are you buying?"

"Yes." Lynda let out a light laugh at the word, the tension in her chest snapping.

"Then yeah." Wil plopped onto the bed instead of the lounge chair.

Lynda almost protested it, but instead, she rang room service and ordered them wine and beer respectively. As she waited for it to arrive, she stared Wil down as if the answers would suddenly come to her, but she wasn't sure how to begin any conversation.

"Are you going to talk to me or stare at me?" Wil raised her eyebrows, her tone harsh, but Lynda suspected there was more teasing in it than anything. Her tone was so different than the vengeful one Lynda had gotten used to.

"Both, I suppose," Lynda mumbled, not sure why she was answering. "About Isla..."

"I thought this might come up, but you should know my answer already. If you want to talk to her, then you should call her. I'm not relaying any messages." Wil crossed her arms, a hard look on her face.

"I know, and I don't expect you to." Lynda folded her hands together in her lap, trying to figure out why she'd really brought up Isla again. She wanted to know the daughter she'd lost, the one she had promised to protect just like Wil was so good at doing. "You're fiercely protective of her."

"Well, someone has to be."

Lynda's lips parted in surprise at that, the old vehemence coming right back from all those years ago. She wondered if Wil felt the change as well or if she was obtuse to it since Isla was still hers to protect. In the end, Isla wasn't the one who needed saving. She'd seen so much of the world by the time Lynda had married Patrick and even more before she'd turned sixteen. She knew what dangers and trauma the world held, and she would never be innocent from it.

"Why would someone need to protect her?"

"Are you kidding me?" Wil eyed Lynda carefully. "Her father died."

"He did." The emotion Lynda expected at the mention of Patrick didn't surface, which she was happy for. She'd worked for years to keep it in and deal with her demons on that front.

"She was left with *you*."

The way Wil said the last word was such an accusation and insult wrapped into one. Lynda had done everything for those girls as soon as she'd known she was going to finish raising them. None of that had been in her plans when Patrick had made her draw up their wills. But he'd been adamant since their mother had died so unexpectedly that they had a plan in case something else happened, and she'd never expected it to come true. She had agreed to it not thinking it would ever happen.

"I don't want to argue with you, not the way we used to."

The knock on the door startled her, but Wil was up before she could manage to figure out what was happening. When she came back with their drinks, the tension in Wil's face had changed. She settled back onto the mattress and nodded at Lynda as if expecting her to continue where they'd left off. Lynda stood up and sauntered over, taking the wine glass and sitting next to Wil, her back ramrod straight.

"None of us expected him to die."

"Assholes with cars do that, but after losing her mother and father? Isla was a mess."

We all were, Lynda wanted to say, but she kept her mouth shut. She'd put on as much of a façade of having her life together as possible. She'd needed to in order to be strong enough for the girls to find their way, and it had worked for the most part. She'd broken down only in private when no one else was around, when no one else could see as she raged in anger that Patrick would dare leave her.

"I was so worried she might do something," Wil murmured.

"Do what?" Lynda raised an eyebrow, looking directly at Wil.

"Kill herself."

That hit hard.

Lynda's heart broke. Those times when Isla would walk through the house, never looking at her, her eyes downcast as if the world was going to end. It very well might have. Those long quiet car rides from the house to school and back. The time she had decided to quit ballet when she had been dedicated to it for over a decade.

Tears brimmed in her eyes as the guilt swam through her, consuming her for the very fact that she had missed the signs. If Isla had chosen to do anything different, if she'd felt any more hopeless.

"Excuse me." Lynda stood up and walked straight to the bathroom, shutting and locking the door behind her. She leaned over the sink, closing her eyes as she dragged in deep breaths to calm her racing heart. She wouldn't have survived losing Isla like that. She would have needed to for Aisling, but it would have been the most monumental task ever.

The knock was gentle but shocking. "Lynda?"

Pressing a hand to her belly, Lynda straightened her shoulders and schooled her features. She had her moment, and now she needed more information. She needed to know everything because while she had suspected decades ago that Isla was struggling with depression, she'd never thought it was that bad. Lynda opened the door and held her shoulders square.

"Are you all right?"

"Of course." Lynda nodded sharply, but her voice had a rasp to it that she didn't expect. She'd done so much research on the psychology of children after the sudden loss of a parent, trying to prepare herself for whatever might happen in the upcoming years, but she hadn't been prepared at all. No amount of research was enough. She'd read about suicide and what signs to look for, but she hadn't seen them with Isla.

They moved back to the bed, sitting on the edge of the mattress. Lynda took her wine glass, swallowing a sip before she set it down. She reached out her hand and settled it on Wil's knee, giving a squeeze. "I wish you would have told me."

"Why? So you could lock her up in a mental hospital?"

"I wouldn't have done that unless it was absolutely necessary."

"You would have done it just to be rid of her."

Lynda sighed as they slipped back into the past habits. She shook her head slowly, keeping her hand on Wil's knee to make sure her point got across. "No, Wil. I wouldn't."

"He would have been so mad at you if you'd done it."

"Patrick?" Lynda pushed, needing to know where all of Wil's anger was coming from. At Wil's nod, Lynda sucked in a breath. "I don't think he would have. If Isla needed it, or Aisling for that matter, he would have supported it."

"No, he wouldn't."

"Wil—"

"You don't understand." Wil's voice rose, the muscles in her leg tensing as her anger flared to heights it hadn't since they'd be reacquainted.

"I'm trying to." Lynda tightened her grasp on Wil's knee again, the warmth of her body searing through the material and into her fingers. Lynda didn't want to let go, even though she knew it was entirely inappropriate for her to be touching her subordinate and for the conversation they were having.

Wil set the beer on the nightstand, and when she turned and looked at Lynda, her face was filled with pain. "It wasn't just Isla and Aisling who lost a father that day. I did, too. Patrick was always that person for me. If I screwed up, he'd yell at me. He treated me like one of his own, and I *lost* him."

Lynda's heart shattered when Wil's voice broke. She'd been so focused on her own girls that she'd forgotten all about Wil. Wil was right. Patrick had always talked of the three of them together as if they were all his. At one point, Wil's grandmother had even approached them about taking Wil should anything happen to her. Lynda had completely forgotten that conversation because it had been only weeks before Patrick had died and then it had never been brought up again.

"I'm so sorry," Lynda said, putting as much emotion into that one apology. "I didn't see it."

"Because *you* didn't want to."

Lynda couldn't fault the accusation. She'd been as wrapped up in her own grief as any, and she'd put as much of her focus into the girls as possible that she'd neatly forgotten all about Wil. The failure was on her. Lynda wasn't surprised when hot tears trailed down Wil's cheeks, dripping off her chin to disappear. She brushed some of Wil's hair behind her ear in a tender move and then drew Wil's gaze up to hers.

"He loved you like his own. I know that he did. He told me as much, and we were in the process of making plans to take you in if anything should happen to your grandmother, but then he died, and everything..." she trailed off.

"Went to shit," Wil supplied.

"Yeah, that." Lynda locked her gaze on Wil again. "But please know that Patrick loved you like his daughter, and I know for a fact he would be proud of who you've become."

Lynda was proud of her, too, but she kept that to herself, not comfortable enough to say it. Wil lost it. Sobs wracked through her. She collapsed into Lynda's arms and pressed her face into Lynda's neck, holding on tight as she cried, letting everything loose. Lynda wrapped her up, not wanting to let go. This had been what she needed, not the confessions, not the tension, but this. Closeness. Human contact. Touch. Closing her eyes, Lynda breathed in Wil's scent, the undertones hadn't changed in all these years.

"He loved you," Lynda whispered one more time before pulling back.

Wil sucked in a breath and wiped her face with her palms. "I'm sorry. I'm so sorry."

Without another word, Wil raced from the room, leaving Lynda on her own. Lynda stayed put, staring at the empty space on the bed that Wil had left. She had broken so many ethical lines, crossing over them without a second thought. A tightness in her chest formed painfully. Jessica's words came back to haunt her. One more violation on her record and she knew it would all be over. Her heart thudded, and she clenched her eyes. She very likely just ended her career. Through it all she hadn't even managed to tell Wil everything.

2007

WIL WOKE WITH A START, her heart pounding. Red and blue lights streamed through her window and into her bedroom. Fear raced through her, the pit in her stomach swallowing it up and refusing to let it escape. If it was a nightmare, she should be calming down. Except she wasn't.

Standing up, Wil moved to the window and pulled aside the gauzy curtains she had left partially open. The heat from the middle of the night was too much so her grandmother had started leaving all the windows open to let the cool air in and the bills down. Standing in the window, Wil looked out at the two police cars parked outside. It took her a minute to realize they were at Isla's house.

Without hesitating, she bolted from her bedroom. Grandma caught her as soon as she tried to go out the front door and wrapped her arms tightly around Wil's middle to hold her inside. "You need to wait."

"What's going on?" Wil asked, still trying to break free from Grandma's grasp.

"I don't know, but you need to wait until the police are

gone."

Wil calmed slightly and stopped straining. Of course her grandmother was right. Running across the street at dawn was not the best choice, especially with police out there. They could think anything of her. Wil opened the front door wide and stepped onto the front steps of the house. She stood and waited. It took hours for the police to leave and for the lights to fade with the daylight.

Grandma came out at one point and rubbed a hand up and down Wil's back, saying something, but it didn't make a dent in Wil's worried brain. She wanted to know what was going on. "Come inside and eat something."

"What?" Wil turned sharply on her grandma.

"Eat breakfast, baby. It's almost time to get ready for school."

"I..." Wil trailed off. Her grandma would make her go to school without answers. Education was so important to her. Swallowing the lump in her throat, Wil folded her arms and stared at the house across the street. "I'm not hungry."

"You need to eat something—your skinny bones—"

"Not today, Nana."

"Fine." Grandma bristled and walked back inside. Wil waited as long as she could, but Grandma wouldn't let her go over there even when the police were gone. With her backpack on her shoulders, Wil walked to the elementary school to catch the bus to the junior high. Isla wasn't there. Wil kept looking for her— on the bus, at the school, in every class, on the bus ride home.

As soon as she got to her house and Grandma was still at work, Wil dropped her bag at the front door and walked across the street. Trepidation was in every single step she took. She was violating something, and she didn't even know what it was. Instead of walking into the house like she normally would, Wil knocked.

Everything held in suspension until Lynda opened the door, her eyes red and puffy, her cheeks pale. Her hair that was usually so properly done up and beautiful was down and against her back. Wil didn't know what to say, but Lynda remained silent. She opened the door wider and pointed back toward Isla's room.

Wil stepped into the house, trespassing through whatever was happening, a stranger in a home she used to think of as hers. It was so surreal. She got to Isla's bedroom and pushed open the door, her heart wrenching when she saw her on the bed, motionless and silent. It was too quiet.

"Isla..." Wil wanted to ask what happened, but she couldn't. Her voice broke on the question, and instead she stepped up to the bed and sat on the edge.

"Wil," Lynda's voice was strong even though she looked anything but.

There was a silence over the house that Wil couldn't name, and when she faced Lynda, she knew. In her heart, she knew what she was about to say. Lynda didn't have the words, but at the same time, Wil needed to hear them. She needed to know and understand.

"There was an accident this morning."

Wil shook her head vehemently. She wasn't hearing this. Tears prickled her eyes, and when she looked at Isla, she knew it was true.

"They said Patrick died instantly, and he didn't feel anything." Lynda didn't even sound devastated. She didn't look like it was affecting her at all.

Wil clenched her jaw tightly, tears streaming down her face. She made the quick decision and climbed into the bed with Isla, wrapping arms around her tightly and holding on to her. She held firm and still as pain raged through her, consumed her.

Lynda might have said something else, but Wil didn't hear it. Wil closed her eyes and breathed in Isla's scent. She stayed there until her grandma came to get her, and even then, they let her stay until the next day. None of them went to school or work except Grandma. The silence hung in the house, over their heads. There was nothing any of them could say.

2023

Wil was emotionally drained. The night before with Lynda had been an absolute mistake, and she'd known it as soon as she had opened that door and saw Lynda standing there in a thin robe that left very little to the imagination. At first, Wil had wanted to toy with her, strip it off, make her feel what Wil had been dreaming of for years, but she'd resisted easily enough.

Lynda's whole mood had been off. Wil had never seen her like that. She'd seen her in so many ways, just woken, exhausted because they had kept her up too late with their chatter and laughter, but there was something in Lynda's eyes the night before that hadn't matched up with any of that.

What they had to do was to remain completely professional from there on out. Wil wrapped her hair up in a tight bun and stepped into the steaming shower. She couldn't believe she had cried into Lynda's shoulder like that. It was utterly embarrassing. Yet that same flicker of emotion crossed Lynda's face, and Wil still couldn't read it.

Letting the hot water seep into her shoulders and her back, Wil stayed put, her mind spinning in a vortex of remembered pain. It took longer than she cared to admit that it had been that same pain reflected in Lynda's eyes the night before. Straightening herself, Wil clenched her jaw. They shared the same pain. It was different, but it was all caused by the same devastating moment.

Patrick.

Wil sucked in a breath and let it out slowly, trying her damnedest not to end up in tears. She didn't want to be reduced to that again. Taking the day by the hand, Wil stepped out of the shower and dressed quickly in a simple black suit with a white button up shirt. She even put on a tie for good measure, one that was a beautiful light mossy green that accentuated the lighter color in her eyes.

She headed down to the Starbucks next to the hotel and

grabbed each of them coffee. She could do this. She and Lynda could pretend like last night hadn't happened, that there was no emotional outburst from either of them, and they could go on with their day as though nothing had happened. Because nothing had.

Wil had thought about it, she wanted to undress her, taste her, touch her, but that had been washed away with the cold memory of Patrick. She hadn't been vulnerable with someone like that other than Isla, and not since Grandma had died. She'd run because she couldn't handle it any longer, the embarrassment at not being able to hold her own was too much. Wil stumbled in her step, but she managed to correct it just in time.

She went back into her room and knocked on the adjoining door. She had no idea why she insisted on using this door instead of the one in the hall, except perhaps it was more intimate, which was not something they needed. She should have gone through the hall.

Lynda opened it wide, already made up for the day in a tight black dress that clung to every damn curve she had. Wil nearly groaned, but she bit the inside of her cheek to keep it in. The cut of material across the top of the dress was at an angle, and Wil wanted to know exactly what was underneath.

Holding out her hand with Lynda's coffee in it, Wil eyed her carefully and wondered if Lynda was going to bring up anything from the night before. "Thought you could use a pick-me-up."

"Thank you." Lynda's voice was rough, as if she'd just woken from sleep or had spent the night crying.

Wil wasn't sure she wanted to know which, but she could easily guess, considering she had an idea of how long it took Lynda to get ready in the mornings. Sipping her hot coffee and ignoring the burn as it touched her tongue, Wil stared Lynda up and down, waiting to see what was going to happen next. She honestly hadn't looked at the schedule of events since they'd arrived, knowing she was going to follow Lynda wherever she went.

Lynda set the cup of coffee on the dresser and walked into her room. Wil leaned against the adjoining doorframe and watched as Lynda grabbed a pearl necklace and clasped it with only one or two failed attempts. She was waiting for something to happen, for a word to be said or a look to be made, and it took her way longer than she wanted to admit what she was waiting for.

The way Lynda's ass moved in the dress, the slight swell that led her eyes directly down to those strong calves and heels. Wil took another sip of her coffee to wet her now parched mouth. Even though she was completely embarrassed by her outburst the night before, by slipping up and not maintaining her put-together persona she wanted to have in front of Lynda, she felt far more connected to her than she ever had before.

When Lynda turned around, fixing a pearl drop earring into place, Wil was sure she caught her stare, and the heated look she was giving. Swallowing that down, Wil stood her ground. She would ignore what happened last night as best as she could and not make a spectacle about it, and they would enjoy their day at the conference and working, as she had no doubt that Lynda would make them work through every meal again.

"What lecture are we going to this morning?" Wil asked, trying to bypass the awkwardness as Lynda stared at her intensely.

"Oh, um, I thought we could go to one about team building."

"Fun." Wil rocked back on her heels and lifted her cup to her lips. "Because that's something we need."

She hadn't meant for it to come out as a dig between the two of them not working well or being forced to work together, but she could see in Lynda's unguarded gaze it had. The team Wil had helped Millie build worked fantastically, and even with the upset of the buy-out they were managing to function well enough.

Lynda stepped in close, her fingers wrapping around the cup of coffee Wil had brought her. Her voice still had that husky tone to it, only this time, when Lynda spoke, it sounded like a just-been-fucked-senseless tone. "Team building is about more than the lowest working together. It starts from the top down."

"I know," Wil whispered. She had to get rid of that image, the sound in Lynda's voice, and she had to give Lynda a reason to change her tone. "But remember, I don't like you."

Lynda frowned, her gaze dropping to Wil's lips and then the cup in her hand before she raised those caramel eyes back up. "I know."

There was that pain again, the same pain that had been in her voice the night before, and all Wil wanted to do was wash it away and take back what she'd said, but just like when she was a teenager, she hadn't been able to stop herself. It wasn't that she didn't like Lynda, they just had a tumultuous past that they'd never managed to get through. "I didn't mean it..."

"You did," Lynda interrupted. "So perhaps team building will be useful for us, Wilda."

"It's Wil," she stated sharply with a pout on her lips.

"Wil," Lynda corrected, tilting her chin down.

She wanted to ask why Lynda kept doing that. As a kid, Lynda had never called her Wilda, but this was the third time Lynda had done it, and each time it seemed so damn intentional. Instead of asking, however, Wil pinned her with a sharp look. Lynda held her ground, and Wil realized just how close they were standing. It would take nothing for her to reach up, clasp a hand behind Lynda's neck and pull her in for a kiss.

Restraining again, Wil held her ground. "Are we working over breakfast again?"

Lynda moved her gaze back down to the coffee in her hands. "I'm not very hungry this morning."

"Good, me either. So are we working until the lecture?"

Lynda's lips parted as though she was going to speak, but then she closed her mouth. Trying again, she said, "Yes."

Instead of leaving the room, Lynda moved to sit in the chair she'd been in last night, and Wil was once again relegated to the small ottoman from the lounge chair. She chose to stand behind Lynda to see the computer she'd left there in her haste the night before. "Have you checked the stocks this morning?"

"Yes," Lynda answered, her voice a little breathier than usual. "They're looking good and holding. I am concerned about the Pickman Portfolio."

"That one was weak to begin with," Wil added, leaning over Lynda's shoulder to move the mouse and pull up the Pickman Portfolio so they could look at it in more detail. "It was the first for one of the junior managers, and not the greatest selection. He no longer works for us, but I've had a hard time trying to convince the Pickman's to shift their investments to something more lucrative."

"Why is that?" Lynda's breathing became rapid, her breasts pushing against the tight material of her dress, and Wil had a hard time not looking at it, daydreaming again.

"They're a difficult couple in a lot of ways. I can set up a meeting with them if you want to try your hand."

"I would like that."

"I'll have Jacob set it up for when we get back." Wil drew in Lynda's scent, the same perfume she'd worn twenty years ago, as if the woman would ever change one single thing about herself. She barely even looked older, though Wil was convinced that was some sort of magic with makeup. But then again, last night, Lynda had been bare, freshly showered, and still as stunning as ever.

"Wil?" Lynda's voice floated up to her, as if she was expecting an answer, but Wil had no idea what she'd been asked.

"I'm sorry, what did you say?"

Lynda tilted her chin up, amusement flashing through her eyes and a twitch at her lips before she repeated herself. "Are there any other portfolios that concern you?"

"Oh, no, mostly just this one. The others perform as expected for the most part."

"For the most part?" Lynda raised an eyebrow.

Wil swallowed hard, sweat pooling at the small of her back, and it wasn't because the temperature in the room was too high. It was her damn body reacting to that look. "There are some I would love to investigate expanding. Millie was adamant about keeping the status quo, but I think we can grow."

Lynda's lips curled upward into a brilliant smile, one Wil had rarely ever seen from her, although Isla's graduation was one of those days, and Wil remembered that day fondly for the few moments like that. The rest of it was a shitshow. Wil found her body sliding forward, and she had to tug it back, mentally and physically. She would never allow herself to do that no matter how much she wanted it.

"I think you'll do well at Jolie Preston."

Wil guffawed and rolled her eyes, straightening her back. The words slipped from her mouth before she could stop them. "Sure, right along with Millie and the rest of the staff you're going to fire through this transition."

Lynda eyed her carefully. Wil wasn't sure what to make of that look, never able to read Lynda no matter how much she tried. Wil shuddered.

"I don't plan on firing you, and I really don't plan on firing most of the employees from investors to managers to admin. Haven't you been paying attention to this conference at all?" Lynda's tone had a bite to it, that carefully controlled anger Wil always envied.

Wil hated to admit the answer was no. Her entire brain had been taken up with this woman next to her, the woman in the tight black dress with creamy smooth thighs, the one she'd sobbed on last night. Shaking her head slowly, Wil raised her gaze to Lynda's eyes. "No."

"Please do today." Lynda's hand landed on Wil's, that firm grasp sending salacious thoughts straight between her legs.

"I'll try," Wil managed to get out.

THE FIRST LECTURE WAS A BREEZE, and Lynda was stopped on her way out by Francine, and a smile lit up her face as she leaned in for a hug from one of her favorite people. "Francine, I'm so glad to see you again. I didn't expect you to be here."

"We're doing some training for our teams." Francine's eyes crinkled in the corners as her smile echoed Lynda's. "I'm glad you were still able to attend the conference this year."

"It was questionable there for a while." Lynda held the strap on her purse over her shoulder, straightening herself so she was at her full height. She used to feel intimidated by Francine until one night two years ago at the conference. They'd both gotten outrageously drunk and needed Francine's beautiful wife to come to their rescue, but she had learned so much in those few hours that she was never willing to forget them.

"And who have you brought with you?"

"Oh, Wil, this is Francine. She's the founder of Shiloh's Home, a safehouse for pregnant teen girls, and someone I'm glad to call a friend. Though it took quite a bit of vodka to get to that point, didn't it?"

Francine gave Lynda a sly look as she extended her hand to Wil. "Good to meet you."

"Vodka?" Wil questioned, sending a sidelong look at Lynda.

Lynda bristled, not needing Wil to know about that, but she'd nearly forgotten she was standing right there. "It's a long story."

"Oh, I'm sure about that." Wil's tone was flirtatious in a way that made Lynda nervous.

Francine eyed both, her gaze flitting back and forth as she stood straight. "Is there history between you two?"

Lynda's stomach flopped. What did Francine mean by that? If she could sense the underlying tension and history between them, surely others would be able to see it as well. And if Jessica showed up in the office—Lynda steadied herself and gave the easiest answer possible.

"Wil was Isla's best friend growing up." Lynda said it casually as if there wasn't a major hurt any time she thought of her oldest stepdaughter, but she didn't miss the shocked expression at her ease of talking about family when she risked a look at Wil. "I've known Wil since she was a kid."

Though Wil certainly wasn't a kid anymore, especially with the conversation they'd had the night before. Though those hurts from the past still lingered. Lynda had found a way to deal with them, and it seemed as though Wil had too for the most part.

"No kidding," Francine murmured, her eyes looking Wil up and down. "I met my wife when I hired her. I'd thought—"

"No, that's not it at all." Wil stepped in, her voice firm as she put her hand out in front of her. "There is nothing going on between us, and there never has been."

Lynda was surprised by Wil's forward protest. She wasn't wrong, but Lynda was straight. She'd been married to Patrick for years and had never thought about another woman in that way. But the way Wil looked almost embarrassed or as if she'd been caught in the act had her attention. Lynda could barely pry her eyes away from the younger woman.

"We just go way back," Lynda said absentmindedly to Francine.

"I'm sure there are some wonderful stories the two of you have to share, but it'll have to be another time. Dinner maybe? Or vodka?" Francine winked at the last bit. "Right now, I have a fire I need to put out."

"Absolutely." Lynda stepped to the side to get out of Francine's way. She was about to walk toward the next lecture hall when her heel caught in the grout on one of the tiles and her ankle turned under.

Flinging her arm out, she started to topple over. Wil's quick thinking and hands around her waist steadied her. Those fingers were warm in ways Lynda missed, not from Wil but from Patrick, from any lover she'd had in the past, actually. She missed human touch that was meant solely for pleasure. Before she could emerge from that thought, Wil's breath was hot on her neck, a firmer arm around her back.

"Are you all right?"

"Yes." Lynda nearly whimpered the word out, but she caught herself just in time. "I wasn't watching my step."

"It's amazing anyone can move in heels that high anyway."

"Practice," Lynda mumbled as she set her ankle right and tested it to see how much pain she would have when moving. Remarkably there was very little, so Wil must have caught her before she completely turned it and subsequently sprained it. Her heart raced, however, and she couldn't figure out why. It surely couldn't be from the simple touch Wil had given her—correction—was still giving her.

Wil kept that arm firmly around Lynda's waist as they moved from the center of the hallway toward the wall. Lynda normally would have told her she was fine and insisted on walking on her own, but that soft simple touch, especially when she knew Wil wasn't very fond of her to begin with, was more than she could have asked for in that moment.

"Thank you, Wil," Lynda finally stated, her voice soft and the look she sent Wil one that was filled with compassion and true gratitude. "I appreciate it."

"Any time." Wil still didn't move, however.

Instead, they walked together down the hall toward the second lecture hall where they were due to be next. As they entered, Wil moved to the side to let Lynda slide into the hard plastic chairs first, just as Patrick would have done all those years ago. She hated that she was comparing the two of them. Wil was easily fifteen years younger than her and her stepdaughter's best friend. She'd literally watched Wil grow up for years, spent hours endlessly in cars as she drove everyone where they needed to be.

Wil slung her arm over the back of Lynda's chair, and she leaned into it happily. The warmth from Wil's body seeped into hers, which was welcome in the cold lecture hall. Strangely, she was enjoying it, probably more than she ought to, but Lynda could think about why later. Wil had grown into a beautiful woman, and she had certainly filled out after high school and was no longer the gawky kid she used to be.

Lynda brought out a yellow notepad and tried to take notes, but again found herself writing notes as she critiqued the lecturer and showing them to Wil in the meantime. Each time she said something, Wil's face would light up with a smile, and she wanted to make it happen again.

At some point, Wil took the blue pen from Lynda's fingers and shifted the notepad on her crossed legs. The point of the pen was dull, but Lynda felt every swipe as Wil wrote something out. Heat rushed to her cheeks when arousal surged between her legs. It was so unexpected. Lynda swallowed hard and almost missed when Wil shifted the notepad back so Lynda could see what she'd written.

I thought you told me to pay attention.

Chastised, Lynda leaned back to stop her taunting but realized Wil's arm was still around her shoulders. Any outsider might think they were more than coworkers, more than boss and employee. That thought churned her stomach slightly. What would Jolie Preston say if they found out, if someone snapped a picture and reported back to Jessica? Shaking her head, she pushed the thought from her mind. No one was there to spy on them, and she had to remind herself of that. They were there to learn, to be better leaders in the long run. That had been why she brought Wil.

"Are you paying attention?" Wil's voice was soft and low, barely above a whisper, but it was right in her ear.

Lynda shuddered.

"Cold?" Suddenly the concern was back, the same concern that had been present when she'd nearly sprained her ankle.

Shaking her head slowly, Lynda parted her lips ready to answer and turned to face Wil, but when she moved, their mouths were nearly touching. When had Wil moved into her? When had she not noticed? She'd always noticed how close people were because she hated it. Patrick had been the only person she'd wanted touching her like this—ever.

"No," Lynda answered pathetically.

"You're shivering, and you have goosebumps." Wil's fingers were on her forearm.

Lynda's breath caught in her throat, and it was a struggle to stay focused, something she definitely needed to be doing right then and there. This was a work trip, nothing else. The loneliness she'd felt the night before must be straying and making her think and feel things it shouldn't. It was all in her head. Wasn't it?

"I guess I must be cold then." Lynda took the offered out. "I'll grab a jacket from my room after this."

They stayed as quiet as possible, not disturbing anyone else around them. Wil, however, didn't seem to care, and tightened her grasp around Lynda's shoulders, half tugging her into Wil's side. Lynda relaxed, which surprised her. She was not someone who relaxed easily, and not since Patrick died. Her heart raced as Wil took the paper pad and pen and put it on her own legs.

"We'll get you some warm coffee when it's done. That's probably better."

Wil's words wrapped around her like heaven. Lynda closed her eyes and tried to center herself. What the hell was going on with her? She'd never had thoughts like this for another woman before. It must have just been what Francine had insinuated, putting ideas in her head that didn't belong there. Yes, that was it.

Comfortable with that explanation, Lynda put all her focus on the rest of the lecture. It was only another thirty minutes until the lecture wound down. When it was over, they all clapped, and Wil helped her to stand.

"How's your ankle?" Wil asked, sincerely.

"Good, thank you." Lynda ducked her chin, not sure she could stand to look in Wil's eyes. "How about we get that coffee?"

"Yes." Wil grinned. She kept her hand on the small of Lynda's back, and again Lynda didn't say anything to stop it. As much as she knew she should, she didn't. She liked it. She loved it even. It felt so...normal.

Sighing, she let Wil lead her as they maneuvered through the crowds down the block to the coffee shop on the corner. They went inside, and Wil ordered for both of them. They settled at a small table in the corner. They were skipping the third lecture of the morning, but Lynda wasn't going to hassle Wil about it. Occasionally time to digest what they'd learned was necessary.

"So how are you enjoying it?" Lynda asked, trying to plod her way through a conversation.

"The conference?" Wil's dark eyebrows rose in confusion.

"Yeah."

"It's good, I suppose."

"You suppose?" Lynda took a sip of the hot coffee, enjoying the burn of it down her throat and into the pit of her belly.

"I haven't been able to pay too much attention, remember?"

"Right." Lynda frowned. "Why is that?"

"No offense intended, Lynda, but your presence is distracting."

Lynda's stomach twisted sharply, and she immediately raised her gaze to meet Wil's. "Excuse me?"

"You come in, take over my firm, and then whisk me out here for a conference with no real explanation, and I don't know where I stand or what we're doing here."

"Oh." Lynda had been sure Wil was going to say something else. "I'm sorry. I didn't realize—"

Wil cut her off. "Add in the fact that you're my best friend's stepmom, and it's not like we had an easy relationship when I was growing up either. I said...well, I was an asshole, and I'm sorry, but I hope that doesn't taint your view of me now."

Lynda's heart was in her throat. She never thought Wil would admit to being part of the problem back then, that she would have enough self-awareness of what happened. She certainly hadn't had it when she was a kid, but this was a different Wil. Lynda only managed one word in response. "No."

"No, what?" Wil looked to be at a loss, but she was so hard to read now compared to when she was younger. As a kid she was all fire, but now, everything was so well hidden behind those dark eyes and rounded cheeks.

"It doesn't taint what I think of you in a professional capacity." Although Lynda wasn't sure how much truth was in that. She couldn't stop thinking about the past lately, about Patrick, and the girls, but also about Wil. The devastation she had when Patrick had died, and the support she'd forgotten to provide Wil. Lynda reached forward and took Wil's hand in hers, squeezing tightly. "I'm so sorry I didn't see it."

"See what?"

"How much you missed him."

At her words, tears sprung into Wil's eyes. It took her a few seconds to mask the look, but Wil's jaw tightened and her gaze became firm again. "It doesn't matter."

"It does." Lynda sighed. "Trust me, it does."

She sipped her coffee again, easing into the conversation. She really needed to stop bringing up the past so much and look toward the future. They needed to see each other now rather than then. Both had to make that switch, and it was hard and easy at the same time.

"For the record, I think what you've done while with Henshaw is amazing."

"You're lying."

"I'm not. I reviewed the files before I started, and since you were placed in a management role, since you started to take on leadership, the company has begun to grow." Lynda meant it, and she hoped Wil took the compliment for what it was. Truth.

"Thank you," Wil murmured before sipping her coffee.

Lynda realized belatedly that her hand still covered Wil's on the table. Releasing her grasp, she circled her cup with both hands—anything to keep from touching and continue the line of the inappropriate. She really needed to get her head on straight.

2007

The first week was a whirlwind. Lynda barely remembered anything of it, barely thought about feeling her way through it. But when she dropped the kids off at school a week after the police had arrived, she was immediately called down to the principal's office. Everything moved slow and fast at that point, and it was so hard to parse out what was her emotions getting in the way and what was just damn overwhelm of information.

As she stepped into the set of offices in the front of the school, she was a nervous mess. She had taken the extra time to get ready that morning, knowing she had to go back to work soon, knowing that the girls needed to have their normal life back as quickly as possible. She'd gotten up early, dressed, put on makeup, and did her best to create the routine they'd once had before...before Patrick died.

Entering the offices was worse than entering the funeral home. They all knew what happened, and they stared at her like she was the pariah, the lost soul who would never find her way again, and perhaps she wouldn't. But that wasn't for them to say.

"Mrs. Walsh." Principal Everette's voice was laced with pity to the point it was sickening.

Lynda swallowed down the bile that wanted to rise in her stomach and held her ground. She hoped he didn't talk to the girls this way. "You needed to talk to me."

"Yes. Come this way."

She was led into his office and sat in one of the two chairs on the opposite side of his desk. He didn't take his normal seat and instead sat next to her. Lynda was stumped by that, but then again, Patrick had handled most of the school issues since he was the biological parent, not her. She'd never wanted to replace the girls' mother.

"How are you doing?"

She hated that question. So many people had asked that question, and she honestly had no idea how to answer it. Wrecked. Torn. Lost. Numb. Angry. Pissed off beyond oblivion. There were so many ways she could go that would be so much more honest than what everyone wanted to hear. "We're managing."

"I'm glad to hear that. I was glad to see the girls were coming back to school today."

Lynda nodded, although she was only at Isla's school. Aisling had already been dropped off with an extra deep breath for help and sanity. "What did you need, Principal Everette?"

"Oh, well, since Patrick is no longer with us—"

Another phrase Lynda had come to hate. He wasn't just not with them—he was dead. He was buried six feet under in a casket made of dark mahogany and in a metal vault to seal the casket and his embalmed body in. There was no coming back. He wasn't just gone—he would never return.

"—there's a small issue of who is going to be caring for the girls."

Lynda raised her gaze sharply. "I am their stepmother."

"Yes, but are you... I hate to ask this... do you have custody?"

Her throat closed, and every already weak muscle in her body tensed ready for a fight. "Yes, I have custody."

"What about their mother—"

"Their mother died when Aisling was a baby. *I* am their mother." She'd never said it like that to anyone before, and it felt so uncomfortable but true in the same breath. She was all they had left for a parent. Instinctively, she knew she had to be firm in this case. Everything had been arranged before Patrick died. He didn't want the girls to go with their grandparents.

"All right, well, when you bring in that paperwork, we'll change over all the contacts for the girls in our systems. And Mrs. Walsh, the sooner you bring in that paperwork the better."

She'd never thought she'd feel this protective of them, not like this. To have the girls torn from her life after losing Patrick was a thought she couldn't bear to entertain. The threat remained in the room, and Lynda was going to snuff it out as soon as possible. "I'll bring it when I pick Isla up from school today."

"Okay, thank you. I appreciate that."

Lynda eyed him with a hard look. "Is that everything?"

"Yes, it is."

"Good." Lynda stood up sharply and walked from the office and out into the hallway.

With fire in her steps, she raced to her car. She pulled out of the parking lot, but she couldn't go home. She couldn't stand to be in the empty house. She couldn't breathe. Pulling over in front of a park, Lynda clenched the steering wheel hard, hot tears streaking down her cheeks, and she let out a wild scream, one she'd never heard herself make before. *Why, Patrick?*

She wasn't ready for this. Patrick should have never trusted her with the most precious thing in his life. She swiped at her cheeks as another sob tore through her. How was she supposed to care about paperwork when her husband was dead, when the girls had barely managed to get themselves to school on time? They were all so broken and the world just wanted to shatter them even more.

"God, Patrick, why did you think I could do this? I can't do this."

The same pain she'd experienced a week before tore through her, the intense hurt and panic twining together to take over all her senses. She knew where the papers were. Patrick had made sure to tell her where he'd kept them at least every few months just in case. But just in case was never supposed to happen. And it had.

Blowing out a breath, Lynda pressed her forehead into the steering wheel and clenched her eyes shut tight. It had happened, and she hadn't been ready for it. She hadn't been prepared for any of this. She wouldn't ever be.

CHAPTER

Ten

2023

THE SCREAM WAS one Wil had heard before, and it touched on the recesses of her mind. It stirred her, waking her up slowly, but Wil thought the sound would get quieter. Instead, it got louder. When she turned onto her back, she heard it through the door. Panic swelled in her chest, and she was out of the bed in a heartbeat.

The door between the two rooms was unlocked. She'd never expected Lynda to leave it unlocked, but she was glad that she had. Racing into Lynda's room, Wil was prepared for anything, for someone to be in there, for it to be the television. What she wasn't prepared for was Lynda thrashing on the bed, the sheets wrapped around her legs, and her eyes shut tight as she moved.

A cursory glance told Wil no one else was in the room. She moved swiftly to Lynda's side, sitting on the mattress and shaking her awake. Lynda's voice immediately quieted, and she looked startled to find Wil hovering over her. Her cheeks were pale, her skin clammy, her hair a mess, some of it plastered to her sweaty forehead. Her eyes were wild with lingering fear before she blinked to take in her surroundings.

"You were screaming," Wil said by way of explanation.

"I was?" Lynda's chest rose and fell, the thin silky tank top she wore pulling to one side, giving as much a view of her breast as the robe had the other night.

Wil bit her tongue. "It woke me up. Are you all right?"

Lynda slid up, her entire body shaking. Wil gripped her wrists tightly, holding her firm to the bed in case she tried to stand up or do anything stupid.

"Give it a second," Wil whispered, taking control of the entire situation. She could tell Lynda had little idea where she was, that she was playing calm when she really wasn't.

The next breath Lynda took was staggering. It hurt Wil's chest just to hear her try to draw air into her lungs. Lynda tried again and failed. As soon as she relaxed in Wil's grasp, Wil shifted and wrapped her arms around her much as Lynda had done for her the night before. She pulled Lynda into her embrace and held on as she tried to breathe. Their chests touched, heat from Lynda's skin searing through Wil's cotton shirt. Wil kept her own breathing steady and regular, their breasts pushing together every once in a while when they matched. Wil stayed still and quiet, hoping Lynda would calm enough to explain what was happening.

They stayed there for close to thirty minutes before Lynda shifted and moved away, putting some distance between them. Wil didn't like how empty her arms felt, but she couldn't force Lynda to stay close either. As the tension in the air eased away, Wil stayed put, needing to make sure that Lynda was okay.

She'd never seen Lynda like this before, this weakness, this much fear and emotion in one single moment. She'd looked for it. Hell, she had pushed to find it every chance she had when she was a kid, but she'd given up that fight somewhere along the way, and now she found it. Running her hand up and down Lynda's upper arm, Wil waited to see what would happen next. Would she be kicked out of the room?

When Lynda said nothing, Wil finally broke the silence. "What happened?"

"Nightmare."

"Of what? Clowns chasing you down Colfax?" Wil tried to interject the humor, break up the tense moment and give Lynda a minute to get out of her own head and gather her thoughts.

Lynda's lips quirked lightly, and Wil was glad that remembering Lynda's fear of clowns was coming in useful.

"No," Lynda sighed the word. "I should say it's a memory."

"A memory of what?" Wil was curious what could cause this unbreakable woman so much turmoil. It may very well give her answers she had longed years for.

Lynda's tongue dashed across her lips, and she wrapped her arms around her knees as she sat on the bed, putting even more space between them. Wil's stomach clenched, not willing to give up the closeness they had found in the last twenty-four hours, the warm underbelly to this cold woman. Wil touched Lynda's thin foot, curling fingers against the arch. Lynda stretched her toes before curling them, but she didn't protest, so Wil kept her hand there.

"The day the girls went back to school. I was so mad at him, you know." Lynda's voice was thick with emotion, but Wil couldn't put her finger on which one.

"Mad at who?" Wil squeezed Lynda's foot, the warmth of her skin centering her and calming her. Just her very presence managed to do that lately when it hadn't before.

"Patrick." Lynda said his name like a curse.

Shock sliced through Wil's chest, landing in the center of her forehead. She'd never seen anything but a perfect marriage from the two of them, and she couldn't fathom it being any other way. Lifting Lynda's foot into her lap, Wil started to massage it and the tension she'd just gathered from her. Lynda let out a light groan and closed her eyes.

"I was mad at Patrick for dying."

Wil swallowed, her ears ringing, but she knew she'd heard

right. She wanted to know so much more, but she couldn't, not just yet. Pushing her thumb in again to the arch in Lynda's foot, Wil sat in the anger that wasn't hers. They had all been mad at him—and Wil had never expected that to be what connected them so firmly together. Dragging in a deep breath, Wil raised her gaze to meet Lynda's.

"It wasn't his fault."

"I know," Lynda confessed. "But that didn't make it easy for me, for any of us."

Lynda raised her gaze on the last bit, making eye contact with Wil, so Wil knew she was being included in that part of the conversation. Wil sighed and dug her thumbs into Lynda's toes, easing the muscles there.

"I was so mad at him that if he had been alive, I would have killed him."

"I never knew," Wil whispered. She'd always thought Lynda didn't care, that she was impervious to any of the grief that was going on in that house. She'd never shown one inkling of pain over what happened outside of that first day.

"I didn't want you to know. I didn't want anyone to know. How awful of a thing is that? To be so mad at my husband for dying in a car accident? Like he ordained it all."

Wil picked up Lynda's other foot and started in on that one, her heart thumping right along with her continued massage. "I don't think it's bad. It's emotion."

"It's chaos." Lynda's muscles tightened, and Wil inwardly cursed, working again to ease them back out, while also sliding her hand up to the lower part of Lynda's calves to work the tight muscles there.

She'd never sat this close to Lynda in a state like this. She was intoxicated by her. Wil's fingers on Lynda's legs were warm, hot, and she kept moving them higher up her calves to ease the muscles, to ease Lynda as a whole. She was so lost in the motions of her fingers and following the muscle line, that she almost missed Lynda's groan of pleasure.

It sent an immediate echo of pleasure through her body, satisfaction that she was able to do something right for once since they'd met again. She kept the motions of her hands, ignoring her own body because this wasn't for her. It was for Lynda, to calm her soul, to relax her from the nightmare of a memory she'd had.

"That feels so good." Lynda's voice was husky and low, her eyelids fluttered shut as if Wil was doing something other than just massaging her feet.

Wil remembered belatedly that there were certain people who could get off by toe and foot massages, amongst other acts. Stumbling in her pattern, Wil recovered quickly enough. Surely if Lynda were getting *that* kind of pleasure from this she would put a stop to it, wouldn't she? Wil had to trust that.

"Do you massage everyone like this?" Lynda questioned, that same distracted tone.

"No, only special people," Wil replied, keeping her voice soft and quiet. She didn't want to jolt Lynda out of the reverie she was in. She seemed so calm now compared to when Wil had first come into the room.

"Where did you learn to massage this well?" Lynda hummed as Wil found a particularly sensitive knot right in the back of her heel.

Soothing her fingers over the tension, Wil teased it from existence as gently as possible. She was slow to answer, distracted by making sure Lynda got the full work up. "My ex-girlfriend insisted on teaching me. She was a masseuse and was on her feet all day. She loved to get foot and ankle massages after a long day. Hand and arm ones, too."

"I imagine." Lynda let out a little sigh. "Ex-girlfriend?"

Wil cringed, not quite realizing she'd let that one slip fully. Usually, she was so careful how she talked about her ex-partners, but she must have been far too distracted by Lynda's beautiful foot and skin to guard herself. And well, at one point, Lynda had known everything about her, so she wouldn't have had to hide anything. "Yes."

"I didn't know you dated women."

"I date men, too, and non-binary and trans. Anyone really, so long as they catch my interest." Wil wasn't sure she wanted to look up and see Lynda's reaction, but when she sensed Lynda's eyes on her for a long time, she couldn't resist finding out what reaction she was going to get.

"You date anyone?" Lynda's eyes were directly on her.

"Yes, so long as it's mutually wanted. I'm attracted to all sex-identities and gender-identities."

"I must be too old because what you just said doesn't make a lick of sense to me."

Wil's lips quirked up slightly. "I don't discriminate, in other words."

"So, you're a lesbian." Lynda said it like she had the answer in hand, but there was a hint of confusion at the end.

Wil shook her head and pressed down on Lynda's calf again, sliding her thumb from just under her knee all the way down to her heel. Lynda moaned, the sound reverberating through Wil's body and enticing her nerves to react. She quietly told them to stop fucking around because fucking was not something that was going to happen.

"I'm pansexual."

"I'm sorry, what?"

Wil grinned and flashed Lynda a knowing look. "Pan meaning all. I like everyone."

"Oh, I get it." Lynda swallowed, the line of her throat moving. "I think Isla is a lesbian. You don't have to tell me if she is, it's her choice whether to tell me, but I think she is. Patrick always suspected."

"Really?" Wil raised her eyebrows, knowing Lynda was right in her assessment, but Isla might find it interesting and helpful to know that Patrick knew as well, even if he'd never said anything.

"Yeah, he mentioned it a few times so we could be prepared for when she did come out."

"Interesting." Wil kept her mouth shut, because like Lynda had said, it was Isla's choice to share if she wanted to, not Wil's place to spill those beans. "I never thought I'd see you again."

"Likewise." Lynda's caramel eyes turned on Wil. "But I'm glad it did happen this way."

Lynda moved, shifting out of Wil's reach, and her hands felt empty without Lynda's skin against them. Without thinking, she turned Lynda by the shoulders, so Lynda's back was to her. Her ex had taught her how to massage feet and hands because she could reach that on her own body. Backs and really any other part of the body Wil had been left on her own. She'd try her best though.

Lynda glanced over her shoulder, a shadow in her gaze, but she didn't move. She reached up, pulling her hair off her back and leaning toward Wil with a slight nod of acceptance. Starting slowly, Wil moved her palms along Lynda's shoulders, sensing where she was most tense and where knots were either out in the open or hidden. Lynda leaned forward, curling in on herself as she drew in steady deep breaths, which had ultimately been what Wil was looking for. Lynda had gone from ready to break to relaxed and in control again, something Wil was pleased with. The other side of Lynda, while enticing and curiosity-inducing, was scary as hell because of the lack of control.

"Tell me about your nightmare." Wil kept her voice gentle, pushing for an answer but not demanding one.

"My memory, you mean."

"Sure, that."

Lynda sighed but remained in place under Wil's hands. "It was the day the girls went back to school, and Principal Everette brought me into his office. He threatened that if I didn't have proof of custody that he was going to call the authorities. I didn't have the paperwork with me."

"He what?" Wil tensed and stopped massaging Lynda's back.

Lynda moved up, turning her head to lock her gaze with Wil's. "I'm their stepmom, Wil. In most states, had anyone biological argued for custody I would have lost, but Patrick was a lawyer, and he knew that, and he wrote up an ironclad will, but I didn't have the paperwork that day. And the threat...it scared the life out of me. I'd already lost my husband, but to lose my children?"

Her children? Wil bit her tongue. Lynda had never claimed them like that before, not in front of Wil at least. She'd never been possessive or protective. Everything Wil had seen from Lynda had been closed off, as though she hadn't loved the girls like she should have, as though she hadn't supported them or cared for them. Yet this story, assuming Lynda wasn't lying, which she had zero reason to do, told an entirely different side of what had happened. "He threatened to take them away?"

Lynda whimpered. "I got into my car and went to a park, and I broke down. Wil, I had done everything I possibly could to remain strong for them. In one breath, Everette took all that power away from me."

"He took nothing away," Wil whispered. "Because there was nothing to take. Isla and Aisling were yours."

A single tear trickled down Lynda's cheek, and Wil wiped it away. "You hated me."

"I didn't."

"You did," Lynda corrected.

Wil clenched her jaw as reality kicked in. She didn't want to just placate. This was a time for sharing the full truth. "Fine, I did, but it wasn't really you I hated. I think you were right when you said you were mad at Patrick. I was mad at him, too. Still am some days."

Lynda gave a wobbly smile. They were so close. All Wil would have to do was lean in and their mouths could touch, but she knew it wasn't the time to test that ground, and she wasn't even sure she wanted to. She may have come out as pansexual in the last few minutes, but Lynda had staunchly remained straight throughout the conversation, never coming out or sharing thoughts about how she might not be straight either. And Isla—Wil wouldn't do that to her again.

Wil dragged in a slow breath and put space between them, needing it to get herself under control. Although she had only felt out of control since Lynda had shown back up in her life, since Wil had heard her voice down the hall. It had sent her world reeling, far more than the announcement Henshaw had made in that conference room.

"We should probably get some sleep if we want to be awake for the lectures tomorrow." Wil put the ball in Lynda's court. If she wanted to stay up and talk more, Wil would gladly oblige her even though she knew it would be wrong. Wil stiffened, staying on the edge of the bed, half ready to leave and half wanting to stay. It would be so easy. Lynda was so warm and inviting, her eyes cleared now, her cheeks still flushed and her lips parted.

But if she wanted to kick Wil out, she didn't want to overstay the welcome. Wil couldn't be the one to choose in that moment, the desires raging through her clashing, the overwhelming need to protect Isla and their friendship, but also the inescapable desire to lean in and take what she'd wanted for years. In that instant, she knew. Wil wanted Lynda to kick her out so she could go take a cold shower so the decision to maintain boundaries didn't have to be hers just one time.

"You're right," Lynda whispered, taking hold of Wil's hand and leaning back into Wil's chest.

Wil bit back the groan of Lynda against her breasts and closed her eyes so Lynda couldn't see what she was doing to her. This was impossible, and every second she stayed there made it worse. She wanted to curl up with Lynda under the sheets so badly.

Lynda said nothing as she stayed in that position. Wil wasn't sure after a few minutes if Lynda had fallen asleep right then and there, but when Lynda's fingers curled around her own, she knew Lynda was still awake. Wil steadied herself, leaning forward to push Lynda off her slightly. Everything moved in slow motion as she pulled everything back in and solidified her decision—the right choice to make. Wil had to keep telling herself that, repeating that this couldn't happen, that it shouldn't.

"Goodnight, Lynda," she whispered, her lips hovering over Lynda's shoulder. Wil moved off the bed and left Lynda's warm body behind.

"Night," Lynda replied, sadness in her tone.

She didn't look back as she walked out of the room, needing the space and the air to clear her head. She shut the door between the rooms and pressed her head against the frame, closing her eyes. *What the hell am I doing?* She was flirting with the lines of decorum and ethics at every turn, and yes, they had history, but that didn't excuse her taking advantage of a woman who was clearly upset. This crush had taken a dangerous turn, and it wasn't just a simple fantasy anymore.

Dragging in a deep breath, Wil pushed away from the door and flopped onto her bed on her back. She stared at the ceiling for an hour before giving up and turning on the television to watch reruns of *The Golden Girls* until it was a reasonable time in the morning to get up and get them coffee.

CHAPTER

Eleven

IT HAD TAKEN Lynda hours to fall back asleep, but she'd managed a couple hours before her alarm had gone off to wake her. She'd taken her time getting dressed that morning, replaying her nightmare memory on repeat. It was one of her favorite methods to work through it, but it also left her absolutely distracted during the lectures that day, to the point that Wil was sliding her odd looks. She hadn't even asked to work through breakfast or lunch like normal.

The noise of the crowd was too much for her brain, and she needed the quiet comfort Wil had offered her the night before. As they reached dinner time, Lynda turned down invitations from multiple people to join them, and when she looked into Wil's dark eyes, Lynda knew she had done the right thing. "I thought just the two of us could grab dinner."

"Like every other night?"

Lynda shook her head slowly, locking her gaze on Wil to check in on her reaction. "No, no work."

Confusion flitted across Wil's face, but her full lips parted as she said, "Are you sure?"

"Yes, I think we need a day off from office stuff. Don't you?" Lynda gripped her purse strap tightly. She'd managed to maintain her distance from Wil all day, well as much as possible since Wil was with her, but there was no arm around her chair, no hand at the small of her back, and strangely enough, Lynda had missed it. "I thought we could have dinner and drinks and relax."

Wil cocked her head to the side. "I didn't think you ever relaxed. Your shoulders and calves told me as much with the number of knots and tension in them."

Lynda's lips twitched as her cheeks heated. "I do, on occasion, rest."

"When forced to?" Wil pushed.

Not wanting to agree with her outright, Lynda switched subjects. "There's a nice steak house just down the block we can go to."

"Sure." Wil's hand was at her back again, and Lynda sighed into the touch.

She would have to analyze that feeling later when she was less raw from the night before. They walked together, slower than if they were going to another lecture because they had the time. The air outside was warm, which was odd for Seattle, but it was still summer. They had missed the rare summer thunderstorm, but the streets were still slightly damp from it.

Lynda's heels were a distant clack as she walked, Wil keeping her hand in place against her back, protecting but not guiding or leading since she didn't know where they were going. As they entered the restaurant, Wil stepped forward to speak with the hostess. "Two of us."

"I just had a table open up." She took them, winding their way through the tables, to the far side and in front of a window.

As she sat, Lynda noted it would be nice to be able to see the sky and outside for at least an hour that day instead of being cooped up inside a building. Wil pushed her chair in for her and then took the chair immediately to her left instead of sitting across from her. Lynda ordered a glass of wine, and Wil —as she was coming to find was typical—ordered a wheat beer.

"Do you not like wine?" Lynda asked as she opened her menu.

"No. It's a little too high brow for my likes."

"Highbrow?" Lynda raised a teasing eyebrow at her.

Wil shrugged. "Nana could only ever afford the cheap stuff in a box when she wanted wine or beer that tasted like piss-water. It took me a long time to like alcohol."

Wil's cheeks reddened and her lips parted as though she was going to say something else but stopped. Lynda wanted to know what that something else was. "What were you going to say?"

"I probably shouldn't."

"Why?"

"Because Isla would kill me." She grabbed the napkin and unfolded it, finding the edge and sliding it through her fingers as her eyes were locked on it.

Lynda chuckled lightly. "Isla is nearly thirty and we don't talk anymore, so I doubt I can do her any harm now."

Wil gave her a hard but unconvinced look before focusing on her menu. "We stole your wine a few times to try it out, and I have to say, no thank you."

Giggling, Lynda crossed her arms over her stomach. She had suspected they'd done that but never had proof, and there wasn't much wine missing either, so she knew they hadn't gotten drunk off it. Kids were allowed to explore and try new things. Reaching out to curl her fingers around Wil's wrist to get her attention, Lynda joyfully leaned in. "What would you say if I told you I already knew that?"

Wil's eyes grew large. "And you didn't skin us alive?"

"No, I didn't. Aisling did the same thing, though I think she was eighteen before she dared to do it."

"She always was more hesitant to try things."

"Always," Lynda agreed. Aisling had stayed closer to home when she'd gone to college and had taken until she was nearly eighteen to get her driver's license. Isla had wanted it the instant she could get it.

"How did you know?" Wil gave her a suspicious look.

"You think I don't notice when I have wine missing? You must not know me that well." Lynda reached out and clasped Wil's hand tightly before letting go as their drinks were delivered and they ordered food.

It was so nice to slip into an easy conversation perhaps for the first time since they'd become reacquainted, yet Lynda still had something on her mind she wanted to talk to Wil about. That tension lived in the bottom center of her chest, just waiting for her to have the right opportune time to dispel it. But she didn't want to ruin the camaraderie they'd finally managed.

"How is your Nana?"

Wil's smile faltered. "She died about seven years ago."

Lynda's shoulders tightened. As soon as the girls had left the house, she'd moved out and rented an apartment downtown. She'd needed to escape Patrick's memory, and it had been the easiest way to do it, especially since Isla was barely talking to her at the time. "I'm so sorry. I loved her."

"She had a good life, but I think once I graduated from school, she finally let go of what she'd been holding on to."

"I can see that." Lynda sipped her wine, sad that she'd brought up such a grief-filled topic again. "I guess you've been on your own ever since."

"I had Isla until she moved."

"Moved?"

"To Cheyenne. Didn't you know?"

Lynda shook her head as her stomach plummeted. She hadn't known at all. Aisling kept her somewhat updated, but the conversations about Isla had become less over the years. It was an unresolved tension they could never seem to escape. Staring into her wine glass, Lynda fought against the regret that ate away at her again. She'd let so much go that she shouldn't have. She didn't know anything about Isla anymore it seemed.

"She moved up there to teach since the pay is so much better. She comes down to Denver every once in a while. I asked her to visit before we left. It's been a few months since I've seen her properly."

"You must miss her." Lynda missed her, too. Most days she was able to ignore that pang of loneliness, but it was only by burying herself in work and ignoring the real world. If she didn't think about it, it couldn't be true—at least that had been her practice for the last few years, but she couldn't escape it. She'd wanted to talk to Wil about Isla, and she was finally getting her wish. Instead of finding a way to reconnect, she was only discovering how much more she had failed to be the parent Patrick expected her to be.

"I do," Wil said, her voice wispy. "But it was the right decision for her to make."

Lynda agreed even though she didn't know the circumstances. The wine was warm on her tongue, the flavor exactly what she needed to distract her for a moment as the conversation paused. "I wanted to thank you for last night."

"Lynda—"

Shaking her head, Lynda eyed Wil and silently told her to be quiet. "I'm serious. I...I needed that more than you might imagine, and I don't often do this, so please listen. Ever since seeing you again, it's been bringing up..." she trailed off, the weight of the moment pressing on her chest and making it difficult to breathe. Her eyes stung like she was going to cry again, and she had to work hard to pull back from her rampant emotions and stay present in the moment.

"Past feelings," Wil supplied. "I know. I've had the same problems. Like we can't escape it."

"Yeah," Lynda agreed, a sad smile gracing her lips. "But maybe it's because we haven't dealt with all of it yet."

"You might be right but doesn't mean that I want to." Wil's eyes were downcast, her brow furrowed as if she was warring with herself to keep the conversation going but also change the topic to a safer bet.

Lynda's eyes crinkled as a fuller smile took over her. "I understand that sentiment, but perhaps it's time. Patrick died sixteen years ago, Wil. That's a long time to live without him."

"Longer alive without him than alive with him," Wil commented.

"Four times as long as we were married," Lynda added, raising her gaze to meet Wil's. "And still some days it feels like yesterday and others as though it never happened."

"How can you say that?" Wil's brow knit together.

"Because it's easier than saying I was widowed at thirty-four. God, I was so young." Lynda sighed.

They fell into silence as their food was settled in front of them. Lynda stared at hers, not sure if she was hungry. Either way she should eat something, if only to help take the edge off the wine she had been drinking.

"But I wanted to thank you. It's been a long time since I had a nightmare like that."

Wil's fingers curled into hers suddenly, tugging her attention so she had to look deep into Wil's eyes. "You know when I was a kid, I always looked up to you. You were so put together, you had a career, you were going places. For years, and I mean decades probably, I wanted to be just like you."

"There's no reason to be like me," Lynda corrected though her stomach filled with a sense of pride. The pain of the reality she knew about who she was then and now wouldn't do anyone any good. "Trust me."

"There are so many reasons I can't even begin to name them all." Wil's eyes were wide, truth and honesty reflected in her gaze, her face relaxed, wanting Lynda to hear what she was saying.

Lynda wasn't sure how to respond. This wasn't a confession she had ever expected to hear, especially from Wil, who had been nothing but a thorn in her side for so many years. Wil squeezed her hand again before pulling away and starting in on her meal.

Lynda had no idea what to say, so she picked at her dinner

and her wine until the conversation tried and sputtered to begin again. She was just about to put a piece of steak into her mouth when Wil's words stopped her.

"You know, if you want to talk to Isla, you should just call her."

Lynda stilled, not sure how to answer that. It had been a distant hope that by working with Wil she would find a way to connect with Isla again, but to have it so blatantly said was another thing entirely. Lynda took a steadying sip of her wine before she focused on Wil, giving as much honesty as she had just received. "I don't even know what I'd say."

"Probably half the shit you've told me since we got here would be a good place to start, but how about just *hello*?" Wil raised an eyebrow, her beer perched halfway to her lips.

Lynda's heart raced at the mere possibility. "You think she would answer?"

"If you want her to answer, I'll tell her to pick up the call." Wil eyed Lynda seriously.

"Thank you," Lynda whispered. "For that and for last night."

"I didn't do anything last night."

"Well, you're very good at massaging then." Lynda's cheeks heated, and at first, she thought it was embarrassment, but after a second thought, she wasn't sure how true that was. Wil's gentle but firm touches on her body the last two days, albeit nothing sexual, had been so welcome, so arousing. She frowned into her wine glass.

"My ex would love to hear you say that she trained me right."

Lynda let out a light laugh. "I'm glad she taught you."

"I still don't understand how you walk in those things and don't break your ankle."

"Practice, Wilda." This time Lynda said her name with a hint of teasing, which surprised herself. She couldn't remember the last time she had so freely flirted with anyone. She had tried to date after Patrick, mostly after the girls had left the house and grown up, but she'd never managed to get beyond the second or third date with any of the men she'd gone out with. Why was she even thinking of dating?

"Practice does make perfect. I remember practicing being so pissed at you that I thought it was the only way to talk to you."

"I remember that, too." Only it wasn't with quite the fondness that Wil had in her tone. Lynda remembered it as being the most painful years of her life, ones she would rather do without in some ways, and in others, ones she knew she could never exorcize from her life. Back then it had felt as though Wil had it out for her, every moment she was in the house was a moment Lynda was waiting to be abused by an overprotective teenager who had little control of her temper. Now, years later, it was beyond pleasant to have a conversation with Wil that didn't involve comments under the breath, outright yelling, or the multitude of different glares she had in her back pocket. "I remember wondering if you would ever forgive me."

"Forgive you?" Wil shook her head. "What did I have to forgive you for?"

"For not being the one who died." Lynda picked up her wine and brought the glass to her lips, looking Wil directly in the eye. "For not being Patrick."

2012

The box wasn't as heavy as the previous one she'd brought into the dorm room, so Lynda stacked it on top of the others and put her hands on her hips. She had dressed down that day because she knew it was going to involve a lot of manual labor, and while the football team was there to help with heavier items, they still had a lot of Isla's things to bring in.

Wil was also there, and it was mostly to annoy Lynda, she knew. Wil had her own things to move since the two of them were going to be living together, but Wil had way less than Isla.

"Fucking pathetic," Wil muttered as she stepped by Lynda, and Lynda knew instantly she was meant to hear the comment.

She tried to brush it off, but years of verbal abuse was too much. They were about to begin their freshman year of college, and her own house would be much quieter with just her and Aisling living there. She wondered if Isla would even come home after Aisling moved out on her own. She imagined until Aisling was eighteen that she would keep that connection with her sister, but something in her gut said Isla would stop being a part of her life, especially if Wil kept up her influence in Isla's life. It pained her to think about, to the point it would stop her in her tracks if she dwelled in those thoughts for too long. She didn't want to think about it, truthfully, because to lose her would be hard. But she was already preparing herself for it, steeling herself against the inevitable.

"I think that's all of it," Lynda said, her voice ringing through the room. "Do you want help unpacking?"

"I think we can handle it," Isla said, her tone over-the-top bubbly, which meant she had also heard Wil's comment.

Lynda shifted her gaze from Isla to Wil and then dropped it to the floor immediately. She needed to control that reaction better. She was a grown woman, and Wil, although an adult, was still very much a child. She had a lot to learn and a lot of growing up to do.

"Good. I'd still like to take you to dinner for your last night if you'd like. Aisling is waiting in the car so we can go whenever."

"Oh." Isla's face fell.

Wil stepped in. "We were going to walk around campus and see if we can find the good places to eat."

Lynda frowned, knowing Aisling had been holding out for that dinner, wanting one last night with her sister before they were going to be separated for a long time. Though the university wasn't that far away, it was a separation, an end to something, and that made it difficult for Aisling who was so attached to Isla. "I'll explain it to Aisling, then."

Wil snorted and pulled herself up on the bed, eyeing Lynda as though she were trespassing.

"I guess I'll see you." Lynda moved in, wrapping her arms around Isla, who hugged her back. She savored that moment, needing it more than Isla probably knew. Ten years with this girl and she loved her as though she were her own daughter, had treated her as such. When she pulled away, her heart broke a little. "Call me if you need something."

"She won't need anything," Wil said, sending one of those infamous glares Lynda's way.

Lynda clenched her jaw to keep herself from frowning. She'd always understood Wil's fierce protection of Isla, but that didn't mean she wasn't tired of putting up with this. She just wished she could solve Wil's issue with her, wipe it out and maybe they could start over like when she was younger, try to find some sort of common ground where they could stand to be in the same room as each other. With her chest tight, Lynda focused on Isla and pushed her heartache into saying goodbye to her oldest daughter.

Isla sighed heavily but nodded at Lynda. "Yeah, I'll give you a call."

Lynda stepped back and toward the door, Wil's voice reaching her on a murmur again. "Go on, get."

As Lynda left the dorm room, her heart shattered. She hadn't prepared for this. She had told herself she wouldn't cry when she left Isla, she'd told herself she wouldn't let Wil get to her yet again, and still there she was, walking down a busy dormitory hallway, completely broken. It was almost as bad as the day Patrick died. The sense of loss, the overwhelming grief, the panic at not knowing what to do or where to go from there.

Tears stung her eyes, and she wiped them away haphazardly. She wouldn't cry in front of all these people. She wouldn't let them see her like this, and she would never let the girls see her like this. They knew her as strong and perfect, and they needed to keep that image in their minds.

For years, her goal had been to raise the girls, to get them to graduate high school and go to college, to set them on the right path to being exactly who Patrick would have wanted them to be. And Isla was finally there. Patrick had missed it all, just like he would miss everything else in her and Aisling's life—the graduations, the weddings, the grandchildren. It was all left to her to be that person for them. And even after all these years, she wasn't sure she could do it.

The ending of her role as stepmother for Isla hit her harder than she'd expected. Yes, Isla would still likely return to her for things she needed and her job wasn't totally over, but college was such a break, such a new start, such a transition in their lives. They could learn to like each other in a completely different capacity, one where they were more friends than parent and child, and one where they could learn to respect where each other came from.

Lynda had been warned by her friends that the transition wasn't easy, and that she'd likely struggle throughout it with more fights in between, but she was ready for Isla to appreciate her and everything that had happened in the time they'd known each other.

Stepping outside of the dormitory, Lynda looked down the row of windows until she found the one she knew was Isla's. She said a silent goodbye to the sweet girl she had known and loved and a welcome to the adult she knew Isla had to be. Then she thought of Wil, and prayed Wil would finally learn to understand what they had all survived and just maybe that she wouldn't be the aim of Wil's abuse any longer.

2023

ALCOHOL BUZZED IN HER EARS, and Wil realized belatedly she should probably stop drinking if she wanted to walk back to the hotel without staggering. But this was a side of Lynda she had never seen before, one she had only ever dreamed of witnessing. Lynda's cheeks had a nice flush to them, her pale skin no longer ashen as it had been for so many years but full of life.

Wil smiled at her, laughing at something stupid Lynda had said, some memory she'd brought up of Isla and her getting caught trying to sneak out of the house when they were twelve. It was a good story, a good memory, and one she had forgotten. Patrick had apparently barely been able to hold in his laughter as he'd scolded them.

"Would you like another drink?" the waitress interrupted them.

Lynda looked genuinely surprised that her glass was empty, and when she looked to Wil, she narrowed her gaze and looked past her. She checked her watch and then focused on Wil again.

"Do you want to have another round here or head back? We can always order up."

Wil's body was telling her something different than her brain was, and the alcohol flowing through her system was not helping to tamp that loud part of her body down. Canting her head to the side, she took Lynda's hand in her own. "It's up to you."

Lynda turned to the waitress. "I think we'll be fine for tonight, if you could bring the check, please."

The waitress ogled their hands where they touched, a grin blooming on her lips before she scampered off to get what was requested. Wil didn't miss what she had assumed, but Lynda apparently had. After Lynda paid for their meal at her insistence and they stood up, Wil found herself drawn to Lynda's side again. She held her hand to the small of Lynda's back, letting her walk a step ahead as they made their way out of the restaurant.

The streets were filled with people, the sidewalks heavy with foot traffic. Wil stayed as close to Lynda as possible, needing her stable form to steady her own since the ground tilted with every step she took. As they got to the hotel, Wil sighed in relief. She could manage to make it upstairs and into her own room, falling into her bed to pass out for the night.

First the lack of sleep wasn't helping any, but the alcohol still buzzed through her brain, making it hard to think clearly. They walked to the elevator, and Wil caught sight of Francine off to the side where the conference rooms were. Francine's face blew up into a large grin before she turned and walked in the opposite direction.

Wil was doomed. Everyone was thinking there was something going on between them when there was absolutely nothing, and she was going to have to correct that when they headed home to Denver in a couple days. Lynda leaned forward to press the button for the elevator, nearly taking Wil with her as she went.

Straightening back upright, Wil bit the inside of her cheek to try and wake her brain up. Lynda leaned into her, her shoulder brushing against Wil's front as they waited for the elevator. She shuddered, heat pooling between her legs as her knees went weak.

"I think a no-work dinner was an excellent idea," Lynda said, her voice huskier than it had been minutes before.

"It was," Wil agreed. She had never seen Lynda so relaxed or been that relaxed around Lynda herself to be honest. It was a perfect evening to get to know each other in a new capacity and work through some of the latent drama of their lives. Wil tapped a random beat out against the small of Lynda's back, the heat from Lynda's body warming her in places she didn't want to admit to.

As the elevator dinged, they stepped inside, Lynda hitting the button for their floor. Wil kept her mouth shut, worried she might say and do something beyond stupid. Lynda turned to her. "Thank you for coming out with me tonight."

"I'll go out with you any time." Wil inwardly cringed at her phrasing, wishing she had a better hold on her tongue, though in all the time she'd known Lynda, she had never managed that for long.

Lynda let out a low giggle. Seductive as it was, Wil had to remind herself that Lynda was her boss, that Lynda was the woman she had despised for years, that Lynda was untouchable. Except Wil had been touching her, more and more as the days passed. She shoved her hands into the pockets of her slacks to prevent that from happening again. *No touch*, she reminded herself firmly.

Lynda turned and pressed a hand to Wil's shoulder, and she groaned, clenching her jaw tight. *So much for that*. Swallowing hard, Wil looked directly into Lynda's caramel eyes and wondered what the hell she was going to fuck up saying next.

"I know it hasn't always been easy between us, but even if we don't get much out of the seminars, I'm glad we came here together, if only to find this."

"Find what?" Wil choked out, Lynda listing closer than

before to the point that it would take nothing for either of them to press their mouths together in a kiss.

"A better balance? Friendship? I don't know, but at least I don't think you hate me anymore."

"Oh, I never hated you," Wil breathed out the words, needing Lynda to know that very thing. Wil had hated who she wasn't.

"You absolutely did."

"I didn't know you." Wil reached up, about to curl her fingers through Lynda's hair and push it behind her ear, but the elevator dinged their arrival on their floor and Lynda moved away just in time.

Relief flooded her. She needed to not have another drink, no matter how much Lynda insisted, and she needed the coldest shower she could possibly manage, not just to sober up but to calm her raging libido. Following Lynda and trying not to stare at her ass was just as hard as ever. Wil kept her hands in her pants pockets and stopped at Lynda's door.

Surprise washed over Lynda's gaze as she put a hand on Wil's arm, half pulling her inside. "I thought we were going to have another drink."

"I'm not sure. I think I've had enough for tonight."

"Then something non-alcoholic."

Wil pressed her lips together hard, unable to resist the call of this beautifully broken woman. And that was just it, Lynda was as shattered as she was, both by the same events, and years of misunderstanding and trying to hold their shit together. Wil wanted to kiss her, the revelation of the connection they shared so strong that it nearly took over the logical part of her brain. More importantly, everything Lynda had done since dinner that night had pointed toward it as well, but Wil couldn't figure out if it was all in her head or if there was more to it than that.

"Please, Wil," Lynda's voice dropped at the end.

Wil had to try so damn hard to remind herself that this was

not an invitation to fuck. It was an invitation to a drink, to spend more time together.

"One drink," Lynda tried again, her fingers tightening around Wil's arm. "I won't keep you up late, I promise."

It didn't matter what they did then because Wil was going to be up all fucking night dreaming about her, maybe even fucking herself to images of Lynda. That soft look Lynda sent her way was her undoing, and Wil found herself stepping into Lynda's room and leaving the cold air of the hallway behind her.

Lynda had already ordered alcohol before Wil managed to get her brain together from the places it was oozing to let her body do the talking. When room service arrived with their drinks, Wil grabbed them and moved to the edge of Lynda's bed. Fuck, she wished there was anywhere else to sit other than where this woman slept, where her scent surrounded Wil to the point she could barely think of anything else.

Lynda sat next to her, their thighs brushing as the wine threatened to slop over the side of her glass. Wil put a hand on Lynda's thigh to steady her and immediately regretted the decision.

"So where were we?"

"Uh...what?" Wil's eyes that were firmly locked on where her hand was on Lynda's thigh dragged their way over her body, the smooth lines of her waist and hips, the gentle curve and swell of her breasts, the way the dark forest green of her dress brought out hints of green in her eyes that had never been there before, to her lips, thin but perfectly painted to appear bigger. Why did she have to like femmes? Why did she have to like Lynda at all? That stupid crush she'd had as a kid had never gone away despite her deep desire to bury it.

"Our conversation," Lynda amended. "What were we talking about?"

"Oh, I have no idea." Wil struggled just to grasp any part of the conversation that didn't involve thinking about stripping Lynda bare and naked. She wasn't going to drink any of that beer

Lynda had bought her. In fact, Wil moved to set it on the night-stand so she would easily forget about it instead of keeping it in her hand where she'd drink it out of habit. "What do you do in your free time?"

Lynda paused, her eyes wide and lips parted slightly, ready for the taking. Wil halted that train of thought. "Oh, I don't have much free time."

"What do you mean?" Wil furrowed her brow.

"I work a lot of hours. I do most of the takeovers for Jolie Preston, so I'm often going into new investment firms with new people and transitioning them to JP's management and way of conducting business. It's a lot of work."

"I imagine," Wil murmured. "When's the last time you took a vacation?"

"When Aisling graduated from college," Lynda answered freely. "And it was only a couple days so I could travel and get back home."

"That was five years ago."

"It was." Lynda sighed heavily. "I've had to take mandated time off, but it wasn't a vacation. It was mandated."

"You should take *vacations* more often. It's good to reboot yourself sometimes." Wil moved her pointer finger in lazy designs on Lynda's thigh and no matter how many times she told herself to stop, she couldn't make herself do it.

Lynda took a long sip of her wine, the red staining her lips more than they already were from the lipstick. Wil was entranced with every change in Lynda, the lines deeper around her eyes and her lips, the subtle yet barely visible gray baby hairs right at the hairline. Her fingers itched to brush against them, see if they were coarse or fine.

"What do you do?" Lynda asked.

"Oh, I read books, go to clubs, mostly."

"Which clubs?"

Wil snorted lightly, not embarrassed to say it this time. "Gay clubs."

"There are gay clubs in town?"

"You really do live under a rock, don't you?"

"Hey, now, I'm very work-oriented, thank you."

Wil chuckled, her voice low with that flirtatious tone to it. She wanted to not have it there, but at the same time, she couldn't believe the situation she found herself in.

"Shit," Lynda mumbled.

"What?" Wil came back to reality and saw Lynda staring at her dress, where she had spilled a good amount of her wine. Sighing, she took the glass from Lynda and set it next to her beer on the nightstand. "I think it might be time to be done with the alcohol."

"I need to rinse this out." Lynda didn't hesitate as she stood up, only slightly unstable in those four-inch stilettos. She tottered to the bathroom and shut the door behind her.

Wil sighed and grabbed the alcohol, moving it to the dresser and far away from the bed and any electronics so that they wouldn't accidentally spill it on anything else. One accident for the night was enough. She was just about to go to her room and leave when she heard Lynda's smooth tones reach her ears.

"Wil? Are you still out there?"

Walking close to the bathroom door and leaning against it, Wil closed her eyes. "Yeah, I'm still here."

"I need some help."

Confused, Wil straightened her back as Lynda opened the door, still very much in the dress with the dark purple stain down the front of it. A lump formed in Wil's throat, making it next to impossible to breathe.

"I can't get the zipper undone. I think it might be snagged on something."

"Oh." Recognition hit Wil hard. Lynda moved back into the bathroom, turning to face the mirror with her hands on the countertop. This was torture. Pure and simple. What she would give to be able to take Lynda here, from behind, to watch every reaction cross her face in the mirror.

Keeping her gaze on Lynda's shoulders, Wil didn't dare look up. She couldn't let Lynda in on what she was thinking, the inappropriate thoughts that had been going through her brain all night, for the last fifteen years. When Lynda turned her head, Wil jolted back to reality, realizing she was supposed to be helping not staring.

Lifting her shaking hands to the top of the dress, Wil smoothed her fingertips over Lynda's shoulders as she eyed the tiny zipper. It didn't look stuck, but she knew those things could be without any sign of them. She'd undressed enough women in her life, not to mention the dresses she'd worn on occasion when she had to.

Lynda's breathing increased, her shoulders lifting as she reached up to hold her sandy blonde hair out of the way for Wil to have better access to the dress. Sliding her hands along the fabric and back to the zipper, Wil shifted to see where it was stuck. Sure enough, the tiny zipper had caught on some of the black fabric in the seam. It took some tugging, some biting of her lip, and some finesse, but she finally managed to get it undone.

Instead of letting Lynda pull it down, which would have been the better option, Wil found her hands sliding down Lynda's back to the gentle swell of her ass. Her heart raced so hard that it threatened to take over everything, but Wil held her ground. And when she let go of the zipper, she glided her fingers back up Lynda's spine, following the trail with her eyes as Lynda's creamy perfect skin was revealed. Freckles dotted along her back, and Wil touched them briefly before parting the top of the dress so Lynda would know that it was undone.

"Wil?" Lynda asked.

When Wil raised her chin, they made eye contact in the mirror, just like she had imagined would happen except then her fingers would be inside Lynda, pounding into her, slowly teasing her, anything to get a look of pure ecstasy on her face.

"How did you know you liked women?"

Wil's tongue dashed across her lips, the words on the tip of it, and there was no way she was going to be able to hold it back. Damn the alcohol for removing her filters. "You. I liked you when I was a kid. Told Isla about it once. But I had the biggest crush on you in high school and it pissed me off to no end that I couldn't make it stop. I wanted to hate you."

Lynda held her ground. Wil wasn't embarrassed by the confession either. She'd always thought if Lynda ever knew that it would be the end of her world. Lynda dropped her hair and turned slowly, her body still against the counter but facing Wil. Wil's hands came to rest on Lynda's hips, her thumbs brushing up and down tenderly.

"You weren't just upset with me because of Patrick. You were upset because you hated and liked me at the same time."

"Yes," Wil agreed. "But I never told anyone that."

"Did you even know it?"

"Not until this week. I used to dream of undressing you like this, all those damn skirts and dresses you had." Wil used one finger to trace the hemline right at Lynda's neck, sensually touching her collarbones in the process.

Lynda's breath caught, and she leaned in like she was going to kiss Wil, but Wil raised her hand and put her fingers against Lynda's lips to stop and silence her. She wasn't done talking yet. She wasn't done confessing, and this seemed like something Lynda needed to know.

"I used to dream of what we'd do. How I'd touch you or you touch me. It was childish dreams, simple things, but as I got older, the dreams—the fantasies—got better." Wil leaned in, pinning Lynda against the counter, their bodies pressed together neatly, hot, sexually. "I used to masturbate to them."

The pulse point in Lynda's throat throbbed, and Wil longed to taste it, but she resisted. It wasn't time for that. It was time to drag this out, to finally say what she'd wanted to say for years but had forgotten needed to be shared.

"*You* are the reason I know I like women."

"When did you stop?"

"Liking women? Never." Wil chuckled lightly.

Lynda shook her head slowly, her hands against the countertop, gripping onto the edge for dear life, as if it was the root that would bring her back to reality. "No, when did you stop dreaming about me?"

Wil looked her dead in the eye. Fear mingled with deep curiosity, and Wil wasn't sure what was going through Lynda's mind at that moment, if this was helpful or if she was playing some obnoxious game that was going to come back and bite her in the ass later. Either way, she'd already started farming out her resume to other investment firms because she knew she was close to losing her job.

"I haven't." The words fell from her lips in full honesty. She didn't want to admit it, but when asked directly, Wil couldn't lie. "I've never stopped thinking about you like this."

Lynda whimpered, and the sound moved straight between Wil's legs. She had all the power in this moment. They both knew it. If she wanted a kiss, she could so easily take one. If she wanted to fuck Lynda senseless, she could do it. When Lynda slid forward, trying to take control back, that simple thing that she had striven for her entire life, Wil wouldn't let her have it. She pressed their foreheads together and closed her eyes, breathing in that scent that was Lynda from the day they had met all those years ago.

"No, we're not going to do that."

Stepping back was harder than she had anticipated, but even her alcohol-riddled mind knew it was the right decision to make, that she had followed her gut and done what was necessary. Taking it one step farther, Wil put even more space between them as they stopped touching.

"I think I should go to bed now. Goodnight, Mrs. Walsh."

CHAPTER
Thirteen

LYNDA BREATHED HEAVILY as she stayed leaning against the bathroom counter. Every muscle in her body was taut with tension, sexual tension, in a way she had never felt before—even with Patrick. Her heart pounded as she stared at the spot Wil had just left. She needed to figure out what the hell that was all about.

She'd wanted Wil to kiss her. She wanted Wil to touch her, in all those ways Wil had dreamed about, and if Wil had tried, she would have absolutely said yes. She would have leapt before she looked. She would have... Lynda groaned. She would have fucked Wil with wild abandon.

She had never, in her life, wanted that before.

Curling her fingers tightly around the edge of the counter, Lynda stayed put. Cold air brushed against her back, bare from Wil lowering the zipper. *Oh God...* she had asked Wil to practically undress her, knowing Wil had a crush on her in the past. What a bitch that made her. *Sure, here, Wil, halfway undress me while I taunt you and don't let you have me.*

Except she would have. Lynda would have gladly let Wil put hands all over her naked body, making her come over and over again. Groaning, Lynda closed her eyes, but she couldn't get the feel of Wil's hands on her hips, the slide of her thumb along her hip bone, against her back, against her collarbones, her chest, anywhere out of her mind. She wanted it again.

"This is ridiculous," Lynda whispered angrily to no one but herself.

Standing up sharply, she squared her shoulders just before the world around her tilted and she had to grip onto the counter again. She was way too drunk to think about this rationally. That was it. The wine she'd had at dinner and after had clouded her judgment, and she wasn't thinking clearly at all.

Lynda stripped out of her dress and hung it up after rinsing the red wine out. She settled her shoes in the closet and took off her bra and panties. The warm water from the shower was too hot, so she turned it down even though she would have loved the heat had she been sober. It was all alcohol speaking, wasn't it?

As she let the water cool her skin, Lynda pressed her lips together and slid her hand between her legs, dipping her fingers between her swollen lips to find herself wet, dripping wet. Her heart raced as she clenched her jaw.

"Non-concordant my ass."

Whatever had happened between the two of them had gotten her body to react at least, in ways she and Patrick had struggled with. Her mind had been all for it five minutes ago. But now? Now she was glad Wil had stepped back and given her the space, the time to think straight. *Not straight*, she corrected before correcting her correction. *No, straight. I am straight.*

Lynda hadn't known anything but men in her dating life. She'd always been with men and never entertained the idea of a woman until...until Wil told her about those damning dreams, about masturbating to them. Since Patrick died, Lynda had even given up on masturbating.

"What am I doing?" Wincing at the pain in her voice, Lynda turned the water even colder. She needed to sober up quickly. Staying drunk and staying in this state was too much for her. She needed to be able to reason herself out of whatever was going on.

Staying in the shower for another five minutes, Lynda finally escaped the icy grasp of the water. Wrapping a towel around her middle, she stared at herself in the mirror. What did Wil even see in her? Maybe it was the beer talking for Wil as much as the wine had been talking for her. She was old, she had been married, she'd raised two daughters into adulthood. She had nothing to give Wil. Not to mention Wil was Isla's best friend. Toying with that could ruin their relationship even more than it already was.

Then again, what was left of the relationship to ruin? No, she had to stop thinking like that. Lynda sighed and left the bathroom to grab her night clothes. She would sleep off the drinks, and in the morning, she would be able to think far more clearly. That was what needed to happen.

But she stopped as she walked by the adjoining room door. She listened carefully to see if she could hear anything coming from the other room, but she was met with only silence. Wil was probably taking a cold shower, too. Was it all a dream? Some random amalgamation of her mind to try and explain away the soft touches, the tender and heated looks.

Changing and sliding under the covers, Lynda stared at the ceiling. Her mind spun with thoughts of Wil, but not just Wil, with those of sex and women and just what that meant for her. It could simply be her loneliness hitting an all-time high, being reminded of how much she loved Patrick before he died, of being thrown back into some sort of relationship with Wil. But it didn't feel like that. It felt like something more than just that.

Turning on her side, Lynda closed her eyes and wished sleep would take her. It was too much to think about, too hard to come to any sort of conclusion that night, especially with what had almost happened in the bathroom, what she had *wanted* to happen.

She slept fitfully that night, hardly resting, but when she woke, she knew it hadn't just been the alcohol talking. The physical memory of Wil pressed up against her was too strong to deny, and Lynda wanted it to happen again, even if she was going to regret it the next day.

Lynda was dressed in a gray skirt, black tank top, and a light green jacket that zipped all the way up the front by the time Wil knocked on the adjoining door. This time, with only one day left of seminars, she knew to expect Wil would have coffee for her. As she opened the door, she gave Wil a smile, one that was as genuine as she could manage considering the circumstances.

Wil raised an eyebrow in a curious look and pushed her hand forward with the disposable cup in it. "Coffee?"

"Yes, thank you." Lynda took it and stepped back into her room to finalize getting ready.

When she went to the bathroom, she expected Wil to follow her and talk like they had done every morning since they'd arrived there, but when she grabbed her necklace and turned to face the door, Wil was nowhere in sight. Her stomach plummeted as fear ratcheted up in her chest. Perhaps all was not as easy as it had once been. Taking hold of the necklace and earrings, Lynda stepped out into the main part of the bedroom where Wil was still standing by the door.

"Were there any lectures you wanted to attend today?"

"No," Wil answered, succinctly.

"Right, then." Lynda set the earrings on the dresser so she could put the necklace on. It was the fourth or fifth attempt at getting the clasp done that Wil finally stepped up and took the necklace from her fingers. Just like the night before, Lynda held her hair to the side. Her hands shook—when had that started? Wil standing so close to her even if they weren't touching was exactly what she wanted.

As the necklace dropped heavily onto her, Wil stepped away,

and Lynda turned around, expecting Wil to be right there, but she was back to standing in the doorway. Lynda wasn't sure what to say, so instead, she grabbed the earrings and put them on. With her purse on her shoulder, she looked Wil up and down. "Are you ready?"

"Yes—"

The ma'am was left off, and she was pretty sure it was for her benefit since they didn't know where they stood with each other after the previous night. Not speaking of it, Lynda nodded toward the door and walked in that direction. Wil followed her dutifully.

All day, she was distracted. She spent hours in lecture rooms, listening to experts talk about leading, and the only thing Lynda could think about was how awful a leader she was to take advantage of her subordinate. Jessica would have her job for this one. They ate lunch with another small group of conference goers, and the distraction and buffer had been welcome.

But even through it all, Lynda caught herself looking at Wil with new eyes. She caught herself seeing her in a new way. It was as if the previous night had shattered the glass Lynda had looked at Wil through all her life, and before her was a woman, someone who had desires and needs, and for some undefinable reason, wanted her. Though she still couldn't fathom why. She was a widow, a single mother of two adult children, and she did nothing for herself but work.

As dinner approached, Lynda made a bold decision. She touched Wil's arm lightly to get her attention. "I'm going to order up dinner tonight. I think I need some time."

Wil ducked her chin. "I can always find someone else to eat with."

"Will you check in with me when you get back?"

"Sure." Wil's brow furrowed. "Is something wrong?"

"No, nothing is wrong. I just want to talk to you before you go to bed."

"Okay. I can do that."

"Good."

Lynda and Wil parted ways for what seemed like the first time all week. She made her way to the elevator, the same one they had taken up the night before, the same one Wil had given her such a longing look and she hadn't even noticed it, hadn't even recognized it as such. But now she knew better.

It was awful of her to make Wil wait for the conversation, but she needed a glass or two of wine in her system to bolster herself for it. She needed the quiet time to ruminate on what may or may not be said and how she wanted to delicately navigate Wil's growing crush. If she was willing to push boundaries that much over the course of a simple week, then who knew what would happen once they got back to Denver.

She barely touched her dinner, but she was halfway through the bottle of wine she had ordered when there was a knock at her door, the main door this time. Standing to attention, Lynda left the glass on the desk and went to answer it, finding Wil standing on the other side. She couldn't read Wil at all.

And that scared her. She was usually good at catching the underlying meaning of what wasn't being said, but with Wil that was so hard to do.

"Come in," Lynda said, her voice low and the merlot she'd chosen lingering on her tongue.

Wil stepped through the door, and when Lynda shut it, she was surprised to find Wil still standing right next to her. Wil was so quiet, probably waiting for Lynda to spill what the conversation was about, but even in the interim hours, she hadn't figured out what she wanted to say or how she wanted to begin.

"Let's sit down." Leading the way to the main part of the bedroom, Lynda sat on the edge of the bed to give Wil the chair.

Wil, however, sat right next to her. So much for space to help her through this. Lynda folded her hands in her lap as she crossed her legs. "We need to talk about last night."

"Am I suspended?"

"What?" Lynda's eyes widened as she shook her head. "No, why would I suspend you?"

"My behavior was inappropriate, Mrs. Walsh."

Oh, the way she said the name. It sent shivers through Lynda, and she knew in that instant the conversation was not going to be about work or how to navigate the tension. "I'm not even going to write you up."

Wil refused to look up at her, her eyes downcast and glued to her hands in her lap. "Then what am I doing here?"

Lynda pulled in on herself. This was not an easy conversation to have, but she needed to figure out how to say the words in a way that would make sense to Wil. "You...you mentioned when you first realized you liked women."

"Yes?" Wil raised a dark eyebrow up, her rounded face turning to the side. "You want to talk about being queer?"

"Yes." Lynda breathed out a sigh of relief, glad that Wil had managed to figure out where she was going with the conversation. "What did you do when you found out?"

Wil's cheeks tinged a dark color, and she reached forward and grabbed Lynda's hand. "What do you want to do?"

God, everything. Lynda barely held back the moan, but her body ramped up the same way it had the night before, the desire to lean in and touch lips. She shivered, her nipples hardening and her breathing increasing.

"Last night was..." Lynda stopped, still not quite sure how to describe what happened in the bathroom. "What happened last night?"

"We almost crossed a line."

They'd already crossed lines, leaving them so far in the distance neither of them could see them anymore. But she knew the one they were talking about, the one they were skirting around without saying, and it was the only one left between them. Clearing her throat, Lynda tried again, "I know that. I...I wanted to."

"All right." Wil lifted Lynda's chin with a single finger. "I guess the question should be, now, almost twenty-four hours later, do you still want to?"

"Yes," Lynda answered honestly, her heart racing. Wil's finger on her skin was so warm, so perfect. She closed her eyes, wishing Wil would move in and kiss her, take the decision from her so she didn't have to make it. When nothing happened, she gazed into Wil's dark eyes. She reached up and brushed fingers against Wil's cheek, down her neck to the top of her chest, finally daring to be the one to initiate touch.

"Mrs. Walsh—"

Lynda snorted. "Wil, stop calling me that."

"Fine. Lynda. Do you want to kiss me, or do you want to kiss a woman?"

She hadn't managed to ask herself that question. All day all she had done was think about Wil. Would another woman be out of the question? She had no idea. What she did know was that she wanted Wil. She wanted to be sandwiched between her and any other surface again, to feel that power drain out of her into someone she trusted.

"You." Her answer was honest. She wasn't going to try to hide anymore. Wil had seen more of her in the last week than anyone had in the last sixteen years since Patrick had died, and she had forgotten how wonderful it was to just be seen. "I want to kiss *you*."

Wil grinned, her face bursting with joy. "Good to know."

Wil tangled her fingers in her hair, and she brushed loose strands behind Lynda's ear before she smoothly moved into cupping Lynda's cheek. This was it. This was the moment she had been waiting for. Wil made eye contact and shook her head. "It's not the time."

Whimpering a whine, Lynda's lips parted in surprise. "What?"

"Lynda, you've been drinking wine again tonight, right?"

"Yes, but I've been thinking about this all day. I've been thinking about how you touched me last night, but also how you've been touching me all week. How your fingers feel against my skin."

Wil stilled, holding Lynda's desperate gaze before breaking it. "It's not the right time."

"What does that even mean? What is the right time?"

"Not tonight." Wil stood up and brushed her palms down her pants as she stepped away from the bed and away from Lynda.

Immediately, Lynda rose to her feet. Wil walked confidently toward the adjoining door, but Lynda didn't want to lose her. She couldn't lose her. Right when Wil reached for the door handle, Lynda covered it with her own fingers, sliding between the door and Wil. She raised her gaze, meeting Wil's eyes in desperation.

"I want this. Now."

The grin wasn't joyful this time. It was wicked. Wil didn't hesitate as she cupped both sides of Lynda's face and pulled her in, their mouths pressing together in a brutal kiss. Lynda tightened her grasp on the door handle, leaning into the door as Wil plundered her. It was everything she had imagined and more.

Pushing back as soon as she managed to catch a thread of her brain, Lynda parted her lips so their tongues tangled. She moaned. Her body writhed. At some point, she'd let go of the door and gripped Wil's sides, tightening her grasp into the fabric of Wil's vest and keeping her as close as possible.

Wil stepped forward, pushing Lynda's shoulders into the door so she was smooshed between the hard metal and Wil's soft but hot body. She needed more. Nothing was stopping the raging burn within her to take, to explore, to fulfill whatever dreams she hadn't even dared to have yet. Wrapping her arms around Wil's back, Lynda threaded her fingers into Wil's hair and tugged hard. Wil groaned in pleasure and jerked her hips into Lynda's, inciting her.

Tugging at the edge of Wil's button up, Lynda pulled it out of her pants until she could reach under it and touch her scorching skin. It was exactly what she had wanted, so soft and hot at the same time. She skated her fingers around the edge to the front and then up and over the material to cup Wil's breast before dropping her hands to the side. Wil nipped at her lip, but Lynda couldn't tell if it was a warning or exactly what they both wanted.

Wil pulled away sharply, breathing heavily as she pressed her forehead into Lynda's shoulder. Silence took over them. Lynda kept her hands on Wil's sides, holding tight to her until her own breathing calmed considerably.

"I need to leave," Wil murmured.

As much as Lynda wanted to tell her to stay, she knew it was a good idea. They worked together. Lynda was Wil's boss, not only that but Wil had looked up to her as a child. They shouldn't be doing this. Except Wil didn't move right away. It was another minute at least before she shifted onto her heels and pulled away from Lynda. Wil reached for the doorknob just to the side of Lynda's body and turned it.

Lynda couldn't believe it. She'd just been kissed senseless, she desperately wanted more, and Wil was going to walk away, and she had to let her go. She had to put that space between them because she needed to get her head on straight. Her heart raced as she stepped to the side and watched Wil walk through the doorway and into her own room. The distance between them was a chasm she had never felt before, and only one she could rectify. God, she wanted Wil. That kiss had been such a moment of passion. It had turned every fire in her on, and she couldn't control herself. With Wil gone, that pull was so much stronger, so damning because she couldn't deny it.

WIL SET her bag on top of her desk in Denver, rolling her shoulders in relief. She had managed to sneak into the office without Lynda seeing her, which considering she was the only other one in there at the moment was quite a feat. She set her travel mug onto the top of her desk and slid into her chair, covering her face with her hands.

Seattle had been a bad decision—everything there had been going fine until she couldn't control her damn impulses again. But that kiss was the kiss to end all of them. No way had Wil been able to sleep that night, and she had vivid fantasies of doing it repeatedly to Lynda at every given opportunity.

But the magic of being secluded and away from the rest of the world was gone, and they were back in the office. Wil swallowed hard, knowing that Lynda was in the next office over already working for the day. The woman was a damn machine. She turned on her computer and grabbed her cup of coffee.

She was just about to get started on the workday when the door to her office opened and closed. Wil cringed, the curse on the tip of her tongue that she barely managed to hold back. When she looked up, Lynda stood there, and Wil could have died.

"Hot damn," she murmured, her heart racing and her body already reacting.

Lynda wore a deep maroon dress that cut across her skin, high on her left thigh and low on her right one. The heels she wore didn't help, and Wil swore they were at least two inches higher than Lynda's normal height.

As she moved her gaze upward, the cardigan was black and hung on her body but did nothing to hide the curve of her hip to waist, waist to breasts. The top of the dress had a mimicking angle before it popped up in the sleeve to modestly cover Lynda's shoulder. Wil couldn't hold back the shudder or the pool of heat between her legs or her itchy fingers to touch, but Lynda eyed her as if she could read every intonation Wil made. Embarrassment rushed through her, and Wil was at a complete loss for words for the first time ever.

They stared at each other, each one daring the other to break the silence, and for one fleeting moment, Wil wondered if this was just as hard for Lynda as it was for her. Wil finally shifted in her chair, and it must have broken Lynda's train of thought because she pinned Wil with a sharp look. "We have work to do today."

"Why else would we be here?" The biting comment wasn't what Wil had intended on saying, but it must have been all the pent-up frustration. She clenched her jaw, wishing she had said something—anything—else. Instead of taking it back, or apologizing, Wil looked at Lynda with as much sexual heat in her gaze as possible.

Stepping forward, Lynda moved to the far side of the desk and slipped three files onto it. Wil hadn't even noticed them in her hand when she'd come in because she'd been too damn distracted by Lynda herself. As she leaned over the desk, Wil had to force her gaze upward to her eyes and away from her breasts, breasts she remembered all too clearly pressed against her multiple times in the last week.

"We're going to be letting these three go today."

"I thought you said we weren't firing anyone." Betrayal filled her, the cold of it grasping her heart. Wil tried to push through it to find the reasoning, the answers to the questions she couldn't even voice yet. Wil grabbed at the files to see who they were losing and how big of an impact it was going to make on the firm.

The top one she absolutely agreed with. Kandi—her actual name—was probably the least fit for their type of environment, not to mention she was consistently late and always had an excuse for it, and not a good excuse. She worked admin, so it wouldn't be hard to replace her, though they would feel the weight without her for a bit.

Next up was Logan Moss. Wil had hired him two years ago, and while his track record wasn't awful, he also wasn't the best employee. He'd skated through by weaving the system for his benefit. It was hard to fire people sometimes. Wil agreed with that one, but the third file made her heart thud loudly.

Jacob.

Wil raised her gaze to meet Lynda's, her heart hammering with fear at the impending confrontation. "Why's Jacob's file here?"

"He's looking for another job." Lynda raised an eyebrow, as if that was enough of an answer.

"As I'm sure half the firm is right now. They think you've come in here to do just this, and that isn't any reason to fire someone. In fact, if they're a good fit, it's a perfect reason to try and work with them to keep them on, to convince them their skills are wanted." Wil folded the file back over and slid it to Lynda. "No."

"There are better options for management than him."

Wil clenched her jaw. Having spent the entire last week at a leadership conference with Lynda where they had both barely paid attention to the lectures because they were so focused on work—and then each other, her pesky brain reminded her—she thought it was damn lofty of Lynda to fire him for that.

"He's new to leadership, and he was just getting his feet wet when we had this takeover. Jacob is a hard worker, he always shows up on time, and he stays late when he needs to."

"He's not smart enough to handle the workload. He wasn't up to speed when we left for Seattle, and there were issues while we were gone." Lynda put both her hands on the desk and leaned over, as if she was trying to use her body to convince Wil to sway in her direction, and while that may have worked two days ago, they were now back in Denver, and Wil was on her home turf, and she wasn't going to make the same mistake twice. No matter how much she might want to.

"What issues?" Wil wanted to stand up, to have the higher ground, but she stayed put and glared daggers in Lynda's direction.

"He wasn't ready to be left on his own."

"That sounds like a management problem and not something we can blame on him. You said yourself that you were worried he wasn't ready for it. I told you I should have stayed here to keep everything going. You're taking out your own pettiness and frustration on him because of *your* failure."

Lynda pursed her lips, quietly controlling her response. Wil had seen her do that so many times that it was impossible not to see this time. "You were supposed to train him."

"So now you're protecting me?" Wil snorted. "Get off your damn high horse. There's no way he would have been prepared to run this place in the week you gave me. Or was this all a trap so you could fuck with his life before dropping him like a bad habit?"

"I'll have you watch your tone with me." Lynda's voice brokered no argument, but Wil had never taken that bait once in her life.

"I'll watch it when you're not being such a bitch about something. It's ridiculous for you to expect such drastic improvement in a week, and I will defend my team every time. That's something you should know by now."

Lynda sighed heavily and straightened her back. She crossed her arms and glanced to the ceiling before leaning over Wil's desk again. "He's not ready for this."

"Then you can fire him on your own. I won't sit in on that. You're being petty."

"Hardly." The warning tone in Lynda's voice should have tipped her off that Wil was navigating far too close to Lynda's limits, but it was too damn early, and she didn't have enough coffee in her veins yet.

Wil dared to stand, leaning over her desk in much the same manner Lynda was. "If you're firing him because he's looking for another job, then you'll have to fire me, too."

Lynda's jaw dropped before she snatched it closed and clenched it tight. Her eyes never wavered from Wil's face as they moved into their second stare down of the morning. Wil had wanted to do nothing but avoid Lynda for the day, or the week if she could manage, and do her work and go home at night to masturbate to that kiss and get it the fuck out of her system, and yet here she was, already having a show down before it was eight in the damn morning.

"Where?" Lynda's voice cracked.

"It doesn't matter where," Wil pushed. "But if you're going to pull this kind of shit, anywhere but here will be preferred. So long as it isn't here *with you.*"

She added the last two words for emphasis but especially after the last week. They'd found a balance for a few days there, but the last couple and especially the flight home and subsequent night before heading back into the office had proved that much to Wil. They shouldn't work together. The break they had made in their relationship eleven years prior was something they needed because nothing good could come from kissing her best friend's estranged stepmom.

"Where are you looking?"

Is that panic? Wil narrowed her gaze to see if she could hear it again or see any sign of it in Lynda's eyes and face, but she couldn't find a trace of it again. Wil crossed her arms, leaning back on her heels as she suddenly had all the power in the conversation, and she liked it. "It doesn't matter."

"Do you have interviews?"

It was there again. The sick satisfaction at the turmoil Wil caused was something she was taking to heart and enjoying far too much. Lying easily, Wil answered, "Yes."

They were back to staring at each other in silence. Lynda finally broke it, reaching for the files on the desk and tucking them against her chest as if the paper could protect her. "When were you going to tell me?"

"When I turned in my resignation." Wil pursed her lips, surprised that the turn of this conversation had taken the wind out of Lynda's sails.

"As soon as Kandi gets in, please bring her down to my office." Lynda strode toward the door, stopping at the sound of Wil's voice.

"Will do, Mrs. Walsh."

It sent a thrill up Wil's spine to be able to get that pure, fear-driven reaction from Lynda. She had seen it. It was only a small second of fear, but she had done it. As she sat back in her desk chair, her heart ached and cold washed through her. Guilt consumed her. She couldn't stop herself, could she?

There were so many ways she could have handled that better than she did. Wil had been fighting herself more than she'd been fighting Lynda, needed to prove that she would do anything to protect those who didn't even know the conversations around them. She knew she wasn't wrong—it was absolutely unfair to fire Jacob like this. He didn't deserve it, and he was an excellent employee and would be even better with some additional training.

Sighing, Wil rubbed her temples as her shoulders loosened. She'd done a shit job of explaining all that to Lynda in a reasonable way, and had the last week not happened, she might have been able to hold her tongue. Fuck, she'd been so cruel. She immediately looked at the door, wondering if Lynda had thought there was more to it than the traditional shift of employees after a buy-out like they had undergone or if she was worried Wil was going to file a formal complaint about what happened in Seattle.

That had never been Wil's intention. She'd instigated it more than Lynda had. She'd willingly put her hands on Lynda's body. They had wanted more—both nights—and Wil had been the one to put a stop to it, but that didn't mean Lynda wasn't worried something else might happen once they got back to Denver.

Wil needed to call Isla. Her mind was a mess of possibilities of what was going on, and while she had grown up with Lynda next door, she hadn't grown up with her in the same house. Perhaps Isla could offer some sort of insight that Wil was missing, something that could tell her exactly what move she needed to make next.

2008

"Isla?" Wil whispered, her heart racing as they laid in her bed. It was nearly two in the morning, but they were getting ready for the first day of school and insisted on trying to stay up every night together until they were forced back into the reality of classes.

"Yeah?" Isla's voice was sweet, but it was also sleep-laden. They'd finished the movie they were watching thirty minutes ago, and the popcorn and pop they'd kept with them littered the bedroom. They'd have to clean that up in the morning before Lynda yelled at them.

Wil wasn't sure how to say the words. She'd gotten Isla's attention for one reason, needing to make a confession, but she still wasn't sure what to say or how. They had only ever talked about boys, but Isla was her best friend. She'd understand, right?

"I think..." Wil started and stopped. It wasn't just that Wil liked girls, it was *who* she liked, and that was the problem. She wanted to talk to Isla about it all, but she had no idea how she would take it. "I'm not sure I like boys."

"What do you mean? I thought you liked D'Ante." Isla turned onto her side, facing Wil in the bed. They were only inches apart, but Wil knew it was a chasm they had to bridge.

Swallowing hard, Wil struggled to find the words. "I know I said that, but...well, there's this girl I like, and I think I like her a lot more than D'Ante."

Isla's eyes were wide, the blue color nearly black in the dark room. Wil was glad, because it meant Isla couldn't see her well either, or the embarrassment she was feeling wasn't too outwardly obvious. "What do you mean you like girls?"

"I like girls like I'm supposed to like boys."

"But you don't like boys?" Isla seemed genuinely curious, and Wil wanted to lean into that, trust that Isla was simply trying to understand and not prodding to take this information and ruin her.

"I don't know. I like boys, but I think I like girls, too." It was the most non-committal answer she could give, and a way that she would be able to take it back if Isla decided it wasn't to her liking or that Wil was some kind of abomination.

"How do you know?"

"Oh, I don't know." Wil buried half her face in the pillow, wishing not for the first time in the last thirty seconds that she hadn't even opened this can of worms. "I guess I just do."

"Like you like her, like her?"

"Yeah." Wil sighed, closing her eyes, not willing to see Isla's reaction. "Yeah, I think I do."

"Like you want to kiss her?" Isla giggled, loudly before she quieted down, realizing it was too loud and might get them in trouble for being up so late.

That was the one part of this Wil wasn't sure she wanted to admit. Pressing her lips together hard, Wil opened her eyes, staring right into Isla's. "Yeah, I want to kiss her."

Laughing again, Isla reached over and gripped Wil's hand. "That's exciting. Who is it?"

Wil's heart stuttered. She was so happy Isla wasn't making a big deal about it, but then the thought of who it was she wanted to kiss, the woman who was sleeping soundly in the next room over, shattered the illusion that it would be accepted.

"It doesn't matter," Wil muttered.

"No, tell me. Who is it?"

"It really doesn't matter," Wil tried again. She closed her eyes, and Lynda's image came to her unbidden, the gentle curve of her body, the confidence she had in her shoulders every time she did something with them, the thin line of her lips that she managed to make look fuller with the magic of makeup.

Wil turned onto her back to stare at the glow-in-the-dark stars Patrick had put on the ceiling, ones that Isla refused to take down even though they were fourteen and it was a bit childish, mostly because it was her father who had put them there. No other reason.

Isla scooted in closer. "Is it me?"

"What? No." Wil shook her head and eyed Isla sharply. "You're my forever friend."

"Just checking." Isla touched Wil's shoulder lightly. "So who is it?"

"You know, I really don't think it matters. Can't we just accept that I like girls and move on from there?"

"I guess." Isla shrugged. "Do you still like boys?"

"I don't know... I think so." Wil wasn't really thinking about that, so her tone was enough to push that part of the conversation aside for then.

They stayed in silence for a long time, and she was pretty sure Isla had fallen asleep on her shoulder. Sighing, Wil turned to face Isla again, trying to shift her out of the way so she could get comfortable for the night.

"You know, you should just tell me who she is. We've been

best friends since kindergarten, Wil. We don't keep secrets from each other."

Wil's heart broke. Isla was right. They didn't keep secrets, ever. "Okay, but you have to promise you won't freak out."

"Who would I freak out over?"

"This one you might." Wil held her ground, her stomach twisting tightly at what she knew was about to happen but couldn't avoid.

Isla grabbed her hand and squeezed tight. "I promise I won't freak out. Who is it?"

"Lynda."

CHAPTER
Fifteen

2023

LYNDA HAD STRUGGLED to focus since that night. She'd taken to referring to it as *that night* because what else was she supposed to call it? That night had been everything to her, and she hadn't been able to stop thinking about it. Not one moment since Wil had walked away from her had she been able to stop imagining Wil's lips against her again.

Wil's body pushing into hers.

Hands against her skin.

Lynda shuddered and blinked to refocus herself for the umpteenth time that morning and it wasn't even lunch time yet. The rest of the team was already in their offices, and she'd warned Wil about the terminations that were going to happen that day, which she hadn't seemed thrilled about.

And with that thought, Lynda realized how long had passed since she had asked Wil to get Kandi and bring her in for her termination. It had been hours. Standing, Lynda walked to the front of the firm and saw Kandi at her desk. Frowning, she immediately turned around and stalked toward Wil's office.

When she entered, Wil was on the phone, so she stood just inside the door, with it shut, and waited.

"Yes, sir. Yes. That will work for me. Thank you."

As soon as Wil hung up, Lynda raised an eyebrow at her. "Job interview?"

"Since you asked so nicely, yes." Wil moved papers around her desk as if she was organizing them, but Lynda saw through the façade. "I put my resume out as soon as I knew there was a buy-out."

Perfect, Lynda thought. She'd wanted to promote Wil, not have to replace her. Walking all the way to the desk, Lynda put a single finger down on it and leaned over, making sure Wil's entire attention was on her. "I told you to bring me Kandi when she arrived."

"And you're just now noticing I didn't? Some boss."

They were right back where they had started all those years ago, small quips, name-calling mumbled under the breath. Lynda wanted to cry and rage all in the same moment. She wanted to drag Wil back into the present and yell at her to stop being such a fool. She'd thought they'd at least made some progress in the last three weeks. All she could do was hope this was a blip on that path. Instead of returning the emotion in kind, Lynda held her hurt in check as best as she could.

"What's wrong with you, Wil?"

Wil snorted, anger flashing through her eyes before she schooled it. Oh, she had gotten better at that through the years, but Lynda could still see it lingering. Wil, wisely, didn't answer.

Shaking her head slowly, Lynda straightened her back. "You can either come with me to do this termination or feel free to clear out your desk. I don't have time for games, and I didn't expect this from you of all people."

Lynda didn't give her a chance to respond as she walked out of the office and toward the front admin part of the firm. She leaned over Kandi's desk when there was no one around. "Kandi, would you come with me?"

"Sure." She seemed jumpy, but Lynda was aware they both knew what was about to happen.

Kandi followed Lynda to the back offices, and Wil stood at hers, waiting and ready to join in the termination. It didn't take long, and Kandi knew to expect it. She even agreed with it, which told Lynda this was not the first time she had been fired for those same issues.

As Kandi left the firm, Lynda steepled her fingers, leaned back in her chair, and eyed Wil who sat directly across the desk from her. Wil remained silent, thankfully, because Lynda was pretty sure if she spoke it was all going to be harsh comments and anger.

"What happened?" Lynda questioned.

"I have no idea what you mean."

Lynda frowned, then pressed her pointer fingers to her lips. She held her position, watching every small change in Wil's features to try and figure out what was going on with her. She looked damn near perfect today, too. Lynda had seen her tousled in the middle of the night, and she had looked just as beautiful then as now.

Leaning into the silence was something Lynda could do. She could sit there until Wil cracked under the pressure and finally spoke. That had been her best weapon when Wil was a child and had thrown these angry tantrums. It all came rushing back to her, even though she had thought they were past this. She hadn't thought they would go right back to it, especially after *that night*.

"Go get Logan."

"Now?" Wil looked slightly surprised.

"Yes," Lynda answered sharply. She wanted to see how quickly Wil would listen to her, how much of a fight she would put up.

"Fucking stupid," Wil muttered as she stood, walking toward the door.

Lynda admired her ass, the curves of which she'd only just begun to learn, but she could feel them in her palms again if she allowed herself to. In the silence, she closed her eyes and parsed through the last few hours. Lynda must have struck some nerve in Wil to toss her back ten years. She'd have to find a way around that and quickly, because the office would devolve if she didn't. But she had to be careful, because Wil ultimately held the power to ruin everything if she wanted to.

It didn't take long, but Wil returned with Logan, and they began the same conversation they'd had with Kandi. His termination went equally as well, slightly more contentious, but nothing Lynda couldn't handle and hadn't handled on her own before. Once again, she found herself staring across her desk at Wil, who eyed her back ferociously.

"Is that all you needed me for?" Wil's voice rang through the room, that same age-old anger right back where it had been before.

"I would like you to stay late tonight." Lynda cooled her tone and schooled her features. If this was how Wil was going to act, then just like before, she couldn't let Wil see how much hurt she was causing. She had to protect herself.

"What for?" Wil's nose wrinkled up.

"We have some extra work we need to do." Lynda shifted to bend over her desk, an obvious dismissal to just about everyone, but then again, Wil wasn't everyone. So, when Wil didn't leave the room, she shouldn't have been surprised.

"Is this about Seattle?" Wil narrowed her eyes, every muscle in her body tense.

Lynda's shoulders tightened painfully. Her back was ramrod straight in an instant as fear washed through her. Her heart thundered, and she had to force herself to look up into Wil's eyes. "What about Seattle?"

"You know exactly what I'm talking about." Wil kept that famous glare in place.

Lynda swallowed, her throat constricting as that fear clawed its way through her. "I'm not sure there's anything to discuss about Seattle." *At least not talked about in the office where everyone else can hear,* but she didn't add that part.

Wil should know better, and she should understand the complications they had run face first into now that they were back in Denver, but maybe she just didn't care. All the progress Lynda thought they had made had gone out the window the instant they had stepped foot in the Rocky Mountains again.

Wil's lips parted in surprise, her look softening for an instant before she hardened again. "Fine."

"You're free to leave and go back to your duties." Lynda needed room to breathe, to figure out just what they were going to do that night, how to navigate around this black hole she had created.

"Are you going to fire me?"

Lynda flicked her gaze up to meet Wil's eyes—eyes that were filled with trepidation. As much as she wanted to offer reassurance, she couldn't. Because if Lynda didn't work there, she couldn't protect Wil, and if Jessica found out everything that had happened in the last few weeks, Wil wouldn't be safe. "That remains to be seen."

"That is so like you, needing a goddamn power trip."

"I'll invite you to watch your tongue, Wilda. The door is that way. You can meet me here once your work is done for the day." Lynda pointed to the door to make her point very clear. She didn't want to have this conversation or argument where the rest of the firm could hear, which would force her to take an even firmer hand with Wil.

Wil stood up angrily and stalked to the door. But just before she wrenched it open, she stopped and spun back around. "My name is Wil, Mrs. Walsh."

Then she was gone. Lynda breathed out a sigh. It was as if the last eleven years had vanished, and they were right back where they started. Lynda traced her fingers over her lips, remembering the kiss, the passion, the control Wil had wielded for that brief time, the control she had taken from Lynda and only allowed her to feel. How were the two the same person? Breathing out, Lynda turned to her computer to try and get as much work as possible done that day.

~

The day had gotten even longer, and by the time the office was quiet, Lynda had struggled to get anything done. She'd gone from daydreaming about *that night* to thinking about Wil's current attitude, which was the entire point of having a conversation with her when no one else was around. The attitude needed to change, and Lynda was willing to do whatever it took to make that happen. But she couldn't let anyone else know that they'd kissed—not without risking everything.

They had been on such good terms for the last week, and semi-good terms the week before. She'd thought they were finally finding their balance, but then Wil had arrived in the office that morning, and the storm she'd brought with had followed her everywhere. Lynda had witnessed the fact that Wil was only angry with her, so it wasn't an all-around attitude adjustment that needed to happen. No, this was something between the two of them and the two of them alone.

She waited, watching to see if the light in Wil's office went off or not, and it was nearing seven in the evening when Wil finally came to her door. Lynda had taken the time to get some extra work done that she had struggled with earlier in the day, and it had been time well spent. When Wil opened her door and shut it, Lynda stood up from her desk and rounded it.

This was not a conversation that needed to happen between boss and employee, but one between colleagues, one between women. Women who had kissed and touched, and oh how Lynda longed for that to happen again. Still, if today were any indication, Wil wanted to avoid that, and it would be good to avoid while in the office proper. Lynda was pretty sure that she wasn't going to be able to get Wil alone outside of the firm any time soon and this was not a problem that could wait.

"Thank you for agreeing to this." Lynda stood on the far side of her desk as Wil stayed by the door. "Take a seat."

Will complied, though her movements were stiff. She probably still thought Lynda might fire her, but the peace had been kept so far that day so there was no reason to initiate a third termination.

"I wanted to talk to you about today." Lynda's stomach was a mess of knots. She'd never been good at navigating this mood from Wil and now was no different than before.

"You didn't fire Jacob."

"I didn't." Lynda smoothed her hands on her dress behind her as she sat down across from Wil. "You were right in that regard, and I have to learn to trust more. However, he's still having some issues I would like for him to resolve sooner rather than later, so you and I will set up an improvement plan with him tomorrow."

Wil remained silent, her lips pressed together hard, her eyes not lifting to meet Lynda's. Whatever was happening between them was something that needed to be dealt with immediately. That much Lynda had gotten right at least.

"Are you going to fire me?" Wil's voice had an unexpected waver to it.

Lynda clenched her jaw, keeping her outward appearance relaxed. She didn't want to sway Wil's thinking on that front because if the attitude kept up, she might have to fire her, even if she didn't want to. Letting the silence drag out, Lynda finally answered, "I think I'll keep you for now."

She thought it would at least get her a smile, some type of sweet response, but instead, she was met with steel. Wil's dark eyes reached hers, and she didn't seem pleased at all. Backtracking slightly, Lynda held her ground.

"Your attitude with me needs to shift, otherwise I may not have a choice in whether or not you stay here." *Or if Lynda was able to stay there.* But Lynda wasn't going to put that kind of pressure on Wil's shoulders. She didn't know what kind of line Lynda was already walking.

"I have an interview…"

"I understand, but that doesn't mean you can treat me with disrespect."

Wil's lips parted, and she shook her head. "I didn't disrespect you."

"I've had enough experience in the past with your attitude and personality to recognize disrespect when I see it." Lynda clenched her jaw and held her ground. She wasn't going to give up on this—she couldn't. Everything weighed on how she managed to walk this line.

Wil softened, the muscles in her face relaxing and her eyes casting down. "It wasn't meant as that."

Impressed with the way Wil managed to pull back, working to slide away from the anger that was so readily her norm. Lynda kept her gaze firmly locked on Wil, the seriousness of the conversation sitting between them.

"Then would you mind explaining what happened today because that's all I see." Lynda crossed her legs, noting that Wil's gaze dropped to her knee that was suddenly revealed, her dress riding up higher on her thigh than normal. Well, there was that at least. Perhaps she hadn't been the only one struggling with that attraction.

"There is no disrespect, Mrs. Walsh."

"Lynda," she corrected. The sliding back into that formality wasn't something she wanted to do. She needed the separation from what their relationship used to be to what it was now. Yes, she might have been Wil's immediate supervisor, but she was no longer her best friend's stepmother, not in that capacity.

Wil seemed surprised by the soft admonition, but she didn't comment on it as she repeated herself. "There is no disrespect."

"Then what is it? Because we haven't really talked since we left Seattle."

When Wil sucked her cheeks in, Lynda knew that was exactly what was setting off the reaction in Wil now. Rubbing her temple, Lynda uncrossed her legs and leaned forward slightly.

"Listen to me carefully, Wil, because this is important. What happened in Seattle can stay there if you want it to be that way, but in order for that to happen you must treat me with respect while we are here. Even if you leave Jolie Preston for another firm."

Wil went to speak, and Lynda held her hand up to silence her.

"I'm not done. If you don't want what happened in Seattle to stay there, then we need to have a frank conversation about what happened. It's your choice, but I won't stand to be treated this way any longer."

Wil held the silence. Lynda kept her gaze directly on Wil, unnerved by how quiet she was. She expected anger, like she had been greeted with most of the day, but this quiet Wil was worse. However, these moments were so similar to the ones right before something had happened in Seattle, and that intrigued Lynda. She wasn't sure if she dared to hope for it to happen again or if it would be good for them to break down those walls.

Lynda stayed in the silence and hoped that Wil would break it sooner rather than later. It was awful to have her own tactics thrown back at her, but it had tossed them into a battle of who had the most patience and who would win out.

Finally, Wil leaned forward, her elbows on her knees as she raised her chin up to meet Lynda's gaze. "How would you like me to treat you?"

Everything Lynda had intended to say went out of her brain at that moment, and all she wanted to say was every dream she had managed to conjure up in the last few days. Her heart thrummed a steady rhythm while she bided her time and an answer. There were feet between them as they sat, but it was almost as if Wil was pressed against her again, the heat of her body clouding Lynda's mind to the point she couldn't think clearly.

"With respect," Lynda finally replied.

Wil canted her head to the side, no doubt calling Lynda's bluff and side-step of an answer. Before she knew what was happening, Wil stood and shoved her hands into her pockets as she stepped toward the door.

"Where are you going?" Lynda found herself standing, her heart threatening to run out of her and follow Wil. The wobble in her voice as she spoke was unexpected, but emotion threatened to overtake her. She couldn't let Wil leave like this, not on bad terms, not on unexplained terms. Touching Wil's arm, Lynda begged her without words to stay. When Wil didn't answer but held still, Lynda whispered, "Stay. Please."

Wil shifted on her toes, turning to face Lynda fully. Panic swelled in Lynda. Why was Wil always leaving? Why did everyone leave her?

"Don't go," she begged. She wasn't sure she could handle it again, that she could stay while she watched Wil walk away without a resolution, without knowing what was going on.

"How do you want me to treat you?" Wil repeated her question from before, and Lynda realized belatedly that she had to answer honestly. She couldn't hide any longer.

With a staggering breath, Lynda pushed the words from her lips. "I can't stop thinking about *that night*."

Wil stayed motionless.

Moving in, Lynda trailed her hands down Wil's arms until she reached Wil's fingers in her pockets, pulling them out so she could lace them together. They stood inches apart, Lynda taller than Wil in her heels, but in that moment, she was the one who had no power. She was the one who was getting on her knees and letting confessions fall from her lips, and astonishingly, she enjoyed it.

"I can't stop thinking about you...pressed against me." She whispered the last bit, ducking her chin as if embarrassed. She pulled their hands together. "I don't want to stop thinking about it."

"Then what do you want?" Wil's question was clear, but it had been the one Lynda had failed to ask herself since they'd left Seattle.

She'd been too scared to ask, too worried about what the answer would change and what it would bring, and how she would handle it. Pulling her lower lip between her teeth, Lynda let it go and looked directly in Wil's eyes. "I want you."

"Are you sure?"

"Yes."

"Are you going to fire me for it?"

Lynda chuckled lightly and shook her head. "I'm the one who should be fired."

Wil let out a grunt, so subtle yet it said everything she wasn't thinking. Before Lynda knew what was happening, she was pulled against Wil's body, the soft curves, the heat. Wil's hand was at the back of her head, pressing their mouths together in a heated kiss. They vied for control, each one pushing the other, which only sped up their momentum.

Lynda groaned as Wil brushed a hand over her breast, her nipple already hard and the shift of the fabric more erotic than she'd ever thought possible. Wil stepped forward, and Lynda had to move backward. She had no idea where they were going, but when the backs of her thighs hit the edge of the desk, she stopped. Wil held her still, hands moving up and down her body as if Wil possessed her.

Not willing to leave Wil out of the groping, Lynda pulled the buttons at Wil's vest, parting the two pieces of material, before she dove in for Wil's shirt. She had the thing completely undone before Wil captured her wrists and locked her hands down onto the desk at either side of her body. Wil's mouth never left hers, and Lynda could do nothing but lean half against the desk and let Wil do whatever she wanted with her mouth.

Finally, Wil released one wrist and curled fingers around the edge of Lynda's dress, dragging it upward onto her thigh to her hip. Lynda wanted Wil's fingers to move between her legs. She wanted Wil to take her, immediately. Wil's thumb brushed right along the line of her panties but didn't stray farther. Eventually Wil pulled away but kept their faces close together.

"Are you sure this is what you want, Lynda?"

"Yes." Lynda held onto Wil tightly, not wanting her to walk away this time, but she knew deep in her bones that was exactly what was going to happen. "Yes, I want you."

She was breaking every single rule she had put into place, every single thing she had told herself that wouldn't happen. They were in the office, they were on her desk, they weren't talking about what it meant. She was going to crash and burn when all this came out, and for the oddest reason, Lynda couldn't bring herself to care.

Wil sighed and nodded slowly. "Tell me that tomorrow."

Without another word, she walked away. Lynda swallowed hard, trying to parse out what had just happened. They had been so close. Her heart raced. Yes, they were in the office, and yes, they still had baggage to sort through, but they had been so damn close to falling completely over the line with enthusiasm. Fixing her dress, Lynda straightened her back and crossed her arms as Wil closed up her office.

She glanced through the window to Lynda's office, raised her hand in a farewell and walked out of the building. Immediately, guilt ate at Lynda's stomach. Wil had been right to stop them. Again. And she had done nothing but cross ethical boundaries and push Wil to cross them. She wasn't just going to end her own career at that point, she was going to ruin Wil's.

Not to mention Isla was still a concern, and while she might not be a huge part of Lynda's life any more, she was in Wil's. Lynda wanted to reconnect with Isla, to bridge the gap that had formed into a chasm and then a world. Lynda frowned as a heaviness sat in the center of her chest. She had to find a way around this, starting tonight.

WIL PICKED her second-best suit to wear the next day. She hated to do it, but she hadn't had a chance to talk to Lynda about leaving for a few hours, so she'd resorted to calling in sick. Not to mention after the threat of firing Jacob, she wasn't sure she wanted to bring that conversation up with her. Wil couldn't afford to lose her job before she had another one in place. But the biggest reason she'd avoided, if she had to admit it, was because she wasn't sure what to say after the previous night.

If she hadn't come to her senses in the middle of everything, she would have fucked Lynda against the desk without any regrets. At least she told herself that, but she knew better. The regrets would come as soon as they finished, and she would have been consumed by guilt. Pushing that worry from her mind as much as humanly possible, Wil focused on her task at hand.

The branch she was interviewing at was easily four times the size of what she was used to. They covered two floors. The position was for a portfolio manager, but the pay was similar enough to what she was earning that it might be worth it to take a step down. If she could pay her rent, she could always make her way back up the ladder again. Not to mention, not having the stress of managing a branch might make her less prone to outrageous bursts of her temper.

Everyone was dressed perfectly here, much like Lynda dressed daily for work. She was glad she'd chosen the plain black suit for the morning. She had foregone the tie, though she wished she hadn't. It would easily show them who she was which would help her judge whether she would be accepted here.

She stopped by the front desk and squared her shoulders. She'd done everything possible to keep her nerves at bay all morning. "I have an interview with Devon McClure."

"What's your name?"

"Wilda Powell." Wil rubbed her thumb across her fingertips down by her hip, using the sensation to center herself. It had been eight years since she'd done an interview.

"Ah, yes, I'll take you to his office." She left her wireless headset on and stood up from the chair.

Wil followed her through the winding halls toward the back of the building. There were no cubicles where she expected them but smaller offices and larger ones. As expected, Devon McClure had a large office in the back of the building, no doubt one with a lot of windows. She kept her shoulders stiff as the office admin knocked on the door.

"Mr. McClure. Wilda Powell is here for her interview."

"Send her in." His voice was much more a tenor than what fit his looks. Wil hadn't expected that when she'd spoken to him briefly on the phone.

She walked in and took the bull by the horns. "Good morning, sir."

"Morning." He held out his hand, and Wil shook it with a firm grasp. He rifled through some folders on his desk and grabbed a yellow legal pad before sitting at a smaller table in the corner. "I was surprised to see your name in my applicant pool."

"Why's that?" Wil eyed him carefully.

"Because you work for Jolie Preston, yet I can't call your current employer."

"I do." Wil knew she was going to have to explain this, and she had prepared an answer. Still the words stuck in her throat a moment before she managed to get them out. "I worked for Henshaw Investments, which was bought out by Jolie Preston last month."

"Ah." His eyes lit up as if there was some recognition. "Lynda Walsh is the manager there, correct?"

"Yes." Wil's stomach dropped. She'd told Lynda they would talk that day, knowing she was calling out sick for the full day.

"She can be a hard one to get along with. Then again, I don't envy her position either. Coming into an already established firm to shake everything up takes a special skill set. I was there the other week while she was on a business trip."

Wil's heart thudded. The reminder of Seattle had been unexpected, but now she remembered where she recognized the name from. Jacob had mentioned him and so had Lynda.

"It does take the ability to walk a lot of lines." Wil had never thought about it like that before. She'd always seen Lynda as the enemy coming in to fire them all. "I haven't told her where my interview is, but she is aware that I have one. I'd appreciate it if she didn't know."

Devon's eyebrows rose in surprise. "All of us managers work together very closely, so it'll be difficult for her not to find out, especially if she looks in our systems and finds your application on file."

Wil understood what he wasn't saying. She needed to tell Lynda everything. "I'll let her know when I get back."

He nodded, eyed her seriously. "Are you ready to begin?"

"Yes, sir." Wil squared her shoulders, more ready now than ever before.

"All right. Let's start with why you're looking for a new position."

Wil cringed. This was going to be her make it or break it moment. Since she was interviewing with a branch of the firm who knew Lynda, no lie would be acceptable—only the truth.

"I'm looking to grow and learn as a portfolio manager. The training at Henshaw Investments left a lot to be desired, and while I think Mrs. Walsh is fully capable of implementing that training, she can't do it immediately. I want to grow now, and I want to learn to be better at my job and management."

"But you're applying for a position below the one you already hold."

"Yes." Wil fought back the urge bolt. "I know it is, but I don't know Jolie Preston's policies and practices yet. I'm starting to learn them, but I would like to have the opportunity to grow without the stress of a buy-out looming."

Devon watched her carefully, his gaze unnerving because she didn't know him well enough to read him. She'd tried to probe Jacob about him, but there had been so much tension in the office the day before that she hadn't managed to get anything out of him.

"I would like to learn the proper way to do my job. I know that's an odd thing to say, and it includes throwing my former manager under the bus, but I want to be as honest as possible. Mrs. Walsh has shared that Jolie Preston highlights leaders and brings mentoring and leadership training full-fledged into its business model. I would love to experience that and to learn from the best in the business."

Wil had to be very careful when choosing her words. She didn't want to get Lynda in any trouble, and she didn't want to get herself in any trouble, especially if she wanted the job. "Mrs. Walsh is an excellent manager, but I think it'll be easier for me to learn without the added stress of a buy-out."

"A mature decision for you to make. Though all the reports I've read about you from Mrs. Walsh have been exemplary. She says your management skills are effective."

Wil wouldn't comment on that. She hadn't expected it either, but to know that they talked about her or that Lynda submitted reports about her work unnerved her. What else was in those files? And Lynda hadn't lied, her management skills were effective, but that also didn't mean they were the best when it came to creating a good work environment. She'd stretched the truth, and that didn't sit right with Wil at all.

"I appreciate you sharing that with me as she hasn't. Still, for now, I'd rather Mrs. Walsh not know I'm interviewing or where I am in the process. I don't want to worry her about being left short-handed at a crucial time."

"I'll refrain from speaking with her for now. And I'm sure Lynda has planned for something like this to happen—Lord knows she plans constantly."

Wil relaxed, a deeper understanding filling her. Lynda was fastidious about researching and knowing what possibilities might happen. She had to anticipate this on some level.

"So, if you advance to the next round of interviews, I will have to inform her, and she'll likely want to speak with you."

"I understand." Wil crossed her legs under the table.

"I appreciate you being honest with me about it. Usually transfers from one firm to another are handled very differently, but since yours isn't in our systems properly yet, I think you've managed to skirt around most of that."

"Thank you, Mr. McClure."

"Well, then, shall we get on with the interview?"

They spent an hour and a half together, and by the time Wil walked out into the warm summer weather, she had a grin on her face and a hope that a second interview would be likely. Even her interview with Millie hadn't lasted that long. She'd been so at ease with Devon, so able to understand what he said and what he was asking, and she'd managed to get some questions answered about Jolie Preston that she hadn't ever thought to ask before then. He was warm where Lynda was cold in management style, and she adored the difference.

Wil checked her watch, wishing she could call Isla already, but summer school wasn't out yet. Instead, she sent a quick text with an update and asked for a call as soon as she got a chance. Wil got into her car and started the engine, a smile on her lips that she wasn't going to get rid of any time soon. She was doing something for herself for once.

She hadn't realized how suppressed she had been under Millie and Mr. Henshaw. She'd worked her ass off and had never been given the grace to grow or take on more responsibility. Breathing out relief, Wil rested in her seat for a moment. It was nearing lunch, and if she hadn't been forced to take the entire day with sick leave, she would go back to work ecstatic. Instead, she had the rest of the day to spend as she wanted to.

Pulling out of the parking lot, Wil drove to the next stoplight. The best part was this firm was still close to her apartment, which meant her travel wouldn't be any worse. She stopped at the light, waiting for it to change. Lynda strolled across the crosswalk, her purple plaid skirt clinging to her hips and her gray blazer smartly buttoned. Wil held her breath, hoping against all hope that she wouldn't look up and see Wil a mere ten feet away.

Lynda raised her chin, her sandy blonde hair falling over her shoulder as a breeze picked it up. Their eyes locked. Wil was doomed. She was out on a day she had called in sick, dressed to the nines in business attire. Lynda's lips parted in surprise, and she faltered in her step before she continued walking. Wil looked down at the clock on her dash. She must be out for lunch —she'd mentioned something on her schedule about a lunch meeting that day. Wil hadn't really paid attention.

Lynda stopped at the end of the crosswalk, turning and facing Wil full on. There was no mistaking that look. Lynda was pissed and confused. Wil's shoulders tightened, all the excitement she had just felt rushing from her. This would only go one way. Wil was screwed.

2009

"Why can't you just get over it already?" Isla screamed, and Wil had no idea what to say to make her stop. She froze on the spot.

Isla wasn't the one who usually got mad. That was Wil's role, and to have this thrown in her face after she'd worked so hard to try and get rid of it was impossible. Guilt ate away at her.

They had never been this distant before, but over the past year, Wil's crush on Lynda had only gotten worse. It had created a void that she'd been sucked into. She couldn't stop thinking about her, and as her crush turned wilder and the fantasies better, she closed in on herself to try and protect Isla from everything. They were nearing the anniversary of Patrick's death, and Wil didn't want to add any extra stress on her.

But it was impossible to hide anything from Isla. They knew each other too well, and Wil couldn't keep secrets from her. She didn't want to. As much as it hurt her to see what this did to her friend, she didn't want to hide any part of who she was.

"I'm so sorry," Wil tried, pleading with her gaze. She bounced in her shoes, needing Isla to understand that this wasn't a choice, that she couldn't control it, because if she fucking could, then she would.

Isla's fury was strong. She pointed at the ground, the bedroom closing in on them. "I need you to be my friend right now. I need you to stop doing things that are pissing her off!"

Wil knew all of this, but she couldn't stop herself. Everything she saw wrong with Lynda and the girls, she had to bring up. She couldn't hold her tongue. Every time she shouted at Lynda, she internally yelled at herself. It was as though she moved out of her body in those moments, seeing herself from afar as she became a person she hated. She had tried so many times to have one pleasant conversation or even to just say nothing, and she hadn't managed it. Grandma had even warned her that it was going to cause issues if she kept at it.

"She needs to be told what she's doing wrong." Her defenses came in full force, and she had to make sure that Isla understood what she was doing and why she was doing it. "Someone has to tell her."

"But I need *you*. Not her. You can't come in here and fight her like that." Isla's voice rang through the room again, nothing was stopping her, and Wil was pretty sure she wasn't even listening to anything Wil said.

Her heart broke at the sorrow in Isla's voice because Wil knew the danger she was in at being banned from the house. She had pushed that line so many times that at some point Lynda would break. It was impossible for her not to. No one could withstand the bullshit Wil put her through.

She tried to step toward Isla, tried to get closer to her so that she would know Wil would always be there for her. Wil put her hands out to the sides so she wouldn't be confrontational, not with her forever friend. They always had each other's backs, and she had to make sure that Isla understood that.

"Stop!" Isla shouted, putting her hand up.

Wil halted, again freezing. Everything moved in slow motion as Isla's cheeks puffed out with each breath, as her nostrils flared while anger soared. Wil didn't know what to do with it. She was stunned, their roles having completely reversed. She wanted desperately to take that away from Isla. She knew viscerally what it was like to be out of control, to have no grasp on what she said or did.

"I'm so sorry, Isla. I've tried—"

"You can't be with her!"

"I know!" Wil shouted, her volume covering up Isla's as the thin line holding everything back snapped. Tears stung her eyes, her cheeks burned, her head pounded as her ears rang. "You think I don't know that! I would never do anything to hurt you."

Isla's chest rose and fell rapidly. Wil tried again to step forward, fear in every second that ticked by. Isla jerked away. "All you've done is hurt me."

Wil crumbled. Every defense she had was gone because Isla was right. She had hurt her in more ways than could be counted, and she had hurt her in the worst way possible. Her heart shattered, and she had to at least try to rectify it one more time.

"I'm sorry."

"You know what the worst part is?" Isla's voice dropped, and she stepped in closer. "You'll never be good enough for someone like her."

She'd known that all along, and she'd never tried anything because of it. She didn't want to even think about it—just the prospect of trying scared the shit out of her. But that didn't stop the damn dreams or the damn feelings. She had tried everything to put it behind her. She'd dated countless people. She'd even had sex with some of them, but she still couldn't stop thinking about Lynda.

"Get out." Isla's voice was dangerously low. "Get out of my room. Get out of my life."

"What?"

Devastation rained down on her. Wil's shoulders tightened into one solid rock, and her feet were glued to the floor. She couldn't breathe. Isla had never told her to leave. Not like this. They had been through so much together, years of friendship.

"I told you to get out of my life!" Isla screeched.

"I..." Wil stopped, shock still ringing through her chest. Time slowed to a halt, and she grasped at every thread of friendship she could possibly hold onto. "I can come back tomorrow, and we can talk about this."

"No. I don't want to talk to you anymore. I don't want to see you anymore. Get out."

Tears streamed down Wil's cheeks, uncontrolled as she stared wide-eyed and open-mouthed at her best friend—her forever friend. Nothing could have prepared her for this, and while she'd known the issues between them had grown significantly in the past couple months, she hadn't ever thought it was this bad. She'd had her head in the sand the entire time. Wil listed forward, as if she was going to take a step and grab hold of Isla's hands and make her listen to some sort of reason.

"I don't understand." Wil's voice shook, no longer strong.

"I can't be friends with you."

Wil's heart tore in two. How was she ever going to be able to come back from this one? She had no one other than Isla. She had no other friends to rely on. They'd always been the pair of them, through thick and thin, through everything. She couldn't imagine her life without Isla.

She cried out, depths of hurt in each syllable, "Isla."

"Listen to me for once in your life. Get out."

Wil shook as she reached for the doorknob. She stumbled into the hallway, Lynda standing awkwardly at the end of it, her hand clasped to her arm as if she was debating whether to intervene. Shaking her head, hot tears spilled off Wil's chin, her eyesight blurred.

"Give it some—" Lynda started.

"Don't talk to me!" Wil pointed at her sharply, knowing that she was falling right back into that same problem Isla was so mad about, but she just couldn't stop herself. She couldn't hold back no matter how much she wanted to, and she finally had the target of all her pent up emotions in her sights. "This is all your fault. You ruined everything."

Wil stalked to the front door, leaving her shoes next to it as she slammed it behind her. She ran across the street barefoot and crawled into her bedroom, collapsing on the bed with her face in the pillow as the real sobs wracked through her. She wouldn't survive. It hurt so damn much.

2023

"I DON'T KNOW what to do," Lynda started as soon as Laura settled across the table from her. She'd only invited Laura today because the complications between the personal and the professional were getting to be too much.

Seeing Wil outside in her car, clearly not sick, and most definitely out for the interview she'd mentioned inexplicably hurt. It hurt more than Lynda ever wanted to admit. Lynda played with the napkin in her lap as she waited for something to happen, for Laura to give her all the answers to all the problems.

"What happened?"

Lynda pursed her lips. She hadn't considered just how much she was going to have to share in order to get the answers that she wanted. Laura was going to tell her to call Jessica again, that much she knew. It was her fault she had let it happen, and the fact that she had allowed it to happen in the office was far worse than the first kiss.

"Wil and I..."

"You what?" Laura sharply commented when Lynda had taken too long to answer.

Sighing, Lynda tried again. "We crossed some ethical boundary lines."

"Lynda, you didn't." Laura's blue eyes softened with pity.

Lynda shook her head quickly. "We crossed the line, but not in that way."

Guilt swam in her stomach. That had been why Wil was so scared to tell her she had the interview today. Lynda just wished she'd known where it was at. She would give her a good recommendation, there would be no reason not to, other than the fact they had only worked together for a little under a month.

"What happened?" Laura reached for her water.

"When we were in Seattle, things got messy." Lynda drew in a shuddering breath to attempt to steady herself.

"Messy how?"

"Are you really going to make me spell it out?" Embarrassment heated her cheeks, and crawling in a hole looked better by the second. She couldn't stop herself. She'd wanted to, many times over, but each time she pushed Wil into acting. It was selfish, and it was so beyond any rules that were in place. She was going to lose her job over this, without contest. She was drowning in a sea of embarrassment, shame, guilt, and desire.

"Yes, if you want my advice. I need to know exactly what happened." Laura pinned her with a serious look, and Lynda knew there was no getting out of it. That had been why she'd called Laura in the first place. She needed someone to tell her what to do because the thought of parsing through all the ways she had screwed up was beyond manageable.

Lynda sighed heavily. Laura was in leadership—she would understand the narrow line Lynda walked—or rather—crossed. And she would understand the fact that Wil was a woman, and that she was Isla's best friend.

"I don't know how it started in Seattle." Lynda started where she could, her heart racing as she tried to pinpoint exactly where she had willingly stepped across the line the first time.

"How what started?"

"It started with touches." Lynda's voice trailed off.

Laura's eyes widened. "Are you saying...did you two...are you in a sexual relationship with her?"

"No," Lynda answered firmly. "Not yet anyway."

"Lynda!" Laura chastised, her drink heavily set on the table. "Give me a minute to soak this in."

Lynda winced. She was coming out to Laura, asking for advice on a very tenuous situation, and she was trying to have her cake and eat it too all in one conversation, and it was too much. But she had no idea where to start.

"She's Isla's best friend. They used to call each other forever friends." Tears stung Lynda's eyes. "How can I do that to her?"

"Lynda, take a breath." Laura put her palm flat on the table. "You need to focus on one issue at a time."

"I can't. That's the problem, it's all jumbled together in a giant mess. What am I supposed to do?"

"You can't sleep with your subordinate. Of all things you cannot do, that is it, Lynda. It'll be the end of your career if you do it and you're caught. You can't risk it."

"I know," she whispered. *But damn, I want to*.

"Lynda, I need you to hear me on this." Laura patted the table lightly. "You can't have sex with her."

But it wouldn't just be sex, would it? Lynda wanted sex, yes, but it would be far more than that. It would be a relationship, and it would be diving headfirst into what both of them had narrowly avoided in the last week and a half. Because she couldn't sexually be with Wil without that first—she'd never managed to do that. In the past few weeks, Wil had gone from someone in her past to someone she couldn't stop thinking about to someone she wanted to be with fully and completely. The shift into the sexual was stark but so very present in a way she had never expected.

Laura clenched her jaw tightly. "I see you *think* you can get away with it."

"No, I know that we can't. I can't." She corrected herself at the last minute. Laura was right. Her career would be ruined in an instant if she did cross that line because she would be the first one to turn herself in.

"Okay, now we've established that, what's the rest of the mess?"

Lynda wasn't sure she wanted to tell her, or what difference it would make. The advice was clear. She couldn't touch Wil again, not while they worked together. "Have you ever wondered about being with a woman before? I know that's a personal question, but I can't ask the others."

"No. No, I understand." Laura seemed to take her time to answer. "And no, I haven't. I don't think another relationship is in the cards for me. After my divorce... Let's just say it's probably for the best."

Lynda sighed. She hated when Laura sounded so down on herself, but she had never shared what had truly happened between her and Rodney. Sure there had been cheating, but Lynda suspected it was far deeper wounds than that.

"I didn't either. Not until last week, not really. I mean, I was so happy with Patrick. We were so in love."

"You were," Laura agreed, lifting her glass to make her point. "You two were the model couple."

Sadness filled her as it did any time she talked about her relationship with Patrick. "But we weren't without issues either. Sex wasn't always easy between us, and I never really understood it. But this past week, I don't know, something's different with her."

"Because it's Wil or because she's a woman?"

"Because she's Wil. I don't know...I don't know if I would want this with anyone else." Lynda had done a lot of thinking on that, because it mattered whether she wanted to be with Wil what her answer was. She was pretty sure she never would have let anyone other than Wil get so close to her. No one would have been able to sneak into her heart like that.

Laura's look softened. "What are you going to do about it?"

"What can I do? She's my assistant manager. I put myself right into this situation. I knew she was going to be working for me when I took the job."

"You didn't know it was going to take this turn, at least. Did you talk to Jessica about it?"

"Not about this part. Only about our shared history."

Laura pressed her lips together firmly. "What physically happened in Seattle, and to be clear, I don't need details I just need the basics."

Lynda's cheeks heated. She was never one to kiss and tell, but she needed Laura to help her form a strategy to navigate this. "We kissed in Seattle—once. It was a whole week in the making though."

"Who stopped it from going further?" Laura tapped her fingers against the tabletop.

"She has. Every single time, Wil has been the one to step back and stop it." Lynda shook her head, knowing it was even more damning for her.

Laura's eyebrows shot up. "Every single time?"

Lynda nodded slowly, her stomach fluttering at the memory before sinking with guilt.

"I'm almost afraid to ask this, but how many times have you crossed that line?"

"Only twice, but I've wanted to do it more than that."

Laura looked devastated. Lynda understood why because the same feeling ran right through her, but that still didn't stop the desire she had, the one she was only just discovering.

"I like her."

"Romantically, to be clear?"

"Yes." Saying those words out loud was far easier than she'd thought they would be. Lynda rolled her shoulders. "I want to be with her."

"Then you know what you have to do, and I'm not entirely sure why we're having this discussion." Laura raised an eyebrow, her face pinched in dismissal.

"Because I've already crossed that line."

"Then stop and fix it." Laura gave her a hard stare, as if nothing of what she was saying was making a dent in Lynda's brain. "If you want my professional opinion, you never should have done it. There's a host of reasons why. She's young. You knew her as a child, so the power dynamics between the two of you are already skewed. She's your employee. You just took over her company when she didn't expect it, so she was already thrown for a loop. You come in and try to protect her and take her under your wing. The number of ways this could and will be interpreted where you're the villain is immense."

"I know," Lynda agreed, fear and guilt slicing through her. It was to the point that it physically hurt, and she wasn't sure she'd ever manage to escape it. When it revolved around work, she was the villain, but when it came to the two of them and nothing else, she was anything but. "I've never wanted something like this before."

"That's something you'll have to contend with."

Laura was dead set against this. Lynda knew she would be, and it wasn't because of the personal side of things. She imagined if the situation were altered and the two of them didn't work together that Laura's advice would be different. Then again, Lynda also wouldn't be asking for her advice.

"What are you going to do?"

"I think Wil had an interview today." Hope instead of devastation sparked inside her.

"Oh? That might be the easiest solution, actually."

"If she gets the job. If she doesn't, then we're right back to square one, where I'm her boss and she's my employee." Lynda had toyed with the different possibilities, from her leaving to Wil leaving. At this point, she was pretty sure there was no way she could fire Wil without facing repercussions from it—not unless Wil did something illegal.

"But it is a hope, especially if she's looking for another job."

"Who wouldn't look for one? I've come in, I've taken over

the entire firm, and no one knows whether their position is safe or not. I've tried to guarantee to them that I'm not firing anyone for the sake of clearing the ranks, but no one ever believes me."

"It's not like you haven't done that."

Lynda's defenses went up in an instant, knowing exactly what Laura was referencing. "It was a toxic work environment. The personalities needed a switch up for the business to thrive. You've been there as well."

"I have." Laura bristled.

Lynda knew about that situation, since Laura had been the one coming to her at that point for advice on how to handle the problems at hand.

"Why don't you try to weasel out of her where the interview was? Then you can figure out how it went and if she stands a true chance at the position."

"That feels manipulative." And she'd just found out about it yesterday. She'd briefly considered it, but she also wanted to give Wil her space, and not antagonize her into another argument if they could avoid it.

"You work together, and you work in the same business. You can't tell me that there's not going to be conflicts."

Lynda frowned. There would be. Even if Wil ended up working at an entirely different firm, they would end up arguing over certain things at some point. Perhaps a relationship with Wil was out of the question. It might not work out in the end anyway.

Laura sighed heavily and grabbed her fork. "It's time to grow up, Lynda. You know what you've got to do, and hashing it out with me isn't going to get you any closer to a resolution."

Lynda scowled. Laura was right, and she hated that.

CHAPTER
Eighteen

WIL GOT to the office early that morning, hoping that she had time to find Lynda before everyone else came in to bother them. She was in luck. The lights were on in Lynda's office. In the last week, Wil had managed to only talk about the professional. Any time she suspected Lynda was sliding into the personal, she found an excuse to run for the hills and get back to work. She didn't stay later than necessary, and she avoided being in a room alone with her. Her nerves were awful, taking over every spare inch of space in her thoughts.

Everything was colliding into chaos, and Wil struggled just to keep a foot in every place she was required to be. She knew Lynda had seen her leaving the interview, but neither of them had brought it up. Devon had told her she'd need to talk to Lynda, but the prospect of that conversation would lead to other conversations, and Wil wasn't sure she could handle any of them without flying off the edges.

Wil had gotten a call for a second interview the following Wednesday and had agreed to go again on Monday. She had no other choice but to talk to her now. The silence was overwhelming, and Wil knew she had to be the one to break it because the deadline to stop running from her problems just moved up.

Wil dropped her travel mug of coffee and her bag in her office before immediately walking to Lynda's. She knocked on the door and shut it behind her, Lynda looking up at her from the desk. Wil's heart raced. The conversation they needed to have was two-fold.

"Got a minute?"

"I hope so, yes." Lynda shifted away from her desk and came around it, evening the playing field between them. Wil always appreciated it when she did that.

They sat in the only two chairs in the office, Wil brushing her sweaty palms on her thighs. "Before we talk about the first issue, you should know I had an interview last week."

"I know," Lynda responded. "Care to share where?"

Wil's lips parted, shame heating her cheeks and clogging her throat. She shook her head, surprised Lynda hadn't figured it out yet. Lynda either hadn't had the time to dig into it or she hadn't wanted to. Wil wasn't sure, but she hoped this wasn't some sort of weird test of her loyalty.

"Did it go well?"

"Yes, actually. I have a second interview later this morning."

Lynda frowned, and she stared at the floor between them. "Feel free to take the rest of the morning if you need to."

"I just need an hour, maybe two." Wil rushed the words, trying to make everything easier since she knew what was coming next was going to be impossible.

"You can have it."

"Thank you." Wil's stomach twisted with nerves. She knew they didn't have long before everyone else arrived, which meant they might not be able to finish out the conversation they needed to have. "I think we need to talk about last Monday."

Lynda raised her gaze, leaning back in her seat and crossing her legs. Her dress rode up on her knee again, and Wil easily pried her gaze away. She wasn't going to give in to that temptation again, not yet anyway. "We need to talk about what happened."

"What exactly *did* happen?" Wil was going to take the offensive on this one. She'd had time to think about it, time to attempt to talk to Isla and never get the words out because of the memories of what happened the last time this conversation surfaced. Before she brought up that tragedy of a conversation again, she was going to need to have confirmation that Lynda wanted this.

Lynda sighed, folding her hands together and unfolding them. *Is she nervous?* They stared at each other in silence, neither willing to talk first, but time was running out, and they didn't have more than twenty minutes if they were lucky.

"I'm not sure—" Lynda started but the phone rang loudly at her desk.

Wil's heart clenched hard before it plummeted. They weren't going to get the conversation. She knew it. They were going to be interrupted again. Wil swallowed hard.

Lynda didn't get up to answer it, and the phone stopped. She focused on Wil again. "I'm not—"

Her cellphone rang, loudly vibrating against the top of the desk.

"Damn it." Lynda stood up and grabbed her cell, her face paling as she lifted it to her ear. "Jessica. What—?"

The energy was sucked out of the room. Lynda turned on her with wide eyes and shook her head, holding her hand up when Wil tried to stand to leave and give her privacy.

"Is he okay? Yes, I know about the planned proposal. Yes, I can do that."

Wil sat in absolute silence, not sure what she could do to help until Lynda told her more about what was going on.

"Yes, I understand. I'll work it in." Lynda nodded and sat on the edge of her desk, the wind taken from her sails.

Wil clenched her jaw, her hands tightening into fists. Finally when she hung up, Lynda blinked tears. She took deep steadying breaths, her chin tilted down before she lifted it, facing Wil full on.

"I thought we were done with drama this week."

"What happened?" Wil was dying to know what that phone call had been about.

"Liam…" Lynda's voice shook. "Liam Martinez is the chief manager at the firm in Boulder. He lives in Denver and commutes. He had a heart attack on his way into the office this morning and crashed his car."

"Lynda."

She looked exactly like she had that day when Wil had finally managed to get to their house after Patrick died. Her skin was pale, her eyes watering, her nose stuffy. Wil was on her feet in a second, wrapping her arms around Lynda's shoulders and pulling her in for a tight hug, running soothing hands over her back.

"I'm fine. I promise."

Wil shook her head, knowing full well that she wasn't. It was likely bringing up everything that had happened with Patrick again. Lynda pressed her nose into Wil's neck, holding tight in the embrace for far longer than someone who was *fine* would. Wil trailed her fingers down and then up Lynda's back, giving her the comfort she could.

"Take some deep breaths," Wil murmured tenderly.

Lynda did as she was told, finally backing away and running her fingers under her eyes. "I need to go to Boulder."

"What?" Wil's mind went haywire. For Lynda to leave on such short notice, she would have to stay there the entire day to keep everything under control. Which meant her interview—

"I need to leave within the hour. Liam was supposed to present to a client, and I can step in for him. It's important."

Wil tilted her head to the side and clenched her jaw, not sure what to say. She wanted to support Lynda, but she also wanted to go to her interview and win over Devon. She wanted the job so that maybe she and Lynda—Wil stopped. They hadn't even managed to get to that part of the conversation yet.

Straightening her shoulders, Wil slid back and put some

distance between them. "If you need to go to Boulder, I'll stay here."

"What?" Lynda's head shot up. "No, you'll go to your interview."

"But I can't leave—"

"Jacob can handle things for a few hours without you."

"Lynda, he's on vacation."

Lynda cursed under her breath. She must be rattled more than expected for her to forget that detail. He'd taken the day for medical reasons, which Wil knew, but Lynda only knew it was a vacation day.

"I can stay." Wil would do anything to wipe that devastation from Lynda's gaze.

"No." Lynda crossed her arms, leaning back on the edge of the desk. "No. I'll figure it out."

Wil watched her carefully, her mind whirring from one decision to the next as she worked through every possibility of how they could get around this.

"I'll need you back immediately." Lynda stood up straight before rounding her desk and sitting in her chair. She pulled up her computer and started typing furiously. Lynda shot her a sharp look, brokering no room for argument. "We're going to have to do this swiftly and carefully for it to work."

"What are you talking about?"

"Do you trust me?" Lynda lifted her chin, still typing on her computer as she looked Wil over.

That was a question too big for the moment and far too complicated for Wil to answer in a split-second decision. They had so many issues in the past, so much history that she wasn't sure they could sweep it all under the rug so she could answer simply enough.

Lynda must have seen her hesitation and fear because she stopped her work and leaned forward slightly, her palm flat against the surface of her desk. "For today, where it concerns your interview and this firm—do you trust me?"

Wil's heart raced, her eyes locked on Lynda's earnest gaze. She swallowed the lump in her throat, knowing that Lynda always put work as a priority, but that she also made her people do that. Wil remembered her taking calls late at night, making adjustments on the fly where she had to go to work early or stay late to help someone out. She hadn't wanted to see it as anything other than her abandoning the girls then, but that wasn't what it was. When it came to work and her livelihood, Wil could answer this. Her heart was a different story.

"Yes," Wil whispered. Lynda understood the business and management better than anyone Wil had met. She knew the nuances so well that it would be nothing for her to navigate this problem.

"Good. Go to your office. I need you to get everything lined up for today. Everything, Wil. I need to run through this proposal so I can be prepared for my meeting."

"Got it." Wil hesitated at her desk another moment.

Lynda locked their eyes together. "Go on. There's work to be done."

Of course there was, because they were never going to get a chance to talk about them. Work was always a priority when it came to Lynda. That was why Wil had found her so many times at the dining room table with her laptop, working late into the night when she was growing up. Then it had been admiration and curiosity, but now Wil knew what it really was—an escape.

Wil backed away from Lynda's desk and walked to her office. She sat heavily in her chair, the cold from the air conditioning making her shiver. Staring across the hall to Lynda's office, Wil shook her head. She should just accept that they weren't going to get a moment any time soon.

Wil checked the clock every five minutes, attempting to get set up for that morning and some into the afternoon, but she remained reticent about Lynda's insane plan to try and do all of this at once. Her foot tapped the floor under her desk as she worked, as she ordered people to go in different directions as they came into her office and were dismissed by Lynda, who was still nose deep in the portfolio she was memorizing.

Knocking on the door, Wil went inside without waiting for Lynda to tell her to come in. "We're all set for the morning."

Lynda lifted her gaze but not her chin before dropping it again. "Good. I think I'm at where I need to be." She checked her watch and clucked her tongue. "I need to be going."

"So do I," Wil reminded her. "Tell me again why you have to go to Boulder and not someone else?"

"I took over that firm last year. They're my people, and they know me, so for me to step in will be relatively easy. I know who is going and how they work, so we can easily play it off like I was supposed to be there." Lynda packed up her bag, shoving her laptop into it and zipping it closed.

"When will you be back?"

"No idea. I'll stop by the hospital to see Liam on my way home if I can."

"Guess I'll see you tomorrow then." Wil shoved her hands in her pockets and rolled back on her heels.

Lynda finally looked at her instead of through her. "We'll talk. I promise."

"When?"

"Now isn't the time to ask that." Lynda rounded the desk and was about to speak when the door opened, one of the lower managers stood in it, looking all the more worried when they both turned on him. "What is it?"

"The Everly Club is here to speak with Wil."

"Damnit," Wil muttered, her heart racing as her stomach dropped that she hadn't managed to do the one thing Lynda told her to. "I forgot to cancel the appointment. I'll go talk to them and be late to my interview. Surely Devon will know what's going on."

Lynda paled, her eyes wide as she stared hard at Wil. "Devon?"

Wil's mouth dropped in shock. She hadn't meant to say that.

She stepped forward with her hand up, every excuse running through her mind in an instant, but Lynda shook her head, a fierceness overcoming her. She checked her watch again and shot Wil a serious look before focusing on the other manager. "Put them in the conference room."

Lynda grabbed Wil's forearm tightly as soon as he left.

"We'll talk about that later. For now, you'll need to go out the back."

"What? You don't know anything about their portfolio or what they're even doing here today." What was Lynda even trying to do? The priority had to be their firm. It couldn't be Wil's interview. The Everly Club was one of their biggest accounts and needed to be treated with that respect. Lynda couldn't put Wil's needs over the company.

"I'll handle it."

"Lynda, this isn't how this is supposed to work. You should have just let me reschedule my interview. He would understand." Energy sparked in her chest, everything moving at the speed of light and the decisions needing to be made coming so rapidly that it made Wil's head spin.

"Devon won't, and never reschedule an interview. There's always a way. I'll see you in the morning." Lynda's tone brokered no room for argument. She stepped in closer, a hand on Wil's upper arm with a gentle squeeze. She pleaded, her voice dropping to barely above a whisper. "You said you would trust me."

Wil frowned, her lips parted with another protest, but Lynda shut her down with one severe look in her direction. This wasn't just about trusting her—it was a giant leap of faith. Wil was about to protest again, when Lynda shook her head, her fingers digging in a bit harder to her arm.

"Go. Now," Lynda ordered.

She didn't want to do it, but what choice did she have? She had to trust it would all work out in the end. With a deep breath and sharp nod, Wil slipped from Lynda's office and into her own to grab her suit jacket. They met in the hallway again, Lynda's laptop still on her desk and her hands at her sides. They made eye contact before the manager from before walked up.

"Wil, you going in? They say they're short on time."

"I'll be handing The Everly Club today." Lynda smoothed her skirt down. He looked absolutely confused, and Wil understood why. No one had ever worked with The Everly Club except her. They never wanted anyone else to work with them, and the meeting that day had everything to do with the buy-out that had happened and assuring them that Jolie Preston could still manage their assets and that Wil would still be in charge.

"Lynda," Wil said to get her attention.

When Lynda's caramel eyes reached her, she changed completely from the frantic woman she had been in the office to a stoic force to be reckoned with. Wil tilted her head to the side, jealous that she was able to tame her emotions that quickly. Wil would struggle with that throughout the entire drive to her interview.

"The Everly Club is here to talk about the buy-out. They're nervous. They never want to deal with anyone but me. This will take you longer than you think it will."

Lynda softened slightly. "Thank you."

Wil faltered in her step, not sure that she was ready to leave when she could so easily stay and help here.

"See you tomorrow," Lynda stated firmly.

It took every ounce of self-control to turn on her heel and walk toward the back hallway. But trust was what Lynda had asked from her for that morning, and Wil had agreed to it. She wouldn't have trusted anyone except her—not even Millie—to handle the situations being thrown at them. Lynda's serious glance helped her move along as she put herself between her and him.

Her stomach raged with nerves but not for the interview. This time it was all because of the chaos happening at the office and within the firm. Devon would surely understand. *Can I show up, explain, and leave?* Maybe he would already know that Lynda was leaving.

She had never seen Lynda go to these extremes for anyone before. She'd always thought she wasn't doing enough, wasn't around enough, wasn't there for the girls enough, but that wasn't it at all. She stretched herself so thin, making everyone happy and keeping herself accessible to the world that needed her. Wil rubbed the ache in the center of her chest. Lynda had been pulled in every direction back then, and Wil hadn't seen it. She had accused and threatened and thrown fits, only adding to that when all Lynda had been doing was what she could. Wil couldn't have been more wrong about the past.

Once she was in her car, Wil put pedal to the metal and sped her way to her interview. Her goal was to make the interview as good and as short as possible. She needed to get back because Lynda needed her there that day, and likely Lynda would need her that night if she ever let herself breathe and come to terms with the news she had been dealt. Wil couldn't imagine that internally she wasn't being affected by the blow they'd been delivered that morning.

LYNDA PULLED into the parking lot outside of Wil's apartment complex and sighed. Weariness settled over her, exhaustion finally hitting her. She shouldn't be there. She should be at home, wrapped in a warm blanket or in the bath. But she stepped out of the car, her feet confident as she shoved her car keys into her purse.

When had it come to this? When had they made the shift that after a day like that she wanted nothing more than to see Wil, to be in her presence, to melt into her arms? Lynda shuddered as she got to the main front door, having already memorized Wil's apartment number from her employee file at the office.

She shouldn't be here. In reality, she should be anywhere but here. The rules be damned at this point. She needed more than what they could offer, and they had already broken so many of them. When had her world started to revolve around Wil?

Lynda took her time on the walk to the apartment, lingering at the elevator and moving slowly down the hall as she tried to find the right door. This was inappropriate. She knew that, but where else were they supposed to talk because if they attempted at work, one or both were interrupted. After the day she had, all she wanted to do was clear the air and ease the tension and find the comfort that she was longing for.

Here it is. Lynda stood in front of the nondescript door and knocked lightly on it four times. Waiting for Wil to open it set her nerves into overdrive. She could only hope that Wil was there and not out being a young adult like she should be doing. Finally she heard someone moving around inside and coming.

Her heart was in her throat. When Wil opened the door, her eyes widened, the deep browns in them sharp in the dim hallway light. "Mrs. Walsh, what are you doing here?"

"Lynda," she corrected, her voice scratchy from the day of talking and crying on her drive home.

Wil didn't seem to even notice as she opened the door wider so Lynda could step inside. The apartment was small, but it wasn't bare. The furniture was aged, but it still looked like it was in decent condition. Lynda immediately recognized the throw on the back of the couch, it had been one that Joyce had made and kept for years. Lynda had seen in the few times she'd gone over to get Isla from their apartment.

"Can I get you something to drink?" Wil stood awkwardly to the side as Lynda perused everything.

"Got a beer?"

"That kind of day?" Wil asked as she shuffled over to the fridge. Though she knew what kind of day it had been—they both did. The week had been filled with random small emergencies that seemed to blow up in Lynda's face to the point she hadn't had a moment to sit and think about anything else.

"Yes," Lynda answered simply, not sure she wanted to elaborate on all that had happened in the last twelve hours. Her back hurt from the drive, but they had been successful in landing the client they'd wanted. Liam would be pleased with that once he returned to work. Her eyes stung at the thought of him, but she brushed that feeling to the side.

Wil handed over a beer bottle, the cap already undone. Lynda held hers up so they could chink the glass together. Wil obliged, and Lynda took a deep long pull from it before sighing and relaxing her shoulders for the first time in what felt like weeks. Just being in Wil's presence did that. She should have noticed it before, but she hadn't put it together until that morning when Wil had stepped in and wrapped her in a hug. She shouldn't be here. Laura would kill her for being here, and Jessica would fire her, but the pull to find that connection again was stronger than anything she had ever dreamed of before.

"If you're busy..."

"No. I'm not." Wil moved to the couch and lowered herself down, still eyeing Lynda suspiciously.

Lynda couldn't fault her for that. She would likely have the same reaction if Wil showed up unannounced at her condo. Following Wil's example, Lynda sat next to her, crossing her legs and leaning back into the soft cushions. She was cocooned in softness, and she closed her eyes in an attempt to truly enjoy the moment of sitting down after a long and heavy day.

"How's Liam?"

Lynda's eyes popped open. "He's in ICU according to his wife. Still hasn't woken up."

Wil reached over and touched Lynda's arm gently. "And how are you holding up?"

She nearly broke. Wil, of all people, would recognize the significance between what happened that day and what happened sixteen years ago. The reminder of how something as simple as a drive to work could turn into disaster.

"Oh, Lynda." Wil shifted and set her beer onto the table. She moved her arm around Lynda's shoulders and tugged her in slightly so Lynda's cheek fell onto her shoulder. "It's normal, you know that, right? For things like this to bring up other things. I'm sure it doesn't help with me being around either."

Lynda kept her mouth shut. Everything had been coming up since Wil had arrived back in her life. Feelings she had thought she'd dealt with resurfaced, and she was struggling once again to get her head on straight. Those last few walls she'd kept in place were gone, shattered in the events of the day, and she was raw. It hurt to be so vulnerable and broken again, but this was Wil. Just like she had asked Wil that morning if there was trust between them, Lynda trusted her to take care of everything. She had no energy to try anything else other than being this broken widow in Wil's caring hands.

"It's not you," Lynda whispered, those words the only thing she could think of. Wil's scent surrounded her, the warmth of her body so welcoming. If she kept her eyes closed much longer, she feared she wasn't going to want to leave that night. If she listened carefully enough, she could hear the steady thrum of Wil's heart. "I loved him."

"I know you did." Wil's blatant and pure acceptance of that was everything Lynda needed in that moment. She completely crumbled in Wil's hands, trusting that Wil would be able to put her back together, piece by piece because that was exactly what she needed.

She sniffled. "He was my world for a very long time."

Lynda struggled to figure out what to say, a way to move to the conversation she had come there to have. She was so stuck in the damn past that it was hard to even contemplate moving forward.

"I'm defined by the fact that I'm a widow, a young widow who never remarried, who struggled to raise two children on her own, and I lived in that reality for so long. I wasn't very good at it, either. I'm afraid I broke them more than they already were." She'd never said that to anyone before. She'd implied it with her friends, but she'd never said it out loud.

Wil remained silent, and Lynda couldn't tell if that was a good thing or not. She wanted her to speak, but she also deeply understood that this was a difficult topic for both. Lynda cradled her beer in her hand, her fingertips cold from the glass, but she was desperate not to move.

"You're my daughter's forever friend." She chose the word they had for themselves, knowing Wil would understand it and her more if she did. She had paid attention, even if Wil hadn't seen it back then.

"Stepdaughter," Wil corrected, a hint of the vehemence that had once been there all those years ago in the undertones. But it sounded different this time, like instead of pointing out the distance already there she was trying to create it.

Lynda cringed, knowing they couldn't avoid this any longer. "Yes, my stepdaughter, but you have to realize, Wil, that I raised her, and I've been her only parental figure for most of her life. Whether or not she talks to me, she will *always* be my daughter, and I'll always be the one who raised her."

Wil tensed, the arm around Lynda's shoulders shifting, and she knew she was about to lose that touch she craved, the closeness she had only just begun to find. Wil leaned forward, her elbows on her knees as she stared at the muted television across from her.

In all the conversations they'd had about this, Isla had been the one elephant in the room they had both avoided. But Lynda couldn't do it any longer. She wanted whatever was between them, and she couldn't ignore this any longer. "You should want to protect her like you always have."

"Do you think I don't?" Wil was angry.

Lynda had been waiting to run face first into this, and she'd found it in her most vulnerable state. There was no more tiptoeing around the issue at hand. They were going to dive headfirst into it.

"I told Isla I had a crush on you when we were kids. I *told* her." Wil's voice cracked, tears filling her eyes as pain etched through the lines on her face, ripping through her.

Lynda wanted to reach over and comfort Wil, but the wall she had put up in an instant was so thick that she didn't dare attempt it. She'd never known that. She had assumed Isla was completely in the dark on Wil's feelings toward her because the threat to their friendship would be drastic. Wil relied on Isla too much.

"Isla was fine with it, she was, for a little while anyway. Then she wasn't. And she couldn't take it anymore, and I can't..." Wil stopped talking, her voice thick with emotion. "I can't do that again. She's the only family I have."

Lynda took her time answering, needing the moment to make sure this was the right decision to make. She wanted Wil, more than what they currently had. She wanted definitions and boundaries around what they'd found together, but she wasn't going to force Wil to make this decision. She couldn't—it would break her. With the answer solidified in her mind, Lynda caught Wil's attention.

"We need to talk to her, and since she's most likely not going to take my call, you need to talk with her. I don't want you to risk your family for a fling." She'd put the ball in Wil's court, letting her decide if this was a mere few nights or more. Lynda knew what she wanted, and it was nothing more than to find the same love she'd had with Patrick in someone else, in a new and different way. She wanted to experience that closeness again.

"I'm not risking it for a fling." Wil cut Lynda a sharp look. "I'm not."

Lynda parted her lips. Not quite sure what to say next. She wanted to push Wil to choose, to make the call right then so they would have an answer in hand, but it wasn't her task to do. Wil had to be the one to talk to Isla—she had so much more to lose.

"I thought that's what this was at first, but it's not." Wil's face relaxed as the realization flooded through her.

Lynda's mouth went dry. She couldn't stop herself from reaching out and running her fingers along Wil's hands, covering them with her own. They were so different and yet so similar at the same time. Both straight forward women who did a lot of internal thinking before the rest of the world heard about it. Wil's skin was soft under hers, the tender touch intimate in a way it hadn't been before.

When they'd kissed, it was all heat, but this carried so much more with it than that. This was something meaningful, tender, something she would keep with her for a long time. Reaching up, Lynda cupped Wil's cheek, turning her so they faced each other.

"I want to kiss you," Lynda whispered.

Pink tinged Wil's cheeks, her eyes still downcast on her hands wrapped tightly together. The light from the television cast a glow on their skin, the shadows flickering across them. Lynda's chest tightened as the moment stretched out. Wil's chin raised, their eyes locking in a new battle, her look utterly defiant.

"What's stopping you?"

Each time they had kissed before, Lynda had been the one to goad them into it, but this time it was a simple ask. Her heart raced. She still held her beer in her other hand, tightly gripping the glass like it was a lifeline she wasn't sure she wanted to let go of.

"You are." Her answer was short, but it was the truth. Wil seemed so unsure of what their future might hold or how it would affect her life, and Lynda wasn't going to be the one to ruin that or bring anymore devastation to all that Wil had faced.

"How am I stopping you?" Wil's brows drew together in confusion, but she leaned into Lynda's gentle touch, her eyes drifting shut.

Lynda ran her thumb across Wil's lower lip, the soft texture tickling her skin. She was desperate to lean in and start the kiss, not only would the distraction be welcome, but she wanted to know what it would be like to kiss Wil when it wasn't all fire—when there was sadness mingled in at the same time.

Her heart thundered, the decision on the tip of her tongue, but she couldn't make it for the both of them. Desperation clung to her because she wanted this so bad that she was willing to risk everything. She broke every rule, every boundary she'd initially set out to keep in place, and now she knew why. But Wil needed to be in this with her for it to work. Wil had to take her hand

and walk through the fire with her because she couldn't do this alone.

Her voice was firm when she spoke, answering the question as honestly as she could. "Do you want this? You now, as an adult, as my assistant manager, as a forever friend to Isla—is this what you really want?"

Wil hesitated. Lynda saw it the moment they locked gazes. If there was any doubt for either of them, then they needed to stop whatever was happening. Her heart broke because she knew it couldn't happen then. They had tiptoed the conversation for so long, and she was so exhausted from holding that line in place. She just wanted this one moment to be it, but it couldn't be. Wil wasn't ready yet. Lynda dropped her hand into her lap and took her beer, sucking down another long pull before setting it on the table and painfully rebuilding those walls as best as she could, brick by damning brick.

Lynda grasped for the threads of what she needed to do even though she didn't want to. Disappointment consumed her. Moving to stand up, she said, "When you can answer that question, then we should talk. I know what I want, but I don't think you're quite ready to tell me your answer yet."

Wil locked her fingers around her wrist and pulled her down hard. Lynda landed in Wil's lap, Wil's mouth immediately on hers. Sparks ignited throughout her body, heating her up as she struggled to catch her breath. Lynda squeaked when Wil flipped her onto her back, pushing her into the heavenly couch cushion and covering her entirely.

The weight of Wil's body on hers was exactly what she needed. She was cocooned in the care and love she'd found, the recognition of everything she had been through and all she was. Reaching up, Lynda threaded her fingers through Wil's hair and held on, desperate to replace the weight of hopelessness with Wil's.

Lynda desperately wanted to part her legs and let Wil sink between them, but she held still as she continued the embrace.

Their tongues slid together just before Wil pulled back slightly and nipped at her lower lip. Wil kissed along her jawline, down her neck, over the tops of her breasts. Lynda kept a hand in her hair. This had been exactly what she had wanted since they'd started this dance, every touch, every caress, but she resisted accepting it into her heart. Wil wasn't ready, and this was her crying out that same confusion they'd been talking about.

Lynda's breathing increased, the short rapid breaths difficult to keep up with. Pleasure soared through her, gathering between her legs, and she had to close her eyes to catch herself. Which was a mistake, because as soon as she couldn't see, all her senses hyper-focused on Wil's touch, on the slide of her tongue along the skin at the tops of her breasts, Wil's hand at her waist as she slid it upward to cup her breast and tease her nipple through the thin fabric of her shirt and bra.

Lynda groaned, the sound vibrating through her as she tried to arch her back. She was desperate for Wil's touch, for more of what she was offering, but that niggling warning bell in the back of her mind told her to stop, and the more she let Wil touch her, the louder it got.

"Wil," Lynda said on a breath. Swallowing, she tried again. "Wil, stop."

She hated having to do this. Pain and hurt filled her chest as she wrapped herself tighter in her resolve. She had to be the one to stop it this time, the one to pull away and put that wall between them again. She hated herself for it, but she had to do the right thing, be the one in control again.

Wil stilled. She hovered over Lynda as she heaved breath after breath. Lynda hated being the one to stop it this time. Compassion filled her knowing that this must be what Wil felt each time before, that painful struggle of do or don't.

"We need to stop," Lynda repeated, making it very clear where she stood.

Wil pushed back, sitting on the couch with her head in her hands. Lynda took two steadying breaths before she shifted upward, touching Wil's hand again. *God, how I want to kiss her.* Keeping her distance wasn't easy, but Lynda knew it had to be done.

"I'm going to go home." Lynda squeezed Wil's hand tightly. "I'll see you in the morning."

She stood—this time fully confident in her decision to end what had only just begun. She left the apartment without saying anything else, her steps firm as she walked down the long hallway toward the elevator. She didn't expect to hear from Wil that night. She did expect awkwardness in the morning until they were able to figure out where they stood with each other and until Wil was able to make a decision. Lynda could wait. She had nothing to lose at this point.

The drive back to her condo was quick, and when she got inside, her body was still on fire from Wil's touch. She knew that if she closed her eyes that she would be able to feel Wil against her, the damp kisses, the firm touches. Shivering in pleasure, Lynda pulled her shoes off to start relaxing.

She had ignored herself far too long, and Wil had pointed that out to her without even trying. When they showed up at work tomorrow, she wouldn't be the same person she had been for years. Her family, her friends—they were her priority. Dare she even like to think that she would make herself a priority again, like when she'd met Patrick all those years ago. Smiling at herself, she settled into that thought.

<h1 style="text-align:center">CHAPTER
Twenty</h1>

THE PHONE WAS warm in her hand and against her ear as Wil waited for Isla to answer. She could still feel Lynda writhing under her, the press of warm wet lips against hers, the heat from her skin as Wil had kissed her way down her neck. *Fuck.* Wil's body was beyond ready, too. After the few kisses they'd had, everything had been chock full of that intensity she'd always seen Lynda to have.

Bouncing on the balls of her feet, Wil waited for the call to connect through. After what had happened that night, there was no way she could avoid this conversation any longer. She owed it to Isla to talk to her first, to explain what was happening, what she wanted. They had to talk because she needed advice, she needed permission, and she needed to be able to go after Lynda instead of being stuck in purgatory.

"Hey, sis," Isla answered.

"Hey," Wil responded, morosely. She should have planned better going into this conversation, but she was pretty sure she knew exactly how she wanted to have it. She paced back and forth around her living room, energy a livewire in her veins. "I wanted to run something by you."

"What's that?" The television echoed in the background, the murmurs of whatever Isla was watching barely audible.

Dragging in a deep, steadying breath, Wil plopped onto her couch and covered her eyes with her hands. "Do you remember when we were kids and I told you that I liked girls?"

"Vaguely." Isla's tone was light, but it held a touch of curiosity in it. Wil knew she remembered, but that she was more curious about why Wil was even bringing it up after all these years.

Maybe this wasn't the best way to start this conversation, but it was honestly the best way for Wil. "Remember when I was talking about liking girls instead of boys when I thought I was a lesbian?"

"Yes." Concern filled Isla's tone and the muted voices from the television stopped.

Wil had to speed up the conversation. "I told you that I knew I liked girls because I had a crush on your stepmom."

Silence greeted Wil on the other end of the line. She wasn't sure how to break it, or what to say next, but she did know that she had to finish her explanation. "I have tried so hard not to. I was such a royal bitch to her, I poked at her, I pushed her and everyone away, and no matter what I did, it never fucking went away."

"You do remember this is what almost ended our friendship?" Isla's breathing was heavy, fear in her voice as she spoke.

Wil cringed. "Yeah, which is why I've avoided it this long."

"And since she's your boss now?"

Wil frowned. "It's...yes, those feelings have been coming back up."

"So you like her?" Isla was so hesitant.

"I do." Wil's voice was barely above a whisper, and she hoped Isla had heard her. The tension in the conversation was thick, and Wil knew she had to be the one to break it. Isla didn't know where she was going with the call. "When we went to Seattle, it got intense and intimate. We kissed. But fuck, it was so much more than that. It was really intense, like I've never felt that way before, and never had that strong of a connection with someone like her."

Wil's heart thudded hard, as if she was confessing to murdering a man in cold blood and burying him in her backyard and needing Isla to help cover it all up.

"I didn't know she liked women," Isla said softly.

Wil wasn't sure Isla's comment was because she didn't know what else to say or if she was mad at them for the entire situation. Her fear of repeating the past ratcheted up another notch, her leg bouncing off the floor. Wil just needed an answer. She needed to know if her forever friend was going to spurn her or not, if this was ruining everything they had managed to keep throughout the years.

"I don't think she knew that."

"What do you mean?"

There. They finally had a place to go with this conversation. "She told me she's only ever been with men, but she seems interested in more than that with me."

"What you're saying is you want to have sex with her?"

Wil clenched her jaw. It wasn't just about sex, and Isla was twisting into that. She had to bring them back to where she wanted the conversation to be. "I want more than that with her."

"You *hate* her."

Sighing, Wil rubbed her temple. There was so much they had to talk about still. She had avoided it. "I don't."

"All you did was hate her through high school and college and even after. You were awful to her, Wil. The things you said... I hated to be around you and her because you were so damn mean. Constantly. There was never a break to it. For years I put up with it, and now you're telling me that you want to fuck my stepmom? What am I supposed to do with that?"

"I know, but it wasn't her I hated, really. It was me. I was mad, Isla. I loved your dad like he was my dad, and he was just gone, and we were left with Lynda, and she didn't care about me like he did. She cared about you and Aisling, but I was just the poor kid from down the road she couldn't get rid of. Or at least that's what I thought at the time, but that wasn't real. It was just my perception of what was happening as an angry teenager who had a fuck-you attitude. But it's been eleven years since I've seen her, and now she's my boss, and the feelings I had that pissed me off to no end when we were kids haven't gone away, and I think... I think she has them, too."

When Isla didn't immediately respond, Wil stood up sharply and paced through her small apartment. It was nearly too damn much. She stood to lose everything if she did this wrong, which was why she was on the phone in the first place.

"I don't know what you want me to say."

"I want you to say that you won't hate me for this." Tears burned her eyes, unbidden and painful. Her chest ached, everything tight so it was hard to breathe.

"For what?" Isla seemed genuinely confused.

"For pursuing more with Lynda. I want more with her." The words flowed so easily, the truth of them left Wil breathless.

"You want to *date* her?"

"I do." It was the first time Wil said it out loud, but it felt right. It was more than just heated kisses. She shared a connection with Lynda that she'd never been able to break, and she wanted—perhaps for the first time in her life—to see where that connection would take them. "I do want to date her, but I won't do it if it's going to fuck up anything between us. I won't."

"Wil..." Isla trailed off. She drew in a sharp breath before she sighed. "I haven't talked to Lynda in five years, and it's not because of you or your relationship with her. If you want to talk to her, then I'm not going to stop you."

"What do you mean it's not because of me?" Wil's head hurt, the whiplash from one moment to the next impossible to keep up with.

"Just trust me, it's not because of you. You were a factor in that decision, but you weren't the cause, and I don't want to get into it right now. Okay?"

"Yeah, okay." Wil clenched her jaw. "But soon?"

"I promise. I'll come down before the new school year starts, and we'll get drunk on tequila and hash it all out."

"Okay." This time when Wil said it, relief washed through her. Silence filtered through the line, and Wil had no idea how to turn the conversation back to where they had started. Her heart raced. "But what about Lynda and me?"

"What do you mean, but?"

Wil shakily went through her cabinets searching for liquor. She needed something to calm her nerves. But Isla wasn't telling her to go away, at least not yet. She grasped for straws, but luckily, Isla interrupted her search.

"I don't know, Wil. I didn't expect this tonight. I love you. You're my sister. I want you to be happy, and if exploring whatever is with you and Lynda is going to make you happy, then do that. But I don't want to talk to her, and I don't want her to use you to talk to me."

Relief flooded through Wil, though there was still a lingering tension of fear that this wouldn't work out. Lynda hadn't tried to do any of that or pry since they had been thrown into this. "I don't think she'll do that. She hasn't once mentioned trying to get back into your life."

"Okay." Isla seemed content, but Wil wanted to verify to make doubly sure.

"You're really okay with this?"

"I will be. I had a feeling something like this was coming."

Wil's hands shook as she leaned against the kitchen counter. "What do you mean?"

Isla chuckled. "You tried to hide your damn crush on her for years and failed miserably. Even Aisling knows about it."

"She doesn't!" Wil's eyes widened, and her stomach plummeted.

"Oh, she does, and I think she'll be way happier than I am that it's happening."

Wil stopped twisting the cap off the vodka. "Hey, do you think you can do me a favor?"

"What?"

"Can you call Aisling and tell her?"

"Why?" Isla dragged the word out.

"Because I want Lynda's home address, and I know you don't have it, but she probably does, and I don't want to get it from the office because that's walking the line on ethics a little too much for me, and I don't want to text Lynda or call her because—"

"You want to surprise her," Isla finished. "Yeah, I can do that. Give me a minute."

Without saying anything else, Isla hung up. Staring at the bottle of vodka in her hand, Wil twisted the cap back on and shoved it into the cabinet. She needed to go into this sober, and she hoped against all odds that Lynda was sober still. They needed to have a talk.

When the text came through with Lynda's address and a *go get your girl* from Isla, Wil raced through her small apartment. She freshened up, then grabbed her keys and wallet and left. It didn't take her more than five minutes to get to Lynda's condo because she surprisingly didn't live that far away.

The lights were on inside, and Wil stepped up to the door. Her body was a live wire of nerves and energy she needed to dissipate quickly. She knew the best way to do that, but they did have to talk first—at least she hoped they would and not just tumble to the floor in a tangle of naked limbs.

Wil knocked.

She raised up on her toes as she waited for Lynda to come to the door. She shoved her hands in her pockets to try and keep that energy confined, to try and not reach out and grab Lynda to kiss her senseless as soon as the door opened. Wil's stomach fluttered.

The click of the lock was loud. Wil's mouth instantly dried up, and when Lynda opened the door, she stood there in her beautiful skirt and blouse she'd worn to the office that day, her feet bare of any heels, and a phone pressed to her ear. Lynda held Wil's gaze intently.

"Yeah. Thank you, Isla. I appreciate it."

Isla? Wil was befuddled until Lynda hung up the call and set the phone onto the small table next to the door. She cocked her head to the side, eyeing Wil up and down with nothing but lust in the look, as if Lynda was going to eat Wil alive for days and they might never emerge into the real world again. She'd told Isla she didn't want to ruin the surprise, and then she called? What had she said exactly?

"Come inside." Lynda's tone was low, a hitherto that Wil couldn't resist. As soon as she had the door closed, Wil glanced down at the offending phone. Lynda didn't give her a chance to ask as she caught the direction of Wil's look. "Isla doesn't break five-year silences for nothing."

Wil's mouth was dry. "No, I don't suppose she does. What did she say?"

Those caramel brown eyes were a mystery most days, but tonight, all Wil saw in them was hope. "She said you were coming, and that she approved."

Before Wil could say anything, Lynda was on her. Mouths pressed together, hotly, Lynda seemed to touch Wil everywhere. Wil stepped forward toward the living area, pushing Lynda back. They needed to go somewhere, standing in the middle of the entryway to have sex wasn't what Wil wanted to happen for Lynda's first time.

Reaching down, Will dragged Lynda's skirt up and over her ass, gripping the supple flesh she found. She didn't know why she was surprised Lynda wore a thong. It made perfect sense with the outfits, but just the thought of it raged through her. Wil nipped at Lynda's lip, biting down a little harder than necessary to try and center them both.

They couldn't turn back now. Heat raced between her legs, compelling her forward as she took another step. The dining area was first, and Wil stopped there, pushing Lynda against the tabletop. She didn't want to wait. It had been years of dreaming of this, and Wil was done holding off.

"Touch me," Lynda murmured, breaking their kiss long enough to say the words before diving back in.

As much as Wil's fingers itched to plunge into Lynda, she wanted to see more of her. She hadn't seen anything of her yet, and Wil wanted skin to skin. She wanted to taste Lynda's breasts, tease her nipples, see exactly what would make them harden. She pulled at Lynda's blouse, tugging it from the waistband of her skirt until she found more of that gloriously creamy skin.

Sighing, Wil ran her fingertips over Lynda's stomach so gently she knew it would tickle. She took her time pushing the blouse up until she pulled it over Lynda's head and dropped it onto the floor. She was sure Lynda would be having an internal conniption that the shirt was left to be trampled on. God knew she yelled at them enough when they were kids for doing the same thing, but Wil was going to make her come even with that thought in her mind.

Lynda reached behind her back and flipped the clasp on her bra, removing it immediately. Wil's lips quirked into a smile, and she dropped her chin to kiss the tops of Lynda's breasts. Freckles littered her chest, pointing Wil's way right down to her hardened nipples. This was heaven. It had to be. Years of waiting and dreaming were finally coming to fruition, and she wanted to bury her face in Lynda and make her come so many times her voice was too hoarse to speak.

Moaning, Lynda cupped the back of Wil's head and leaned down so her back was on the table. Wil licked a small circle around one supple nipple while she reached up and pinched the other. Lynda arched her back off the table, her lips parted in ecstasy.

This was the Lynda Wil had dreamed of, the one who had no barriers holding her back, the one who was all passion and heat and fire. Popping off one nipple, Wil moved to the other. At the same time, she lightly scraped her nails down Lynda's body to her knee and back up on the inside of her thigh.

"Yes," Lynda hissed.

Wil kissed down Lynda's stomach as Lynda reached up to play with her own breasts, teasing her damp nipples all the while staring at Wil directly. Wil's heart hammered a little harder, the connection between them unbreakable. Her own body ramped up, and she swore she felt exactly what Lynda did. Wil kissed over the lump of material that was Lynda's skirt and then took small nips of her thigh, swirling her tongue as she got closer and then farther from where they both wanted her to be.

"Please," Lynda begged.

The sound was so sweet to Wil's ears. That had been what she was waiting for, the sweet surrender of a woman in power. It was perfect and exactly what she needed to hear to reach forward and slide the fabric of her thong out of the way. Lynda smelled glorious. It had been a long time since Wil had fucked anyone, but Lynda's scent was perfect, musky, sweet, with a hint of spice. Wil could only imagine at that point what she would taste like—if it would be similar to her scent or different. Either way, she knew she would savor it.

Lynda's hips rocked up as if she was trying to get Wil to her sooner. Risking a glance up, Wil checked one last time just to confirm that this was happening, that this was what they both wanted. The look she received was unadulterated passion. The sizzling energy between them palpable as she held their locked gazes.

No doubts—they both wanted this.

Wil intended to start slow. She pressed her tongue against Lynda's swollen lips, but as soon as that pure flavor hit, she couldn't resist. She plunged her tongue inside as far as it would go. Closing her eyes, she focused on only that. In seconds, she moved up to tease with the tip of her tongue while sliding one finger inside slowly, stretching and testing to see how much Lynda could handle.

The soft whimper Lynda let out spurred Wil on. Lynda's hands roved all over her own chest until Wil added a second finger. Putting all her concentration into Lynda, Wil fucked her with wild abandon. Years of built-up tension releasing in an instant as she swiftly brought Lynda to orgasm, and then took her up again, and again. By the third time, Lynda was halfway sitting, her hand behind to support her and her fingers threaded into Wil's hair as she held on.

When she crashed this time, Lynda tapped Wil's forehead, indicating she wanted Wil to stop. Standing up straight, Wil kept her fingers inside Lynda's pulsing pussy, enjoying the clench of her muscles and the spill of her juices against her skin. Lynda pulled Wil in for a long, slow, sloppy kiss. As they parted ways, Lynda put her head against Wil's shoulder and steadied her breathing.

"Bedroom. Now."

"Yes, Mrs. Walsh." This time, the teasing tone Wil had was perfect for the moment. She helped Lynda off the table, pulling the zipper on her skirt and pushing it down along with the thong so she could watch Lynda walk in all her glory toward the bedroom. It was the sexiest thing Wil had ever seen.

As they went, Wil slowly undid the buttons on her vest and her shirt, pulling the fabric apart and undressing so that by the time they got to the bed, they could roll onto it and be ready to go. Lynda eyed her hungrily. Wil moved her hands to her belt, but Lynda stepped forward and stilled them. "Let me."

Wil said nothing as Lynda slowly slid the belt open, then the button and zipper. Lynda moved with precision and practice, something Wil hadn't expected when she'd never been with a woman before. Reaching up, Wil curled Lynda's hair behind her ear and cupped the side of her face as Lynda pushed her pants over her ass and hips. Stepping out of the material after toeing off her shoes, Wil stood in front of Lynda in nothing but her boxer briefs and sports bra.

"What do you want me to do?" Lynda asked, gliding fingers over every inch of exposed skin.

"Whatever you want," Wil replied, pulling Lynda in for a quick kiss. "I'll do whatever you want to try."

Wil sat on the edge of the bed and lifted her hands to pull her sports bra off. Reverently, Lynda touched her. Her fingers were soft, smooth, barely there until she pushed in more. Wil pressed kisses against Lynda's skin whenever she got a chance, encouraging her silently.

"I want to taste you."

"Then do that." Wil shifted backward on the bed and pulled her boxer briefs off as she went. As she got to the center of the mattress, she spread her legs wide and moved her fingers between them. Lynda stood utterly entranced with what Wil was doing. It took her a minute to snap out of it, and she finally followed Wil, laying down between her legs. She took her time, kissing around Wil's hand and observing, but as soon as she went in, she went all in.

Lynda's fingers replaced Wil's, and she latched her mouth firmly on Wil's clit. Sucking. Soothing. Flicking. Tingles floated through Wil's body and her mind as everything she had was focused on that moment. Lynda stayed where she was, drawing in deep breaths as she curled her fingers upward. Wil had been waiting for this, waiting for the moment when she could let loose and not look back.

She reached down, sliding her fingers into Lynda's hair and tugging lightly. Tilting her pelvis upward to give Lynda a better angle, Wil groaned. She pushed lightly on Lynda's head, urging her without words to give her more. "Little harder. Fucking perfect."

Wil moaned on a breath, her words escaping her. She urged her body into Lynda's, holding the tension as her orgasm built, wrapped around her, and pulled her down into the sea of pleasure.

Her mind was bliss. When she opened her eyes, Lynda was

pressed against her side running soothing hands over her body. Wil turned onto her side and pulled Lynda against her, dropping kisses into her hair.

"I suppose we should talk."

Lynda hummed. "I guess we should. Tomorrow. I'm too tired tonight."

"You did come three times."

Giggling, Lynda tickled Wil's sides. "I'm not complaining."

"If you did, I'd have to punish you with another one."

"Don't tempt me." Lynda moved in, kissing Wil's lips and sucking the lower one. "Because it's really tempting."

Wil tingled everywhere, the flush running back through her before pooling between her legs again. "Well then, let me show you what else I can do."

CHAPTER
Twenty-One

WIL LEFT EARLY in the morning to go home and change. Which left Lynda by herself, staring at the table Wil had fucked her on three times over the night before. With the coffee cup perched at her lips, Lynda sighed. The phone call from Isla had been so unexpected, and she almost hadn't answered it. Though she was so glad she had. Isla had left the call with a promise to talk later that week, but she'd wanted Lynda to have time with Wil.

However, she and Wil hadn't even talked since she'd rushed to her own apartment for a change of clothes. They'd promised to talk that morning, but they'd been up so late that when Wil had rolled out of bed it was nearly time for them to leave. Pursing her lips, Lynda finished her coffee, grabbed her purse, and headed to the office. They were going to need to find that time soon.

As she got out of her car, later than she normally arrived, Lynda's body ached, a sweet ache she hadn't experienced in far too long. Making her way into the office, her step was lighter. She and Wil had at least worked out some of their problems, and that was a welcome reprieve from what the last week had been.

Within minutes of her arrival, Wil stepped into her office

and settled a disposable coffee cup on her desk and smiled down at Lynda in her chair. Lynda's heart pattered, and a smile lit up her face at the familiar peace offering.

"Hey there." Wil said, her voice scratchy from last night.

"Morning," Lynda answered, a slight tease to her tone and her cheeks heating with the memory of what they had spent hours doing. Something about this day was already different in a way she was ready to enjoy.

"How was your night?" Wil asked so nonchalantly, even though she knew the answer.

Lynda glanced out of her office, checking to see if anyone was in yet or in the vicinity. With no sign, she stood up and slid against Wil, pressing their mouths together in a chaste but heated kiss. When she pulled away, Wil smiled up at her.

"I take it that your night was good."

"It was better than good." Lynda's voice dropped, barely above a whisper. "And I would love to have another night like it."

Wil's lips curled. "I think that can be arranged."

Lynda stepped away from Wil before she gave into temptation again and before someone saw them. She sat in her desk chair and pulled over the coffee Wil had brought. She'd enjoyed the extra attention Wil had given her while they were in Seattle, and it seemed as though they were back to that level of intimacy, something Lynda was grateful for.

"We have a lot of work to do today," Lynda started. "We need to put together an improvement plan for Jacob and implement some trainings."

"What are we starting with?"

"Both, actually." Lynda pulled up her computer and opened the email. "You tackle the improvement plan. I'll begin with the trainings."

"Why do you want me to deal with Jacob?"

"You need the experience if you're going to move up in the business."

"Oh?" Wil raised an eyebrow. "Too much work for the lady in the red dress?"

Lynda's eyes crinkled in the corners at Wil's flirtatious tone. "You want to move up and learn more, and you're interviewing with Devon. If you want a leg up with him, you'll do the planning work."

"I know." Wil sighed, staying right next to Lynda.

"Get to work, Wilda."

Wil's nose wrinkled at the comment, but a thrill ran up Lynda's spine at the reaction. She was oddly playful today. She remembered vaguely being this playful with Patrick when they had first started dating, but it was so long ago, and there was so much heartache in between that she must have forgotten about it.

Wil stepped out of the office, and for the first time in days, Lynda was finally able to focus on work. She was halfway through her day when she got a phone call, the one she had been waiting for. Checking to make sure her office door was shut, Lynda answered it and leaned back in the chair, remembering the email she had sent first thing that morning. It had taken her the better part of the last week to craft it, and with what happened the night before, it needed to be sent immediately.

"Jessica," Lynda said by way of greeting. "Did you get my email?"

"I did." Jolie Preston's CEO was not someone Lynda talked to daily, but she was familiar enough with the woman to have an idea how this conversation would go. And it would take her most tactful presence of mind to make sure it turned in her direction. "Care to explain it?"

"I told you how Wilda Powell was my stepdaughter's childhood best friend, and we've been running into some conflicts of interest." Lynda's stomach fluttered in anticipation of where the conversation was going.

"Has it gotten worse since you mentioned it before? Because it wasn't an issue then." Jessica still sounded confused.

"Right, normally it wouldn't be, but Wil and I had a contentious relationship for years, and our past keeps getting in the way of moving forward."

Jessica paused. "Your report from Seattle seemed positive."

"It was, and it gave me great insight into Wilda's ability to run this branch. I think she's ready, and I don't think we should hold her back any longer."

"But she's a finalist in the interview process for Devon. I'm concerned about someone so willing to leave as soon as change comes."

Cold rushed through her. She hadn't realized the interview process had gotten that far or that Devon had made up his mind yet. She should have talked to him first. Her mouth was sticky with fear when she found another reason to keep her request in line with what she wanted.

"He's not hiring for a manager—not to the extent Wilda is capable of. She won't be using her full skillset to work with him." Her argument sounded weaker by the minute. "I think it would be best for her to remain here and take over my position. I can fill in for Liam until he's fit to return."

Jessica paused as she took in what Lynda wasn't saying outright, and Lynda's heart skittered with fear. "You're resigning?"

Lynda bit her lip, reminding herself why she was doing this. She might lose everything she had worked for, but Wil would be worth it, and she deserved it. "If necessary, though, I would prefer to be reassigned elsewhere."

The silence was long. Tension riddled along Lynda's arms and spine as she waited to hear what Jessica had to say. For once in her life, Lynda was glad the CEO was a woman because this conversation would be much more difficult to have with a man, and she would have taken a completely different tactic. But she and Jessica knew each other well, so she had a good indication on what would be said.

"What's the real reason?" Jessica murmured.

Lynda stared out through the glass window into the hallway as Wil walked down it. "For years after Patrick died, I focused on two things—raising the girls and making sure I had a job to put food on the table and keep them in that house. It's been nine years since Aisling moved out to go to college. It's been five years since she finished. They don't need me in that way anymore, and meeting Wilda again for the second time has put some things in perspective."

"What things?"

"That I want to be happy." The weight that had been pushing down on her released, and Lynda dragged in a breath of fresh air easily as relief flooded her.

"I'm not sure I understand."

Lynda smiled to herself. "You probably never will unless you've lost a spouse, and I hope that never happens to you. But Jessica, I don't want to put work first this time."

Another long silence greeted her, and just when Lynda was about to probe Jessica to speak, she finally answered. "I'll see what I can do."

"I would appreciate it sooner rather than later, because I don't want to come in here beyond two weeks, and if you can't find something for me, consider this my two weeks." Lynda's words were firm and confident, the knowledge settling into her chest of how right her decision was.

"You're playing hard ball, Lynda."

"I know." Lynda smiled. "But I have a feeling it'll be worth it in the end. It'll all work out. I promise. And Wilda will become the next chief manager?"

"I'll see about her. Her resume was impressive, but I still have some concerns."

"You'll have to snatch her up. She's already farming it out beyond us." Lynda assumed that was true, but she hadn't confirmed it with Wil, and it would add pressure to Jessica to make a swift decision.

"I'll look at her."

"Don't waste time on it. She's not one you want to lose. Trust me."

"You aren't either, Lynda."

That warmed her. Hanging up, Lynda went back to work, leaving Wil in charge. She would spend the next few weeks making sure Wil was as up-to-date on Jolie Preston's policies as possible, that way, Wil would have the best chance at being her successor.

~

The coffee was warm as it slid down Lynda's throat, and she bided her time while she waited for the opportune moment to talk to Camryn about the problems she was having. Finally, Camryn wasn't having any more of her avoidance.

"What's going on?"

"What do you mean?" Lynda pushed back, wincing as she avoided out of habit.

"You don't usually call me up and ask for an emergency coffee date."

It was true. She'd done it often after Patrick had died, but not many times in the last few years. Lynda turned her cup in her hand, staring at the brown liquid as it moved. "There are so many things coming up lately, I'm not sure where to start."

"Which one is the bigger thing?"

Lynda gave Camryn a desperate glance. "That's the thing. I don't know."

Camryn hummed. "Love or life?"

"Love or love." At Camryn's confused look, she tried again. "Since Wil, I can't stop thinking about Isla. I shouldn't have let it go this long."

"Do you want to talk to her?" Camryn reached out and covered Lynda's hands to still them. "It's been what? Five years?"

Lynda nodded. "I should have pushed to resolve things

sooner. I'm the adult in the relationship, and I should have made sure we had good communication."

"Oh Lynda." Camryn squeezed her fingers. "You were widowed so young and thrown into raising two teenagers, or almost teenagers, without any warning, and you and Isla are both incredibly strong-willed. There was no way the two of you were going to survive those transition years into adulthood without some bruises."

"This is more than a mere bruise. I let her go five years without even trying to talk to her." Lynda's face fell, guilt eating away at her. She'd known she'd been wrong so many times, but she hadn't made changes or fought for what she wanted, or what Patrick would have wanted.

"You haven't done anything?"

Lynda swallowed the lump in her throat. Patrick would hate how far she had let them all fall. He had trusted her to take care of his family, and for the last five years, she hadn't even talked to one of his daughters. She hadn't checked in, she hadn't attempted to even contact her. He would be so disappointed in her. "No."

"And why do you want to do something about it now?"

"Because of Wil." Lynda wasn't afraid to admit that. Having Wil back in her life brought forth everything she had done wrong in the past years—from the time the girls were younger until now. She had made so many mistakes. She wanted to rectify them, but she hadn't even known where to begin. Hiding away from that was so much easier than facing it, but when Wil's name had been thrown her way as being part of Henshaw's firm, she knew it would force her to look at her relationship with Isla in a different light. So she'd taken that opportunity. "They're still best friends."

"So? What does that have to do with you?"

Lynda slid Camryn a sharp look, glad to see Laura hadn't gossiped about her in the meantime. Everything slammed together in ways she hadn't expected, to the point that it was impossible to untangle things. She had worked so hard to keep her distance from Isla, not to press Wil into being in the middle of all the drama she had avoided for years, but it was impossible. She'd realized that when Isla had called her, a wobble in each word. Isla hadn't called her because of her. She'd called because of Wil. "I had sex with Wil."

"You what?" Camryn's eyebrows disappeared into her hairline at the shock.

Lynda wasn't going to say it again. She waited for Camryn to fully comprehend, turning her cup in her fingers again. She wasn't embarrassed by it, not really. But the fact that Wil was Isla's best friend never escaped her attention, and there was a tension between them that needed to be resolved. They both needed to be able to talk to each other about their lives, and Isla was such a large part of Wil's that if they were going to continue to be together in any capacity, Lynda would need to be able to create that space.

"I want to be with her. I called Jessica and told her that I wanted to transfer—"

"Lynda!" Camryn interrupted, putting her hand on Lynda's to stop her from talking. "You're resigning?"

"No, I want to transfer and let Wil take over my position."

"After you've had sex with her? Have you even thought about this?"

"She deserves it. She can handle it." Every one of Lynda's defenses went up. It was time for her to make more drastic changes than she had thought possible. It wasn't about her job anymore—it was about the family she had been given and then lost.

Camryn blew out a breath. "You're favoring her too much, and you need to talk to Laura about this. She'll be able to explain this so much better than I can. Look, I'm all for you talking to Isla if that's what you want to do. You two need to work through whatever this block is, and if it's for Wil, then fine."

Lynda knew the big problem was coming next. Her stomach dropped, and cold washed through her. "And Wil?"

"If you want to be with her, then be with her. I don't have a problem with it." Camryn dropped her tone, whispering. "But you can't have sex with your employees and then try to give them a promotion."

Lynda heard the words, but it didn't sink in. "She can do the job, and she deserves to be in a position that could use her skills."

"Even if that is true, and I'm not doubting it is because I trust your evaluation of her skillset, it's such a conflict of interest that no one will see her for her abilities. They'll see her because of you."

Lynda didn't want to believe it even though Laura had essentially told her the exact same thing. Wil was one of the most skilled assistant managers that she had ever worked with when taking over a company. She was such a quick learner and a go-getter. Lynda stared down at her coffee again, not quite sure what to say or how to maneuver through the rest of the conversation. Was she guilty of favoring Wil? Absolutely. But when that favor was deserved, did it matter? Devon saw her skills since he wanted to hire her, even Jessica had commented on them.

"I can't believe you think this is a good idea."

Lynda kept silent, thoroughly chastised. She'd already done it, unfortunately, and she was going to follow through with it if she could. Wil deserved a promotion, and Lynda was going to do everything in her power to make sure she got it.

"What do you think about Isla?" She changed the topic, avoiding the one she knew they were going to have conflict on. Isla was as wrapped up in this mess as she and Wil were, but at the very least, both of them wanted to protect her.

Camryn gave her a hard look, knowing exactly what she was doing but going along with it. This was why Lynda liked her so much. "I think you should call her."

"What if she doesn't answer?" Fear filled her in a way she

hadn't ever allowed before. It hurt so much to have that distance between them, to put Aisling in the middle of the drama. Lynda had pulled back on that relationship in order to save Aisling any more hurt, but that had been the wrong decision. She should have fought for her daughters harder, fought to give them everything they needed, the family they deserved.

"Then you'll deal with it then, but you can't make her do anything. Give her a call, tell her you want to talk with her and listen to her. Hear me on that one, Lynda. You need to listen far more than you need to talk. That girl has a story to tell, and you need to hear it."

Lynda squared her shoulders and clenched her jaw, the last of her defenses going up. "I was there for it."

Camryn glared. "Hear it. She won't see what happened the same way you did."

Lynda nodded slightly, knowing Camryn was right, even if she didn't want to fully admit it out loud. "Okay."

"And be patient. Every ounce of patience you have and more, you're going to need it."

Lynda had already suspected that one. She lifted her coffee cup to her lips and took a long sip with unsteady hands. "Thank you."

"Anytime, but really, give up trying to get Wil a promotion."

Lynda wasn't going to do it. She wanted Wil to thrive, and their relationship shouldn't have any bearing on that. Even then, she knew they should have waited. But she hadn't been able to resist. As soon as the temptation was there and it was an actual possibility, Lynda had wanted nothing more than to find out what it was all about. She wanted Wil. It had been the exact same when she'd met Patrick. She'd known as soon as she opened her heart to him that she loved him.

"Look," Camryn quieted down again. "You're going to do whatever you want. I know you are, but please, be careful."

"I'll try."

"I saw what Wil put you through for years. It was almost impossible to watch you go through that."

"I know. It was so hard, but she's not that person anymore, and I'm not that person anymore. I've worked through my grief."

"I know you have." Camryn straightened her back. "Doesn't mean I don't worry about you. That's what friends are for, you know?"

"I know." Lynda had worried about Camryn and her husband more times than she cared to admit, and still worried. Even though Camryn tried to convince everyone they had found some sort of balance, Lynda was pretty sure it was a farce. "Thanks for coming today."

"Any time."

Twenty-Two

CAMRYN HAD ENCOURAGED IT, but that didn't mean Lynda wasn't nervous. She stood in her kitchen, leaning against the counter with the open bottle of wine next to her. She'd poured herself a second glass as she stared at her cellphone. She knew she was going to have to be the one to make the call, but why did it have to be so hard still? Laura would tell her to get it over with.

Lynda smiled at that thought, knowing her friends had her best interest in mind. She'd thought giving Isla the space she so clearly craved would bring her back around, but it hadn't. It had only increased the distance between them. Lynda thumbed her phone, the debate still raging within her even though she knew the solution. She had let things fester without any type of reparations far too long.

Before she could change her mind, Lynda hit the number Isla had called her from and lifted the phone to her ear. Her entire body vibrated as she waited for Isla to answer and for her sweet voice to say *hello*. When it reached voicemail, Lynda's heart shattered.

"Hey, this is Isla Walsh. Leave a message, and I'll get back to you."

She almost hung up. She almost threw the phone across the room. Swallowing her pride, Lynda started after the beep. "Isla, it's Lynda. I was hoping you'd want to talk and maybe—"

Her phone buzzed loudly in her hand. Removing it from her ear, Lynda stared down at the incoming call. *Isla.* Her lips twitched as she answered. "Hello?"

"Hi." Isla's voice always had that pure quality to it, the intonations perfect for someone who had no emotional baggage. Lynda had envied that on occasion, but she knew they both carried more weight than either wanted to admit.

"Hi," Lynda replied, not quite sure where to start now that she was finally on the phone with her. She stared at the wine, wanting it to bolster her but also needing her wits about her to make sure she heard and explained clearly. She hadn't planned any of this. "I hoped we could talk a bit."

"About what?" Isla was on the defensive, and Lynda couldn't blame her. For her the call would be out of the blue, but she'd not only answered, she'd called back. That gave Lynda some hope at least.

"About a lot of things." Lynda sighed, lifting her wine glass to her lips but not taking a sip. "But really...whatever you want to talk about."

The pause in the conversation was loud, the silence reverberating through Lynda's chest to the point she had no idea where to go with it or what to say. Isla was always the hard one to pull threads of conversation from. Aisling was easier, much more emotional and like her father, but Isla had always kept everything close to her chest unless she was breaking.

"Mostly I want to listen," Lynda tried again. "I want to get to know you again, who you are now, and maybe we can find some kind of thread of a relationship."

"Relationship?" Suspicion filled Isla's voice.

That had been the wrong choice of a word. Lynda clenched her jaw, chastising herself. She set her glass down and straightened up, staring at her front door and then the window outside.

"I'm not good at this, Isla. I was never good at this. But I do love you, and I want you to know that."

Again, she was greeted with silence. Lynda clenched her fist hard, wondering where she had mis-stepped this time, what egregious error she had made this round. Hope drained from her rapidly, replaced with the cold sweat of fear and devastation.

"I know." Isla sounded so small, as if admitting that one thing took everything in her. A rush of air left Lynda's lips and tears of joy welled in her eyes. She hadn't thought Isla knew that.

Lynda's lips curled upward slightly. They were still talking, and that was a start. "I know you don't really count me as your family. You always made that clear. But you and Aisling are mine, and I would like to attempt to work on whatever happened between us. If you're willing to try."

"Why now?"

It was a good question, one Lynda had asked herself several times over already. She grabbed her wine glass and made her way to the couch, sliding onto the cushion. "Because of Wil, I'll admit that. Not because of any influence she's had—she's been very practiced to maintain boundaries when it comes to you. But being around Wil again has brought up a lot of memories, a lot of the past, and I've always regretted how our relationship ended up. With her around, I can't help but think of you."

"She didn't tell you to call me?"

"No, she doesn't even know that I am."

Again, Isla took her time answering. Lynda wished she could see her face, read in between what Isla wasn't saying and what she was.

"I'm under no illusion that this is going to be a quick fix." Lynda pulled one leg under the other. "I also know we can't work on this unless we're both in it, but I want you to know that whenever you're ready, I would like that."

Lynda waited for Isla to respond, giving her the time to think since she always thought a hundred things before she answered.

This time around, however, she had hope that something was different, if only because of Wil.

"I think I would too." Isla's voice was soft, still a small amount of hesitation, but if there was one thing about Isla, she never said anything she didn't mean.

"Yeah?" Lynda's eyebrows rose in surprise.

"Yeah," Isla agreed awkwardly.

Lynda couldn't stop smiling. She hadn't expected this. She had hoped for it, but she had never anticipated it might happen. "I figure at the very least we can be on speaking terms, and that will help relieve a lot of stress for Aisling."

Isla snorted. "And Wil."

Lynda hadn't thought about that, which forced guilt to settle into the pit of her stomach. "Is Wil stressed about it?"

"I think she feels guilty."

"Why?" Now Lynda was all kinds of curious, needing and wanting answers to questions she'd never thought existed.

Isla sighed, but the tension that had been present at first seemed to have vanished. "She thinks she's the reason we don't talk."

"What?" Lynda shook her head. That was far from the truth from her understanding. "Does she really?"

"Yeah, because you were the cause of a lot of the problems with her and me in high school, and a bit through college, but I think she honestly just felt guilty for having a crush on you."

Lynda wasn't quite sure what to do with that. "Isla, you've always been your own person, and while I did believe Wil had influence on you, I never thought she was the reason you weren't speaking to me. I always thought it had to do with a difference of opinion in how I raised you."

"She's not, to be absolutely clear on that. And you might call it a difference of opinion, but I call it being an absent parent."

Lynda's heart shook. She'd never gotten this far in a conversation with Isla before, and as much as she wanted to explore it, test it, pursue it, she didn't want to push her luck. "We should both probably tell Wil that. And then, if you want, perhaps we can talk more and I can listen about what really caused us to fall apart."

"Probably a good idea."

Lynda relaxed, the quiet in her condo not as fraught as it had been a mere twenty minutes ago. She held her wine glass firmly. "So how do you want to do this?"

"Do what?"

"Begin to learn who we are again."

"Oh. I don't know." Isla took a deep breath. "Are you busy next weekend?"

"I won't be if you want my time." Lynda tried to tamp down the hope in her chest that threatened to bubble up.

"Want to meet for lunch in Fort Collins?"

Relief flooded her, taking over all of her senses. The air rushed from Lynda's lungs and every muscle in her body relaxed. She had never dreamed this was possible and certainly not this quickly.

"I would love to." That hope took over. She closed her eyes and reveled in the feeling of it. Seeing her daughter again for the first time in years was actually going to happen. She'd never thought it was possible, but two phone calls in and they were going to see each other.

"Just...don't tell Wil. I don't want her to know yet."

"Oh." That was going to be hard, but Lynda could manage it. "I'll do that for this first time, but I don't know how long I'll be able to keep it from her."

"Me either, but I'd rather this first time just be the two of us so we can clear the air—hopefully."

"I understand." Lynda finished her glass of wine. "I'll make it happen."

"I'll text you the details."

"Sounds good." The conversation was winding down, and as much as Lynda wanted to continue it, she knew that she had to let go. It was one of the hardest things she had to learn as a parent. "I'll see you soon."

"I'm looking forward to it."

Isla was the one to hang up. Lynda glanced at her phone and relaxed into her couch cushion, a smile lingering on her lips. No matter what happened when they went to lunch, she had tried and Isla had tried, and that was more than either of them had done in a very long time.

~

Wil stepped into Lynda's office Friday morning and shut the door even though it was the end of the workday and half the team had left already. "Got a minute?"

"I do," Lynda stated as she flicked through a few more screens on her computer, not looking up. "What's going on?"

"I need your full attention."

Lynda stopped suddenly, tension in her shoulders and her heart thudding wildly. That tone said everything and nothing at the same time. "What is it?"

Wil handed her an envelope with her name scrawled across the front of it. Lynda didn't want to take it. She knew what it was because there was literally nothing else that it could be. She stared at it, dumbfounded, and refused to take it.

"I was working on it." Lynda grasped at the straws she still had.

"You were what?" Wil shook her head, a deep line in the crease of her brow.

"I was working on promoting you into my position, and I would move back to Boulder. I thought that's what you wanted."

Wil gave her an understanding look and shoved her hand forward with the letter still in it. "Your plan isn't going to work, and honestly, what I want has changed."

Lynda glanced at the closed door and the empty hallway. She

didn't want to be blamed again for not doing everything possible for her. "You have to be patient."

"I've been patient, and this is the best choice for me to make." When she didn't take the letter, Wil dropped it loudly on the top of the desk. "And I'm tired of waiting for the right moment and the right opportunity. I'm going to make things happen in my life. I'm not going to wait around for them to just magically happen."

"Wil," Lynda started and then stopped. "Jessica said she was working on it."

"She's not going to promote me." Wil put her hands on her hips. "You have to know that. She doesn't know anything about me or how I work, and it would put you out of a position. She's not going to let you resign or transfer either. Who else could come in here and turn this place around?"

Instinctively, Lynda knew Wil was right. No one had really wanted to do what she did. Others did it as a stepping stone to their own branch, but Lynda thrived in it. But she couldn't bring herself to let Wil do this to her career—it was such a risky step backward. "She can't force me to stay."

"This is stupid." Wil's voice rose, the power in her words bowling Lynda over.

Lynda had known it from the start, but she'd been desperate. She wanted Wil to get what she deserved, and she wanted their relationship to flourish. It couldn't with the confines placed on it by being Wil's boss. And she knew that as soon as she told Jessica what happened that it would be the end of her career. Resigning was easier than being fired.

"I won't let you step down to a lower position when I know you've worked so hard."

"You don't have a choice." Wil's voice powered through the room. "It's *my* decision, not yours."

Lynda tentatively reached forward and slid the envelope into her fingers. She stared at it, pain ricocheting through her chest as she struggled with what to say and do next.

Wil left her office with a storm in her wake. Her heart sank. This was Wil leaving her again, but in a way that Lynda had zero control on the possibility of getting her back. She had worked hard to put something in place so Wil had every opportunity, all the ones she had missed when they'd first known each other. Her plan would never work now. She was crushed. Two weeks and Wil would be working with Devon.

He didn't know her, though. He didn't know or understand her ticks or appreciate the temper. Lynda slid the letter opener through the paper, ripping into it. She took a deep breath before she pulled the letter out. She wasn't even sure if she could read it. It would be simple, because Wil didn't like flourish. Lynda pressed her hand to her mouth and steadied her racing heart.

Ultimately, Wil had been right. This was her decision, and instead of forcing her into a position she didn't want, Lynda should trust her. She didn't think this was the right choice to make, but it wasn't hers to choose.

Devon would be a good manager for her. He had a temper of his own that he had learned to tame years ago. Lynda barely remembered it anymore. But sticking the two of them in a room together when the going got rough would be like putting two livewires too close together. She opened the letter up, read the simple words on the page, double-checked the dates and sighed.

Cringing, Lynda did the only thing she could. She got into their systems and approved the transfer request. She watched as Wil left the office, hitting the lights before she walked down the hall without even a look in Lynda's direction. Rubbing her temple, Lynda closed her eyes and leaned back in her chair. This hadn't been what she wanted.

CHAPTER
Twenty~Three

WIL HATED walking into the office Monday morning. They'd attempted to talk through some of the issues throughout the weekend, but between their schedules it had been difficult to find time, and impossible to find any type of resolution. At one point, Wil had hoped Lynda would be able to give her some advice about working with Devon. Instead, it seemed she was going to be left entirely on her own.

Lynda perched at her desk, buried in work when Wil came in. It was now or never. Dropping her stuff at her desk, she slid into Lynda's office with the coffee she had bought on her way in. It seemed like an olive branch of sorts, and she could only hope that Lynda saw it that way. Wil took a steadying breath as she set the coffee on the desk and waited for Lynda to look up at her.

"Morning."

Lynda raised her chin, dropped her gaze to the coffee, and straightened her back. "Have you reconsidered?"

"No," Wil answered honestly. This was the best decision for her to make, and she knew that with everything in her. Going with Lynda's plan wouldn't be ideal for anyone, and at the very least, when their relationship did come out to the firm, it would be seen as favoritism and wouldn't go in either of their best interests in the long run.

"I wish you would." Lynda still didn't take the coffee cup.

Wil frowned inwardly, trying to hold up her end of stoicism while they were on the job even though no one else was quite in yet. "This is the right decision to make. You digging your heels in because it's not what you want isn't going to help anyone."

Lynda bristled, staring at the coffee cup again. It was as if once she took it that she would be admitting Wil was right and was using that to continue to control the conversation. It was petty, which wasn't something Wil had ever seen from her before. This was so new.

"You're being ridiculous," Lynda muttered.

"No, actually, you are, for once." Wil furrowed her brow. "And why is that, exactly?"

Lynda huffed, her gaze dropping once again to the coffee in front of her. She snatched it and cradled it between her palms. "I don't like it."

"Like what?"

Lynda's tone had changed, so Wil took a softer approach. She leaned against the desk, half-sitting on it as she eyed Lynda over her laptop.

Lynda wrinkled her nose. "You've earned a promotion or at least an equal move."

Wil nodded slowly, everything clicking in an instant. Lynda wanted what was best for her, much like she had wanted for the girls for years—this was how she showed her care. Pressing her lips firmly together, Wil tried a different tactic. "I hear you on that, but here's something else to think about—I can't work with you."

Lynda was absolutely affronted. Her lips parted, her eyes widened, and she paled visibly. "You can't work with me?"

"No, and I knew this going in. It's a huge part of why I sent out my resume. It's not just our past, but it's our present. What are we doing?"

Lynda's breath hitched. She glanced toward the door, but Wil didn't dare to follow her gaze. Either they were going to talk about this or they weren't, but she needed to have some sort of resolution. The tension was worse than when they were in Seattle.

"What are we doing?" Wil repeated.

"I don't know," Lynda finally answered, her breath nearly gone.

"We've had sex, so we've already broken the rules, but since then? Nothing. Communication stopped. I need to know what we're doing. You said it wasn't just a fling."

Lynda dashed her tongue across her lips. "I want to be with you."

Wil was about to respond until she really thought about that tone, the lust underlying every single word of it. Making eye contact, she looked into those caramel brown eyes, trying to decipher exactly what Lynda wasn't saying. When her eyes shone brightly, Wil was pretty sure she understood.

She stood up and walked to the door, shutting it. It would give them one more moment of warning if they needed it. Instead of stopping on the far side of the desk, Wil walked right around to where Lynda was perched. She took the coffee cup from her fingers and nimbly set it on the desktop.

"As in commitment," Wil stated, but it was also a question. She wanted to be doubly sure what the two of them were talking about here.

"Yes."

Butterflies flew around in Wil's stomach. She put her hands on the arm rests, leaning over Lynda to get into her space. "As in we're together and with no one else."

"Yes," she whispered.

"And Isla?"

Lynda's face went lax, and she raised her gaze to Wil's eyes. "That's where I was this weekend."

"What do you mean?"

"Isla and I met for lunch in Fort Collins."

"Really?" Hope lit up suddenly. If they were talking again, then perhaps the tension and fallout wouldn't be as awful as she had planned. "Did it...did it go well?"

"It did." Lynda grinned broadly, her eyes lighting up. "We had a really nice lunch."

Wil dropped her head, smiling even bigger than before. She'd never thought that would ever happen. Relief flooded her, and she relaxed her shoulders. All of the tension that had been filling her vanished in an instant, replaced with the possibilities for what the future held. Her heart raced, and she couldn't wipe the smile from her lips.

"I'm so happy for you." Wil was just about to move and straighten up when Lynda touched her hand. Wil froze in place. "What is it?"

"None of this would have happened without you."

"That's not true. One of you would have broken eventually." Wil knew that once Isla settled down a bit or when Aisling started having a family, they both would have come running to Lynda. Neither of them knew what value there was in that relationship yet, but when they couldn't deny it, they would have begged for it.

"I doubt that. But to answer your question..." Lynda lifted her hand to Wil's cheek, caressing her tenderly. Wil closed her eyes, leaning into the touch. "I want to be with you, and I want to see where our relationship will take us."

Wil nodded slowly before whispering, "Then I *can't* work with you."

"I know," Lynda answered. "But we have two weeks."

"Not if you let me transfer sooner."

Lynda was petrified. Wil had never seen her like this before, and she wanted to rectify it in an instant, take it back and stay if only to wipe that fear from her gaze. Lynda's hand fell away, and Wil got down onto her knees, taking hold of Lynda's hands and clasping them together.

"What's got you so frightened about this?" Wil slid her thumbs back and forth along Lynda's hands.

"It's not the job. I can handle that." Lynda's voice dropped, and she didn't lift her gaze to look Wil in the eye.

"Of course you can." Wil tried to smile at her to ease the tension, but she was pretty sure she wasn't successful. "So, what is it?"

"I'm not... I've never done this before."

"Lynda, you were married." Wil was as confused now as she was before.

"I loved Patrick with everything I had, but we had problems. We weren't the perfect couple."

"Every couple has problems. You dated other people—you should know that."

"I know." Lynda nodded and swallowed hard. "I'm not explaining this very well. I'm not sure how to."

"Take your time." Wil tightened her grasp on Lynda's hands but continued the soothing stroke of her thumb against the side of Lynda's hand. She'd seen Isla do this so many times throughout the years that she knew exactly what to do—wait.

"We don't have time. That's what I'm saying. I have spent most of my years struggling to get through to the next day, from losing Patrick to raising the girls, and now, I don't have any of that weighing me down anymore. I don't want to waste time."

Wil wished she understood better, that it was easier for them to talk to each other, but that had always been one of their major issues. They never listened well, and communication was always an issue. Wil repeated Lynda's words in her head but still was unable to parse through them. She chose what she said next carefully. "I'm not sure I understand."

Lynda bent down, clasping Wil's cheeks and brought their mouths together. "I want the best for you. I always have."

"Okay."

"So yes, I'll approve your transfer—I already did. And if you want this to be your last week and Devon agrees, I'll approve that, too."

Wil's heart jolted, her muscles tensing as she met Lynda's eyes. "But you fought so hard against it."

"Because everyone leaves me one way or another." Lynda trailed her thumb across Wil's lower lip. "But I think I have to let you go to love you."

"I'm not leaving you," Wil whispered, pressing a kiss to Lynda's hands. It hurt her heart to think that was all Lynda was afraid of. They might be going their separate ways for work, but it was to allow them to be together in the way they both wanted.

"I think I know that. But change like this isn't something I deal well with—not this kind anyway."

"You asked me once if I trusted you." Wil kissed Lynda's hands again before bringing their gazes to lock together. "I do trust you. Do you trust me?"

"Wil." Lynda's gaze softened, and she leaned down to press their lips together tenderly. "I love you."

"You love me?"

"Yes." Lynda smiled.

The door to her office opened sharply, and Lynda sat up straight, a mask in place. She kept her hand on Wil, keeping her on the ground. Wil ducked her head, hoping against hope they weren't about to be caught.

"Hey, have you seen Wil? Her stuff is in her office, but she's not there."

"I think she went to the bathroom," Lynda answered swiftly.

"Oh," Jacob answered, his voice trailing off. "I guess I'll wait a few then."

Lynda nodded at him, and they both relaxed when the door shut. Lynda giggled lightly, another surprise to hear from her. Wil stayed kneeling on the floor, her hands in Lynda's lap. They kissed again but quickly.

"You won't have much time without him coming back in here looking for you."

"Do you want me to tell him he's getting a promotion?" Wil stood up and moved away from Lynda, hoping the distance she was putting between them would help her want to keep her hands off.

"I think you deserve that right."

Wil smiled. "Friday?"

"Yes, Friday will be your last day as my assistant manager."

"But not as your ass li—"

"Wilda Powell."

Wil laughed heartily as she walked away from the desk. She was going to have fun with this one, that was for sure.

Friday the crew had given her a sendoff, and Lynda had even shown face during the party. She'd left soon enough that people wouldn't suspect but stayed around long enough to also make sure they knew she was there for them all. Monday morning rolled around faster than Wil anticipated.

Jacob was so nervous about working with Lynda, and unfortunately, Wil couldn't give him too much advice on that front. Their working relationship was so desperately tainted by the past and their current situation that she couldn't even begin how to explain it. But it was Monday, and she had to leave Jacob behind and move forward.

She was getting dressed, having brought her clothes to Lynda's that morning so she wouldn't be as rushed to get home and changed. She was working on the buttons on her shirt, when Lynda stepped up in front of her, the shift of her robe revealing far more skin than Wil wanted to see at that moment. She didn't need to be distracted. She was nervous enough as it was.

"Here, let me." Lynda's hands were sure as she took over the buttons.

Wil dropped her chin and stared down at Lynda's dexterous

fingers, but it took her longer than she cared to admit to notice that Lynda wasn't doing them up. "Lynda."

"You have time."

"Lynda," Wil repeated and grabbed her hands. She held Lynda's wrists tightly, bringing them up to her chest. "I don't want to be late for my first day."

"You won't be late, and even if you are, I'll make an excuse."

Wil snorted lightly. "What are you going to tell him? Sorry, Devon, but I needed Wil's specialized skill set for an hour this morning."

Lynda chuckled low. "If you think that'll work as an excuse."

"No, it won't." Wil shook her head. She bent down and kissed Lynda firmly. "I don't want to screw up this job."

"I can't imagine you as a screw up."

"Somehow, I don't think you always thought that."

Lynda shook her head slowly, her eyes widening. "I never thought you were going to screw up your life. There were certainly decisions you made that I didn't agree with, but they weren't so far off base that I thought you were going to ruin your future."

Wil was shocked. She'd always assumed Lynda had thought the worst of her. Lynda must have caught on because she stepped in closer, their bodies pushed together with their hands locked between them.

"Do you remember sneaking into Isla's room? It was the first anniversary of Patrick's death, and you jumped the fence into the backyard and snuck in through her window."

Wil jerked her head back. "How did you know that?"

Lynda's lips curled upward. "It was my house. You think I didn't know when you three were in it or out of it?"

"So you know when we snuck out of the house to go down to Poppy's to smoke pot?"

Lynda paled, the color rushing from her cheeks, and she stiffened in Wil's grasp. "You didn't."

"Oh, we absolutely did. Multiple times junior year."

Shaking her head, Lynda stepped back, but Wil followed her. She pushed Lynda into the wall, moving her hands above her head and pressing in.

"It seems you don't know everything." A sly smile tugged at Wil's lips.

Lynda's breathing picked up. The robe parted, revealing more creamy skin for Wil's pleasure.

"I bet there's still a thing or two I can teach you."

"I have no doubt of that." Lynda's voice was husky, breathy, as if she was getting exactly what she wanted.

Wil cringed inwardly because she was. Holding firm, Wil dropped one hand and reached for the tie of the robe, pulling it hard so that it parted. Lynda was completely bare underneath, the same way Wil had left her when she'd woken up that morning.

She palmed Lynda's breast, teasing her nipple. Lynda arched her back, seeking more touch, but Wil wasn't going to give it to her. She was going to hold off until that night because there was no way she was going to be late on her first day at a new firm. Bending down, she took Lynda's lips in a heated kiss, circling her nipple as it tightened into a hard little nub.

Lynda groaned right as Wil pulled away and dropped her hands. She took two steps back, her hands at the buttons on her shirt again as she did them up.

"Now that's just cruel."

"I think you like a good tease."

Lynda pouted, and Wil snorted back her laugh.

"Oh if you could see your face right now."

Immediately, Lynda schooled her features. Wil finished with the buttons on her shirt and started on her vest. She walked toward the bedroom to grab the tie she had brought and threw it around her neck. Lynda followed her bare feet silent on the carpet. When Wil turned around, Lynda was right there, her robe still wide open and giving Wil the view of a lifetime as she took over tying the knot.

"It took me years to learn how to do this. How amusing that I should find a woman who looks dapper in a tie." She pushed it against Wil's neck, making a few small adjustments before stepping back. "You look amazing."

"As do you, every day." Wil winked as she snagged her shoes and started putting them on.

Lynda hummed. "Today is going to be so quiet without you."

"You'll have Jacob. He likes to talk."

"To you." Lynda stood still, watching every move Wil made. "He doesn't know me well enough to be comfortable."

"Not yet, but that's part of what you have to do, get to know your staff."

"I did get to know my staff. Then she decided to find a new job."

Wil rolled her eyes. "You can't hold this against me forever."

"I won't. Just today. And maybe tomorrow."

"When will you tell Jessica?"

Lynda pursed her lips, tensing. "I don't know."

"She needs to know."

"You don't work at my firm anymore."

"We work for the same company."

"There's no more conflict of interest," Lynda defended. "If I tell her now, then there will be inquiries into everything else."

Wil sighed heavily. "I don't want to hide this."

"I don't either." Lynda pressed her lips together. "You need to be there at least a few weeks before I'll feel comfortable talking to Jessica. I want to support you through this, but I'm trying to think of the best way to work this so neither of us ends up in trouble."

Wil knew Lynda would bear the brunt of the consequences when it came to this. The transfer might help, but she could see the benefit of waiting a few weeks to a month to announce company-wide that they were dating. Wil tugged the bottom of her jacket into place. "I want to be with you, Lynda."

"I know." Lynda's face softened, her lips twitching up in a smile. "I'll figure it out."

"Soon. I know you said you don't want to waste time." Wil leaned in for a kiss. "Now, I've got to get to my new job."

"Nervous?"

"Yes, and excited."

"Good. Oh, and don't bring Devon coffee. He doesn't drink what he calls muddy water."

Wil let out a light laugh. "Duly noted, but for the record, I only bring my favorite boss coffee."

Lynda's cheeks reddened, and Wil didn't stick around for anymore conversation. As soon as she was in her car, she let out a breath, centered herself, and went to start the first day of the next part of her life.

LYNDA SET the candles on the table Friday evening. The office had been so quiet, and while Jacob was decently pleasant to work with, he was still awkward around her. It was making it difficult to get to know him and fully understand how he worked, but then again, they had only been at it for a week so far.

Rolling her shoulders, she stared at the table. The food was in the kitchen, staying warm while she waited for Wil to get to her condo. Nerves rolled around her body, though she couldn't pinpoint the cause. The play of them along her skin and on her heart and stomach was hard to keep control of. Lynda stood in the center of her small condo and waited for something to happen, for the other shoe to drop.

That was how it always happened in her life. Something good would be going along and then something disastrous would come in to replace it swiftly. She hadn't seen Wil all week, but they had talked sporadically when they could. But not seeing her, not having that time to look into her eyes and make sure that they were still on even footing and in the right place drove her wild.

The knock jump started her heart into high gear. Lynda

started toward the front door, her heart hammering with each step she took. She hadn't managed to get changed yet because she'd been so worried about the set up for dinner. She opened the door, finding Wil on the other side, looking handsome in her suit and tie.

Lynda couldn't resist. She reached forward, pulled Wil by the tie directly to her so their mouths could meet. She sighed into the kiss, reveling in the feel of Wil against her, the shiver of being held and touched even if it wasn't meant to incite just yet. She had hopes for that too, but for now, she just needed Wil's presence. When that desire had turned to need, she had no idea, but it was new, and she enjoyed it as much as it scared her.

Wil turned her to the wall, kicking the door shut and pressing her between the hard surface and her body. It was exactly what she'd needed, and somehow, Wil had known. That or they were both stuck in the throes of desire. When Wil finally slowed and pulled away a little, Lynda smiled up at her, a hand on her side.

"How was the week, truly?"

"Not awful. Steep learning curve on some things, so I think it was a good choice to take the job. I'm learning a lot."

"Good. Devon treating you right?"

Wil's lips quirked slightly. "Are you going to spank him if he's not?"

"Perhaps." Lynda found the humor Wil had aimed for. "I've missed you this week. It's been so quiet."

"No one to argue with?"

Lynda's lips curled upward. "No, but Jacob also has a steep learning curve and big shoes to fill."

"He'll manage. Give him some time."

"He won't look at me when he talks to me."

Wil snorted, pressing her forehead into Lynda's shoulder as her body rocked with her laughs. Lynda was at a loss for what was wrong or what possibly could be funny.

"What?"

"I think he has the same problem I do."

"What problem is that?"

Wil hummed, the low tone sending shivers straight from Lynda's nipples to between her legs. Wil eyed her with hunger, and Lynda dragged in a deep breath, ready for whatever Wil was about to do. Wil touched her cheek lightly with one finger, sliding it down over her collarbone and then her breasts, teasing her nipple through her green dress, the same one she'd worn *that* night.

She hadn't even realized when she'd gotten ready that morning. Wil leaned in, an arm pressed into the wall right by Lynda's head. She skimmed her lips without kissing across Lynda's jaw. She kissed Lynda's neck, the gentle touch more enticing than if she'd sucked her skin. Heat flared through Lynda's body, touching all over her as she waited to see what Wil would do next.

"You look amazing in this dress, have I mentioned that before?" The hot air from Wil's mouth skittered along Lynda's skin, goosebumps forming in its wake.

"I seem to remember something about you liking this on me." Lynda tried to follow along with everywhere Wil touched her, but it was impossible. Closing her eyes, she listened to the sensations in her body, the gentle press of Wil's fingertips into her skin, the wetness that pooled between her legs, the tingles that ran along her legs and spine.

"Yes." Wil dragged out her answer. "I seem to remember it has a zipper that likes to get stuck."

Lynda smiled slightly. "It does."

"Should we see if it gets stuck today?"

Humming, Lynda kept her eyes closed, her shoulders pressed into the wall, and she was about to let Wil do absolutely anything to her.

"Turn around," Wil commanded.

Lynda's eyes flew open, but she listened to the words. Slowly she leaned forward and slid around, pressing her palms into the wall to hold herself up because she knew she was going to need it. Wil gently touched the edge of the dress across her back, sliding her fingers just under the material before she found the zipper and tugged it.

"Seems to be working just fine." Her breath was at the back of Lynda's neck, startling the little hairs there.

Lynda sucked cold air into her lungs, hoping it would steady her, but she couldn't manage to keep her mind in check. She wanted Wil to touch her already. Everything since they'd finally broken down that final barrier had been fast and quick, but this was drawn out teasing, so very reminiscent of when she first rediscovered who Wil was and learned who she had become. Wil's hands were at her hips, sliding around her front and dragging the bottom of her dress up. Cool air touched her thighs, and Lynda let out a little moan of pleasure.

"That's it," Wil whispered. "Let me know what you're feeling."

Lynda struggled to catch her breath, everything Wil was doing was erotic and solely for her personal pleasure.

"If you want to know what Jacob's problem is," Wil started, and Lynda tensed at the shift in conversation.

She didn't want to go back to talking about work and definitely not to talking about Jacob. Wil pressed a kiss to the top of Lynda's shoulder, her fingers finding the edge of fabric to Lynda's panties, slipping just under it before sliding away to cover over it, rubbing slightly. Lynda groaned, falling more into the wall as pleasure coursed through her.

"He hasn't had what I've had, but he wants it."

"What?" Lynda meant it to come out with a bite, but instead the words slipped out on a groan when Wil circled her clit firmly.

Wil chuckled, her chest pushing into Lynda's back as she

skated her palm upward to cover her breast. "He's attracted to you, and I can't say I blame him. You're quite a catch."

"Hardly," Lynda said, though she wasn't quite sure which part of Wil's statement she was disagreeing with. Her breath caught when Wil moved to slide her hand in the top of her thong, two strong fingers on either side of her clit, scissoring back and forth. "Wil."

"Oh, he likes you all right. Wants to do exactly what I'm doing to you."

Lynda shivered. "I won't."

"I know you won't. I had a hard enough time getting you here." Wil nipped the same shoulder she'd kissed earlier, her teeth biting into soft skin.

Lynda lost her ability to focus. Everything became about Wil's hands, her body, her breath, her next action, what she would continue and what she would stop. Lynda rocked hard back into her, seeking more contact, more pleasure, more everything.

"I love you," Lynda whispered, the words falling from her lips in the most unexpected way. She was flooded with a wash of warmth and connection between the two of them, the string between them tightening and thickening. "I love you so much."

"You're right where I want you," Wil murmured into her ear. "I want you to come."

Lynda shuddered, her orgasm building to the pinnacle before ripping through her. She cried out, her cheek pressed into the cold wall, the perfect contrast that she needed to keep her wits about her, to keep her thoughts in the moment. Her heart was full when she turned around, relaxing against the wall as she pulled Wil toward her for a sloppy kiss.

"I have a surprise for you," Wil whispered.

Lynda shivered as Wil gently pushed the sleeves of her dress over her shoulders, the material pooling at her hips before she slid it down to the floor. Lynda stepped out of the circle of material, but Wil pushed her against the wall again swiftly. Her bra was off, and Wil's fingers inside her faster than she could catch her breath.

"I was supposed to surprise you." Lynda's eyelids fluttered shut with a groan as Wil pressed into her firmly.

"Oh?" Wil halted her movements, pulling a whimper of displeasure from Lynda. She didn't want Wil to stop whatever it was she was doing. Lynda's eyes flew open to catch Wil finally looking at the dining room table that was set with candles burning and a present wrapped in a box at one of the settings. "Should I open it now or wait?"

"Wait. Definitely wait." Lynda dragged Wil back, kissing her tenderly. "Your fingers are already wet, so why bother stopping and starting."

Wil laughed. "You really did miss me, didn't you?"

"Of course." Lynda started at the buttons on Wil's jacket, needing to have skin against skin. Wil distracted her, fingers slowly easing in deeper while her thumb played over her already sensitive clit. "I've been thinking about this day all week."

Wil shook her head but said nothing as Lynda continued to undress her. As soon as she was in her sports bra and pants, Lynda started on her pants. Wil stilled her fingers.

"You're about to find the surprise, and I really hope you don't mind."

Lynda furrowed her brow in confusion. "What are you talking about?"

Wil hesitated. She lifted Lynda's chin to look in her eyes before she spoke slowly. "I have a strap."

"A strap," Lynda repeated, still not quite understanding.

Nodding, Wil kept Lynda's hands still. "A dildo."

"Oh! Oh." Lynda eased against the wall, her stomach fluttering with surprise, curiosity, excitement, and a hint of apprehension. Everything mingled together in a way that she wasn't quite sure she could figure out which emotion would win out. "Well then."

"I wasn't sure what you'd want, but I thought you might like it."

Lynda tried to smile, but she knew she failed. She honestly hadn't thought about it, and it hadn't even occurred to her to ask.

"I can take it off."

"No," Lynda stated firmly, excitement and intrigue winning out. She slid her gaze from Wil's face down to her crotch and back up again. "Let me see."

Wil finished unbuttoning her pants and pulling them down along with her boxers. Lynda immediately grabbed for the strap, sliding her hand along the smooth rubber.

"How do we do this?" Lynda whispered, her eyes glued to the toy.

"However you want."

"Here?" Lynda asked. For some reason, one of her favorite places was to be smooshed between a hard surface and Wil's warm body.

"I'd say the table, but..." Wil slid her gaze back toward the beautifully set table. "Maybe the floor would be best."

Lynda dropped her gaze to the hardwood floor, not relishing the idea of the wood against her knees or back and getting up when they were finished. Pursing her lips, she met Wil's gaze. "Couch."

"Done."

Wil took her hand and led her toward the sofa. The straps slid up her ass on either side before hooking to the one around her hips. The way they moved with her was so enticing. Wil sat down first and pulled Lynda so she straddled her. The cushions would be easier on her knees, but she had a feeling she was going to regret this decision come morning. Still, she was intrigued by how this was going to feel.

"Move as slowly as you want. You're certainly wet enough, but if you want lube, I brought some."

Lynda gave a small smile as she held the toy and slid down

slightly. The bulbous head pushed against her, the thick girth stretching her in ways she hadn't felt in years. She sighed as she pulled up and pushed back down.

"That's it," Wil encouraged.

Lynda let out a small moan, closing her eyes. Wil's hands at her hips guided, but she wasn't rushed and pressured into moving any faster than she was comfortable with. When Lynda finally sat fully on Wil's lap, she buried her face in Wil's neck, breathing in her scent and steadying herself. She wanted to move, but at the same time, comfort surrounded her in the form of Wil's arms, fingers tracing patterns against her back.

"Whenever you're ready," Wil whispered.

"Okay." Lynda dragged in a breath, finally pulling herself together enough to move. She lifted and pushed down, pleasure spearing through her. Wil snaked her hand between them, flicking her clit back and forth each time she plunged down.

"I love you, Lynda," Wil stated so clearly.

Lynda could have wept, her movements faltering in the rhythm. Leave it to Wil to throw her yet another unexpected surprise. She hadn't even known she'd been waiting to hear those words, waiting for Wil to finally tell her. Tears brimmed in her eyes, but she pushed forward, writhing on top of Wil as her pleasure built up again. She'd never thought this was possible before Wil, had never dreamed she could experience this kind of ecstasy.

"Wil," Lynda breathed out her name.

"I've got you."

Wil was always so in control when it came to this. Lynda could cling to her every time she was falling apart. Rutting her hips against Wil, Lynda closed her eyes and focused her full attention on her body. Wil reached up and cupped her breast, toying with her nipple before skimming her hand back down to her hips all the while never stopping the tease on her clit. Lynda held on tightly, heat rising in her chest and cheeks.

"You've got this."

Lynda welcomed her orgasm, convulsing as she fell into Wil's arms and held on tight. She was so lightheaded, and her face so hot. She wasn't sure when she would feel normal again or be able to catch herself enough to return what Wil had so graciously given her.

"Touch me," Wil begged. "I'm so close."

Lynda dragged herself up, leaning back on her heels so she could weave her hand under the toy. She found Wil's clit, swollen, hard. In silence, she played with her, she teased her, she rocked into her when Wil pushed, she pulled away when she relaxed. She followed every movement Wil gave her, every groan, every breath.

Wil scrunched her face as she came, her nose wrinkled, and her body tensed. Lynda bent down, pressing kisses gently over her cheeks, her lips, her neck. She wanted to touch everywhere she could reach, and she never wanted to let go. Wil lifted her up and turned her onto her back.

"You're absolutely beautiful when you're spent."

Lynda snorted lightly, far too happy and satiated to think. "Then I'll leave you to plate up dinner."

"Are we going to sit at the table naked and eat?" Wil winked, that devilish gaze back in her eyes.

Giving a chastising look, Lynda shook her head. She couldn't even imagine doing that, but she was pretty sure Wil would barely give it a second thought. "No."

"Pity. You got my hopes up." Wil leaned in and sucked hard on Lynda's nipple, grinning the entire time.

Lynda groaned, her fingers in Wil's hair in an instant as she dared herself to think she might be able to go another round. Glee filled her as she teased back, "You should know better."

Wil laughed and kissed her hard. "Fine, I'll get your robe."

"Thank you. Because I'm not sure I'm able to walk just yet." Lynda glanced down at her red knees, her thighs still trembling from the force of her orgasms. She was pretty sure if she did stand, they would be jelly.

Wil bent down as she moved to get up, licking her way firmly through Lynda's folds. Gasping, Lynda shivered as the last legs of pleasure were pulled from her.

"Sorry," Wil said, though she didn't look it. "Had to have a taste."

Lynda giggled as Wil stood up. She had never been happier.

CHAPTER
Twenty-Five

ONE YEAR LATER...

Nerves rushed through Lynda in a way they never had before. Her heart thundered, and she could barely keep still. Wil sat next to her as they waited in the restaurant, and Wil knew. She had to know. They'd talked about it on the entire drive up without even saying the words.

"I'm scared," Lynda mumbled, half-hoping that Wil didn't hear her but knowing she fully would.

"I am, too," Wil whispered back, "But I don't think she's going to be surprised."

"I'd hope not." Lynda twisted her hands together in her lap. She needed to get this over with. They'd wanted to tell her first, and so they'd kept it a secret—somehow—for the better part of two weeks until they'd found the time.

"Hey." Isla's sweet voice filled her ears, and Lynda shuddered.

They had spent the last year slowly getting to know each other again. Lynda worked hard to not play the parental role she sometimes wanted, but to simply be there as a support when Isla needed it. She sat across the table from them, her eyes that same stunning blue as Patrick's. It always brought a spark of grief and love whenever she saw Isla in person.

"Hey," Lynda answered, her voice no longer the same firm tone she usually held. She could never really keep that when the girls were around. "How's everything going?"

"It's good. We go back to school next week, and I get in to set up my classroom in a few days."

Lynda nodded along, but she was so distracted by the entire reason they were there. She tried to pay attention to the conversation happening at the table, but she was lost in her own thoughts.

"How's work?"

"It's good." Lynda cleared her throat. "Finally finding a balance of work and play. My assistant manager has finally found his stride, I think."

"Jacob's a good kid," Wil teased, but Lynda couldn't stop looking at Isla. She looked amazing and healthy, and oh so very comfortable with the two of them there. The first time they had done this, it had been anything but relaxing, and this was such a drastic change from that.

"He is. He's done well to learn and take over for Wil."

"Good." Isla gave a beautiful smile, the gleam reaching her eyes.

"There, uh...was something we wanted to talk to you about," Wil started the conversation, the entire reason they were there, and Lynda was so thankful for Wil's ability to get straight to the point.

Isla cocked her head to the side, sipping the water she had ordered, but there was a tension in her face that wasn't there before. "What?"

Wil sent Lynda a look, clearly tossing the conversation into her court. Taking a deep and steadying breath, Lynda dove in. Her stomach fluttered with nerves because this could very well be the end or the beginning. "We're getting married."

Isla didn't flinch. Nothing in her was readable. Lynda looked for any sign of any reaction, but she was met with nothing. She swallowed hard because they had already agreed that unless Isla and Aisling could handle it then they wouldn't. Her mind raced with thoughts, and she had to stop herself from speaking, had to give Isla the time to think and respond. She'd been practicing that a lot over the last year.

Isla stared down at her drink before flicking her gaze up to meet Lynda's. She didn't even bother to look at Wil. She cracked a smile, her grin broadening by the second, and the tension rushed from Lynda's chest and shoulders as she nearly melted in her chair.

"You are?" Isla finally looked at Wil, so much love reflected in her gaze.

Wil nodded, echoing the sentiment. "We are."

"When?"

"Not one fucking clue," Wil answered on a loud laugh. "We wanted to talk to you first."

Isla stood up suddenly, the legs on the chair scraping from the sharp movement. She came around the table and wrapped her arms around Wil's shoulders. "I'm so excited for you."

"Are you really?" Wil asked, tugging Isla into her before she stood to give her a proper hug.

Lynda stayed put, joy soaring that everything seemed to be working exactly as they had hoped. She stayed put, her hands in her lap, as she watched two forever friends have so much joy for each other. That was love at its purest, and she'd always envied their connection with each other.

"I am," Isla answered, containing a squeal as she bounced on her toes and clenched her eyes tight.

Lynda relaxed even more, the last bit of tension releasing. They could handle this. It wouldn't be the end of the world. She was shocked when Isla rounded Wil and hugged her, her firm arms around Lynda's shoulders, a kiss to her cheeks. A tear slipped from Lynda's eye and down her chin as she buried her face in her daughter's hair for the first time in six years.

Isla's scent had changed over the years, but the feel of her, the warmth of her personality, the heartache that had been caused between them so many times over dared to sew together a little more with each second that Isla clung to her. Lynda dragged in a ragged breath and tried to hold back the tears of overwhelming happiness that filled her.

She'd never thought this would be possible again. She'd never thought she'd love again or find her kids again. Her heart warmed as she let Isla go and wiped her cheek. She reached for Wil's hand, curling their fingers together. She didn't know where to look or what to say. All they needed was Aisling and it would be perfect.

"When are you going to tell Aisling?"

Lynda's lips quirked upward. "I was just thinking the very same thing."

"Today?" Isla's eyes lit up.

"Maybe tomorrow."

Isla clapped her hands together. "I can't keep this a secret for long. She's going to be so happy. Oh, don't let her plan the wedding."

Wil intervened, thankfully. "We were just going to get the paper signed, I think."

Isla's face pinched, and she focused on Lynda. "No. We were all there when you married Dad, and we'll be there when you two get married."

"Nothing big," Lynda added in. "I've already done all that."

"But Wil hasn't." Isla pointed a finger at her before she walked back around the table to her chair. "And don't you think she deserves all the hoopla?"

Before Lynda could answer, Wil jumped in, the rapid fire conversation picking up like it had never stopped. "Since when have I ever given the vibes of someone who wants a big to-do for a wedding?"

Isla snorted, indignant, but a smile graced her lips in an

instant. "Fine, but I'm going to be there—Aisling, too. Just tell me when and where."

"We will," Lynda assured, more than happy that the future plans were being made. It meant Isla truly was happy for them, that she was comfortable with the way they were progressing. "I promise."

Isla shifted her gaze from Wil to Lynda. "And you said you wouldn't ever get married again, so I'm shocked on one level. But damn, I'm so excited! Wil deserves this."

"She does." Lynda cracked into a smile, unable to hide her happiness any longer. "I did say that at one point. It wasn't a priority then, and honestly, it wasn't ever a thought in my head until this last year. I guess sometimes the past sneaks up on you."

About the Author

Adrian J. Smith has been publishing since 2013 but has been writing nearly her entire life. With a focus on women loving women fiction, AJ jumps genres from action-packed police procedurals to the seedier life of vampires and witches to sweet romances with a May-December twist. She loves writing and reading about women in the midst of the ordinariness of life.

AJ currently lives in Cheyenne, WY, although she moves often and has lived all over the United States. She loves to travel to different countries and places. She currently plays the roles of author, wife, and mother to two rambunctious youngsters, occasional handy-woman. Connect with her on Facebook, Twitter, or her blog.

facebook.com/adrianjsmithbooks

twitter.com/adrianajsmith

instagram.com/adrianjsmithbooks

tiktok.com/@sapphicbookmaker

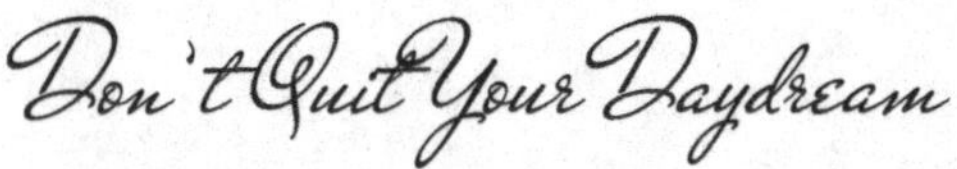

Don't Quit Your Daydream

What happens in the elevator doesn't stay in the elevator.

When Laura's business partner hires Skylar to bring their company to the next generation, Laura sees red. An obnoxious millennial isn't someone she wants to work with—they're known for failing their side hustles. Since Laura gave up everything for Solace Inc to succeed, including her dreams of marriage and family, she's not willing to risk it on just anyone.

Skylar vies to succeed in her first big contract and won't let Laura's sour personality get in her way. Each day she finds something else intriguing about Laura and all the fronts she puts up. With a dash of humor and hope, Skylar bets on her sunny disposition winning Laura over. What she doesn't expect is her growing crush on a straight woman to go anywhere.

Skylar has to remember...don't fall in love with the grump down the hall.

Releasing April 2023

Also by Adrian J. Smith

Romance

Memoir in the Making

OBlique

Love Burns

About Time

Admissible Affair

Daring Truth

Indigo: Blues (Indigo B&B #1)

Indigo: Nights (Indigo B&B #2)

Indigo: Three (Indigo B&B #3)

Indigo: Storm (Indigo B&B #4)

Indigo: Law (Indigo B&B #5)

Crime/Mystery/Thriller

For by Grace (Spirit of Grace #1)

Fallen from Grace (Spirit of Grace #2)

Grace through Redemption (Spirit of Grace #3)

Lost & Forsaken (Missing Persons #1)

Broken & Weary (Missing Persons #2)

Young & Old (Missing Persons #3)

Alone & Lonely (Missing Persons #4)

Stone's Mistake (Agent Morgan Stone #1)

Stone's Homefront (Agent Morgan Stone #2)

Urban Fantasy/Science Fiction

Forever Burn (James Matthews #1)

Dying Embers (James Matthews #2)

Ashes Fall (James Matthews #3)

Unbound (Quarter Life #1)

De-Termination (Quarter Life #2)

Release (Quarter Life #3)

Beware (Quarter Life #4)

Dead Women Don't Tell Tales (Tales of the Undead & Depraved #.5)

Thieving Women Always Lose (Tales of the Undead & Depraved #1)